Brandy, Ballad of a Pirate Princess

By Dan Hendrickson

ISBN: 9781734518764

Interior design by booknook.biz

Dedication

This one goes to my youngest daughter Donna.
Sweetie you are a hopeless romantic just like your father.
Remember the time you saved that baby bunny from that
big scary dog? Well Brandy is just like you!

TABLE OF CONTENTS

Chapter 1

Mother's Pride

Caribbean Sea between Jamaica and Southern Tip of Florida, 1829

"Hold your guard up and widen your stance. You're not on solid ground. The sea is a tricky old bitch and she'll test you."

The Scarlet Mistress presses her attack, causing her fifteen-year-old daughter to step back, barely able to meet her mother's lightning-fast barrage of slashes and jabs with a rapier and dagger. The Scarlet Mistress never allows Brandy to practice with more than one blade at a time. Telling her if she can't protect herself with one blade, then she has no right to live. The English man-of-war cutter rolls slightly back, forcing the mother to lean forward to adjust her balance, which causes her to press hard with the thrust of her rapier. Brandy sees the opening and brings her rapier up and in a slight arc, catching the attacking blade.

She then twists her rapier downward, causing her mother to lose control of the weapon. Brandy grabs it from her with her free hand. Before her mother can counter, Brandy takes both rapiers and brings them down on the dagger with a vicious stroke that sends it flying across the deck before it bounces up and over the rail and into the ocean. Using her right foot, she sweeps her mother's front knee, causing the woman to fall back and land on her bottom.

Brandy crosses both blades and steps in close, putting the two razor-sharp edges against her mother's throat, and yells "Yield!" Mother and daughter stare at each other with the same intense green eyes. The deck is stone silent as two mates and the rest of the crew wait to see what will happen next. The Scarlet Mistress's temper is legendary among the crew of *The Red Witch*. Many pirates and sailors alike have had the misfortune of being on the lethal end of her wrath. Few can match her skill with a blade or her lust for her enemy's blood. She—along with her husband, Captain Eric Erasmus, aka "The Plague"—have sailed and marauded together for a quarter of a century.

"Take those blades from my throat, you little whore," the Scarlet Mistress says as she slowly stands.

Instead, Brandy presses the blunt sides of the rapiers harder into her mother's neckline.

"ARGH!" her mother screams. Her spittle sprinkles her daughter's face.

"That's enough out of both of you. Kat, concede. Brandy bested you fair and square. You'd think her own mother would show pride in having such a lethal daughter."

Brandy drops her blades, and Katrina Mooney nods and yields while everyone on the deck turns to acknowledge *The Red Witch's* captain.

He steps out of his cabin, stretching his arms and yawning. Eric Erasmus has jet-black hair, a full mustache and beard, and deep blue eyes. He is a massively muscled man standing six feet, three inches tall and weighing 240 pounds. His forearms are almost as thick as his biceps and shoulders, after spending the last thirty-five years at sea working ropes and rigging as much as a rapier and dagger. He looks around the deck. He cups both hands around his mouth and yells up to the lookout nest some fifty feet up the main mast. "Skinner, do you see anything in the shipping line? They told me in Jamaica a whole convoy of merchant ships should be coming this way."

"Nothing yet, Captain, but I got me eyes open!" Skinner shouts.

"That sea goat can't see past the end of his nose. Why do we let him do lookout every morning, anyway?" Erasmus says to no one in particular.

"Because he likes the exercise, Captain. Says it's the reason he's the best arm wrestler in any port. Says the winnings he gets makes up for the lack of profit-sharing from his favorite cousin, our beloved captain."

Erasmus smiles at his first mate, Don Lomoche. He shakes his head and points his chin back up to the lookout nest. "That boneheaded rat lacks for nothing because of me. He'll get his due when you all do. *The Red Witch* did not come cheap, you know. They say this redwood is the hardest in the world. We've never been bested." Erasmus looks over at his daughter. "Brandy, make yourself useful. Climb up there and help your uncle find me some bounty."

Brandy throws a half salute. "Aye aye, Captain!" She looks around for something, and then looks at her mother.

"Don't look at me. You just threw my favorite dagger into the ocean, which I have half a mind to take out of your hide."

Captain Erasmus reaches in his belt, pulls out a six-inch blade and tosses it to his daughter. She easily catches it by the handle, then clamps the blade between her teeth and climbs the main rigging up to the lookout. Like Skinner, she does not use her feet to climb but pulls herself up by the strength of her arms while holding the dagger in her teeth. Many a time while boarding another vessel, a pirate will have to put his blade in his teeth while climbing so as to not get it tangled in the rigging. Whenever Brandy has to climb, her mother and father insist that she have a blade in her mouth to perfect the skill. Not using her legs when she climbs is her Uncle Skinner's idea. That, coupled with the constant sword-fighting lessons from her parents has endowed the girl with considerable upper-body strength. She puts most of the male crew on *The Red Witch* to shame.

Captain Erasmus watches his daughter climb the rigging. The hot Caribbean Sea breeze makes her long, red hair swish through the air like wild flames dancing. He looks over at Kat. "You're the only one I have ever seen climb the rigging like that, but not in a while. I fear she will someday outdo both of us."

The Scarlet Mistress looks at her husband with a sneer. "She still has a long way to go. Once she's down, send her to me. She'll replace that dagger. I'll be in our cabin." She turns and grabs the two rapiers that her daughter threw to the deck earlier and strides toward her quarters. Just before entering she takes a sideways glance up the main mast and sees Brandy standing in the lookout nest with her uncle, and her intense green eyes twinkle with enormous pride. She grabs the latch to the cabin doors and mutters under her breath, "Nicely done, Brandy. They've begun to fear you like they do me."

Brandy stands behind her uncle and shades her eyes with her right hand as she looks out over the early-morning eastern sky. Skinner has the frame of a gorilla. His arms are long and muscled. He sports a bright blond beard and a mustache that accentuates his blue eyes and has long blond hair that he wears in a ponytail. Many a maid in port has lost her heart to his infectious smile, and many a man his gold to the strength of his arm.

The sun shows it to be around 8:00 a.m. Brandy knows they are looking for a convoy of merchant ships that left New York harbor two weeks ago and are headed to New Orleans. Her father's plan is to catch the last one in the line and overtake it while the others flee to safety. The ship, its crew, goods, and passengers will be brought to a secret

Caribbean pirate port where everyone and everything, including the ship and the people aboard, will be divided up and sold. It is the pirate's way of life; the only life she has ever known.

She was born right on *The Red Witch* fifteen years ago during one of the biggest hurricanes anyone can remember. Captain Erasmus thought to get his wife to the mainland in Florida to give birth to what he then hoped would be a son and heir. Brandy did not oblige him on either count. She was brought into this world below deck while Erasmus and his crew struggled to save *The Red Witch* during the storm. The crew still talks about how when the first cries of the newborn daughter of Captain Eric Erasmus and the Scarlet Mistress sounded out, the storm died down and calm seas ensued. The timing of the ship entering the eye of the storm and then making port and hunkering down through the rest of it is thought by its crew to be a miracle and an omen that Brandy was a gift of good luck from the sea.

She taps her uncle's shoulder. "Uncle Skinner, I see something off port. It looks to be ships, but they're too big to be merchants."

Skinner lowers his spyglass. "Aye, Brandy, those be ships all right— full-blown English man-of-war Royal Navy warships. I count five so far. They don't sit as low in the water as we do because we're made of the heavier redwood, which also means we can't outrun them and there's too many to fight off. I've been watching them. They'll be on us soon."

Brandy rebukes her uncle for not sounding the alarm, but he puts up a hand. "Your parents and I have plans for something like this. You sound the alarm, and when you get down, do exactly what your mother tells you to do."

Brandy does not hesitate. She puts her hands to her mouth and yells, "Captain, English armada off port, five men-of-war! Thirty minutes out." She looks back at her uncle and says, "Why did you wait?"

Skinner reaches up and wipes the tear from his niece's eye. "I only spotted them when you and your mother were dancing around down there, trying to kill one another. If I had said anything then, your father might have tried to run and keep them at bay with our aft cannon. But it'd been useless. Those ships are much faster than we are, and it's a two-day sail to the nearest friendly port. It be best we surrender and pray for mercy from their admiral."

Down on the deck, Captain Erasmus points his spyglass in the direction Brandy had just announced and feels an unaccustomed cold wave of panic. The Royal Navy usually leaves him and his ship alone, unless … they finally figured out who his wife really is. Then he knows there could be a real fight. His mind races for the best strategy. If it were two or even three ships, he would have a fair chance of taking out the first one and making a run for it while firing back on the others. The superior durability of his cutter's redwood might tip the odds in his favor under those circumstances, but with an armada of five, he knows he is facing the entire Royal Navy fleet stationed in this part of the new world. Though he might take down one or two in the battle, the remaining ships will send him and his crew to the bottom of the sea. His only hope is to hide his wife and surrender.

"Stand down and wait for them. Lomoche, send up the white flag."

Before he can draw his next breath, Captain Erasmus feels a burst of intense pain exploding into his back. When he looks down at his chest, he sees the protruding end of a rapier stained with his own blood sticking six inches out of his sternum.

A hand reaches up and grabs a fistful of hair from the back of his head and pulls his face backward so that he can see his first mate, Don Lomoche, sneering at him. "I am glad you chose to cooperate, Captain. Me and my boys did not want to have to explain to Admiral Bennets why we were firing on him."

He pulls his rapier from Captain Erasmus's dying body and lets the bulky man fall to the deck. Three men separate themselves from the rest of the crew and take positions around Lomoche with their rapiers drawn. He looks around at the rest of the crew, holds his own bloody blade out and points it at the approaching armada. "If any of you want to live through this, you'll do nothing. I have Admiral Bennets's personal guarantee that he will spare any man who sides with me. Not only will they allow us to live, but we will be free to sail away on *The Red Witch*. We will be part of his personal fleet here in the Caribbean, but we will be alive and free to seek a fortune far greater"—he points his rapier at the corpse of Captain Eric Erasmus—"than this ignorant son of a whore ever let us do. Now, who is with me?"

Before anyone can respond, a flash of red flame flies from above and into Lomoche with the power of a cannonball. Having released herself while halfway down the rigging she is descending from, Brandy slams the heel of her foot into his jaw, sending him crashing to the deck. With her father's dagger in hand, she lands on her feet and storms toward the man at unbelievable speed. Lomoche barely has enough time to stand up and hold his blade out in defense. She parries it and steps inside his perimeter, turns, and brings her own blade down, and with a strength and speed born from pure rage, she severs his hand from his body. The severed hand and the blade fall to the deck. She takes the hilt of her dagger and rams it into the right eye of Lomoche so hard that the eye bursts. He falls to the deck, and she is immediately on top of him with her knees pinning his shoulders and arms. She raises her blade high with both hands, and with tears streaming down her cheeks and screaming a series of curses at the man, brings the blade down, aiming to thrust it straight into the maggot's heart. Before the blade makes contact, a voice screams out, "Brandy, stop! We need him!"

She turns and sees her mother standing beside her. In her hands are the two rapiers they were sparring with earlier, both dripping red with her victim's blood. At her feet sprawled out on the deck of *The Red Witch* are the corpses of the three men who had stood with Lomoche. Brandy stands up and screams. "He killed my father! I will carve him into little pieces and feed him to the sharks!"

The Scarlet Mistress softly rebukes her. "What do you propose we do about them?" She raises her hand and points to the rapier she is holding at the armada of ships. Stunned, Brandy numbly looks at the enemy and quietly sobs.

"Skinner, where are you?" the Mistress yells.

"Right here, Kat." She turns to see her husband's cousin standing behind her, rapier in hand and waiting for her orders. She shakes her head. "There will be no more fighting."

Brandy steps back defensively and glares at her mother. "What do you mean no more fighting? I—"

Before she can finish, the Scarlet Mistress steps in close and with the rapier still in her grasp, backhands her daughter so hard across her cheek that she slinks to the deck unconscious. She then walks over to Lomoche, bends down, and backhands him, knocking him completely out. She stands and drops both rapiers on the deck and says, "We are beaten, and your captain is dead. Get to your stations and prepare to be boarded."

As the crew leaves, she looks around the deck to three she trusts, quietly motions them to her, and scans the immediate vicinity to see no one is left on the upper deck. She motions her chin to Skinner, then her daughter, and whispers, "You know what to do." Skinner nods his head, picks Brandy up, hefts her over his shoulder and makes his way to the lower decks. Kat watches him go and then looks back to the other three, "Juan, Pablo, and Briskett, when they board us, you will tell Admiral

Bennets that you sided with Lomoche, and after my daughter tried to kill him you attacked her, slit her throat, then killed her and her uncle, and dumped them into the sea. Brandy has a legal claim to this vessel. You know that Captain Erasmus only preyed on American merchant ships, so this English admiral would be honor-bound to uphold that claim. But he made a deal with this devil"— she points her hand at the unconscious Lomoche— "and I believe he would kill her to take *The Red Witch* and give it to him."

She looks them all in the eye with an intensity that makes them step back and gasp. She points at Lomoche. "When this maggot wakes up, you will all swear your allegiance to him. None of you will leave this ship. You will call him your captain and you will care for the daughter of Captain Erasmus's inheritance until she comes back to claim it by taking Lomoche's miserable life. Now swear!"

In unison, the trio answers, "We swear, Mistress!"

As the crew is preparing for the armada to send skiffs to board, a scream is heard from the upper deck and then two bodies fly over the railing and into the ocean. They hear the Scarlet Mistress scream, "You traitorous bastards, you killed my daughter!" Several ascend to the upper deck to find Juan, Pablo and Briskett holding her by the arms as she thrashes and kicks to be released.

"What's going on here?" one asks as they stare at the trio.

Juan steps forward and says, "If you think we are going to hang for this sea bitch,"—he points his chin in the Scarlet Mistresses direction—"you're all mad. Brandy and Skinner are now shark food. When Lomoche wakes he will be our new captain and we will do as he says. Now get back to your station and prepare for the English Navy to board."

As the crew disperses again the Scarlet Mistress sighs and releases herself from the men. She turns and says in a hushed tone, "Briskett, bind Lomoche's wounds and cauterize that miserable stump before he bleeds out. Juan and Pablo, come with me." She leads them below deck to Skinner's cabin where they find that he has laid Brandy on his bunk and is cutting her long red hair. The puffy welt forming around Brandy's cheek and eye is already starting to turn black. Skinner is almost done, and the Scarlet Mistress reaches over and grabs a small bowl of thick black liquid from the small table next to Skinner's bed. She dips a combing brush in it and brushes the hair dye into her daughter's now boyish-looking hair.

"Be sure to work it in thoroughly, Kat. We have to make sure her roots look as black as the depths of Hades—and hurry."

Once done with the hair, Brandy's mother asks the men to wait outside the cabin. She takes off her daughter's fancy black boots, leggings, leather belt, white blouse, vest, and black scarf. She replaces the fine clothing with a simple pair of trousers and torn burlap blouse tied together with old rigging rope.

Brandy opens her eyes and tries to sit up but is still dizzy from the blow her mother gave her earlier. She lies back down and looks into the face of the woman whom she both loves and hates. "Why…?"

Her mother picks up a sponge and cleans the still fresh dye from Brandy's forehead and neckline. "Brandy, we have little time. The Royal Navy will board in moments. Lomoche must have told them who I am. They have been looking for me for a long time. When I was two years younger than you are now, the captain who brought my family over from Ireland was a black-hearted devil. He killed my mother and father and sold me into slavery. There is still a standing order signed by the king himself to execute me. That is why you must sneak off this ship when they arrest me. Lomoche knows you have a legal claim to this vessel, and he would try to use my arrest to cover for killing you." Brandy sits up, but her mother stays her with her hand. "Brandy, there is no other choice. You can come back to claim what is yours someday. But ..."

"But what, Mother?"

"But you can also leave this bloody life and this hell a pirate lives at sea, and go live your life like my father wanted his family to do."

A loud pounding comes from the other side of the cabin door and Skinner sticks his head in. "Kat, they've boarded. I have to get her down with the others."

The Scarlet Mistress places her hands on her daughter's cheeks, and with tears running down her face, she says, "Brandy. Please. Your father and I planned for this day a long time ago. He would want you to run to fight another day. I want you to run and live. Whatever you choose, please, darling, do what Skinner tells you."

She then stands and orders the two others who came down with her to bind her hands and escort her up to the deck. Brandy stands and follows her uncle to the lowest level of the ship where they hold the prisoners from previous raids before offloading them to the slave markets at different ports around the Caribbean.

When the Scarlet Mistress returns to the deck of *The Red Witch*, she sees about twenty Royal Navy marines and three officers. One of them is an older, pudgy man who has stuffed most of his bulk into the belly of his uniform, but the admiral insignia on his lapel distinguishes him as Bennets. The other is obviously a ship's physician attending to Lomoche. She bursts away from the two men escorting her and makes her way to the admiral. Several marines aim their muskets at her, but she ignores them.

"Do what you want with me, but keep me away from those two rodents. They killed my daughter and her uncle and then threw them overboard."

The admiral pauses for a moment and directs his attention to Juan and Pablo. "Sided with Lomoche, did you? Too bad you were not in time to save the others. But all's well though, because we have the Scarlet Mistress, and his Majesty King George will finally get satisfaction for the death of his cousin. With her daughter and husband dead, there will be no unsightly squabble over the ownership of this wretched vessel." He looks back at the doctor. "Lieutenant Smyth, see that when Lomoche wakes up he is told that *The Red Witch* is his."

"Aye aye, sir."

Bennets clasps his hands together and rubs them greedily. "His Majesty will be very pleased to hear of your execution, my dear. The Bennets family has not enjoyed the royal gratitude in many a year. Your death may earn me a governorship appointment." He directs his voice to the seamen. "Hang the Scarlet Mistress on her own ship."

The marines grab her and force her to a plank that leads out over the deck to the ocean, where a noose is already set. They put the rope around her neck and pull it taut. As they are about to push her forward, the third officer sees movement from the hatch and calls the admiral's attention to it. A ragged group of vagabonds ascend onto the deck, led by the marines.

A sergeant runs up to the admiral and salutes. "Admiral, these are the prisoners we found in the lower decks. Some of them claim to be British citizens emigrating from England to settle in the Caribbean."

Bennets looks over at the thirty-some men, women, and children and scowls. "Captain Thompson, I thought Erasmus only preyed on American Colony ships! Why would there be English citizens with this lot?"

The officer steps forward and answers with a quiver in his voice. "Yes, Admiral, that is so, but when some of them are dropped off at our main port in Puerto Rico, they take passage on local transports to gain access to the rest of the Caribbean."

Bennets looks over the crew of *The Red Witch*. "That may have been a technicality to your departed captain, but my orders from Admiralty are to hang any pirates caught preying on English subjects." He puts his hand to his chin and rubs it thoughtfully. "But I am also under strict direction not to aid colony ships. Captain Richards, see that these people are transported to one of our ships scheduled to dock at the closest English-controlled port, and be sure they are all processed as English subjects. Since we caught and executed the woman responsible for the king's cousin's death, and having killed Captain Erasmus, that should smooth over any objections from Admiralty of my having confiscated this ship and put her into my own company's service."

Before Richards can respond, the Admiral holds up his hand. "Wait. They have incarcerated these poor people in the belly of this beast for God knows how long. Let them stay to see the execution of their captor." He looks to the men holding the Scarlet Mistress with the noose around her neck. "You may proceed with the hanging."

They push her out again. The rope around her neck extends up to a piece of sail mast that protrudes out over the sea, and they give the rope enough slack so that when she is forced over, the fall will break her neck and kill her. She steps up on the plank, but before proceeding she turns and looks at the prisoners. In the middle of the group she sees Brandy and Skinner. Brandy now has jet black hair and looks like a boy. Skinner has shaved off all his blond hair and has removed his earrings and jewelry. They both look the part of prisoners on a pirate ship.

She stares directly into Brandy's eyes. "Take a good look, all of you. Thirty years ago, I was one of you. Only I was not so fortunate. They took me and sold me into slavery." She points her chin at Admiral Bennets. "They sold me to a pig like him. At thirteen years old, he forced me to feel his grubby old hands on me for over a year. One night I took his own dagger and slit his miserable throat. Then I ran from His Majesty's justice and joined a pirate ship. I offered myself to any man strong enough to keep me for his own. Eventually, Captain Erasmus took me as his woman, then his wife. Since that day I ran from the governor's house, I've killed, marauded, and pirated all over the Caribbean. I've sent countless vagabonds like yourselves to the bottom of these rotten oceans; others I have sold into slavery and profited on their misery. Count yourselves truly blessed that the admiral here is forced to protect you now. Go, live your lives and stay off these cursed waters."

She then looks at her former crew. "I curse you miserable braggarts for not protecting your captain and for what they did to my daughter. You all will spend the rest of your days on this devil's spawn of a ship, sailing the cursed waters. Know this—only an heir of mine can release you from this curse and since you killed my only one, I hereby damn all of you to this hell!" The Scarlet Mistress then turns and runs off the plank, throwing herself downward. She dies instantly.

Brandy feels an ice-cold numbness course through her spine. Violence and death have been realities she has dealt with her entire young life. She feels the old pull in her gut to attack and kill those who are killing her crew, but a firm hand comes over and clasps her shoulder from behind. The familiar voice of her now only living relative speaks softly in her ear. "Kat wanted you to live, Brandy. She was right. Your father would have you bide your time and plan your revenge. With him, the trying meant nothing without the succeeding. We have no chance here. Play the part and let's get off this ship, then we can figure out what to do next."

"Why did she curse the crew? They all did exactly what she said, and no one has sold us out yet."

Skinner sniffs, wipes a tear from his eye and gently pats his niece on the back. "The Scarlet Mistress was a sly one, for sure. Pirates be a superstitious lot. Most, if not all, will stay on this ship for the rest of their lives. Juan, Pablo and Briskett will keep them here and wait for you to return and claim it. In the minds of the rest, your mother sealed their vow to her with her own blood. If you ever come back, Lomoche won't know what hit him. That be certain."

The marines help the prisoners climb into skiffs sent over from one of the man-of-war ships that will be heading back to a port in Jamaica. Brandy can't help but notice the wretched faces of the prisoners they are riding with. Most have not seen the light of day in weeks, and all are suffering from dehydration and malnutrition. Brandy never paid them much attention in the past. Her father used to say they were casualties of war and knew the risks when they set out on these waters. A deep pang of guilt hits her heart when a beautiful, young, dark-skinned mother tries to comfort her crying daughter. She knows that once they get to an English port, they will be processed as slaves and sold to the highest bidder. She sees that the mother has traces of a blackened eye and older bruises on her arms as she puts her little girl on her lap. Brandy reaches up and touches her own black eye and bruised cheek from her mother's strike earlier and realizes that she did it to help her daughter blend in with the rest of the prisoners. She looks over at her uncle. "How could we look at these people like they were just stock to be sold?"

Skinner puts a hand on Brandy's shoulder. He looks down and in a hushed whisper says, "We be pirates, Brandy. That is how we live, by spoiling others of all that they have, including their lives."

Brandy takes a moment to watch the only home she has ever known sail away under the command of a mutineer who stole it and her life away.

CHAPTER 2

LIFE NOT AT SEA

Kingston, Jamaica, 1844

At thirty years of age, Brandy is a single woman living and working in the major port city of Kingston, Jamaica. Her Uncle Skinner turned out to have quite a stash of gold in that city and used it to buy a tavern just off the main docks. He named the tavern *Katrina's*. Brandy kept her hair dyed black, and Skinner never let his grow back. Skinner changed his name to Skynyrd, but Brandy kept hers. She ran the front of the tavern and he ran the back. Like her mother, Brandy grew into a strikingly beautiful woman. Also like her mother, she was not small of stature, standing five feet, ten inches tall and weighing one hundred fifty pounds, full-figured, and still athletic.

Her arms and back are still like iron because of the hard labor of running a tavern and keeping up on her sword practice with her uncle and an employee named Zhang Yong, a Chinese immigrant they hired five years ago. Her hair is now as long as it was before she left *The Red Witch*. Being jet black, it always seems in contrast with her vibrant, green eyes. Those same eyes have quite the hypnotic effect on the regular seafaring patrons of her uncle's tavern.

Katrina's is considered a friendly place for lonely sailors to pass their time away. Because of Skynyrd's, Brandy's, and Zhang Yong's proclivity for keeping the peace in the place, people feel comfortable and at ease. Fights, conflicts, or arguments rarely break out because one of the three will usually end the situation quickly.

Many a sailor thought they had found the woman of their dreams in Brandy, but she would always make it clear that she wanted nothing to do with sea life, nor did she want to pine away at home waiting for a sailor to return. Other suitors over the years from different stations in life around the island tried their hand at winning her affection, but Brandy always found them to be lacking. Skynyrd was worried that she would never find a companion. Not a few women her age around the island were already experiencing the joy of being a grandmother.

It's 4:00 p.m. on a warm June day and the Caribbean sun is setting in the western sky, giving the crystal blue waters of Kingston Bay a beautiful sparkle. Brandy stands at the edge of the balcony on the second floor of her uncle's tavern, folding towels and bedsheets she's taken in from drying in the breeze. *Katrina's Tavern* has ten rooms for hire on the second and third floors. She and some other girls who work in the tavern take turns caring for them and the patrons who occupy them. They are comfortable and clean, having a bed, night table, two chairs, a small sofa, wash table with a jug of fresh water, and a bowl for shaving and cleaning.

Outside in back and fenced in around a small courtyard, there are three sets of outhouses and two shower stalls that, if paid for in advance, can be supplied with several buckets of heated water. The tavern's rooms are usually occupied by ship's officers who can afford to pay Skynyrd's prices for the accommodations. They currently occupy five of the ten rooms, and the tavern below is already starting to fill up as the exotic Asian-style music Zhang Yong is playing on his harp-like instrument draws in curious sailors. Brandy finishes folding the last of the bedsheets and hands them to one of the girls who works at the tavern with her. "Davonte, please take these to the rooms not occupied and make them up with fresh water and towels in each. Thank you."

"Right away, Mistress Brandy," the dark-skinned Jamaican girl answers with a sweet smile.

Brandy smiles back. "Davonte, remember to get some supper from the kitchen before you go to serve tables. Something tells me it will be a long night. Every berth in the harbor has a ship in it. A lot of hungry and thirsty sailors will be headed our way."

"Yes, Mistress Brandy. Thank you!" She curtsies and heads off.

Brandy grimaces. "Davonte, please just call me by my name. You're not a slave anymore. You're a legitimate employee of my uncle Skynyrd and no one's property."

Davonte grins from ear to ear, exposing brilliant white teeth. "I know, mistress ... uh, I mean Brandy. Old habits die hard. I'm working on it."

Brandy turns her head away as she shudders from the old guilt of having profited for the first half of her life off terrible institutions like the buying and selling of human beings. She walks over to the stairs on the side of the building leading to the fourth floor where there are two small apartments—one she occupies and the other her Uncle Skynyrd occupies—and raps loudly on his door. She heard Skynyrd return home late last night after she closed *Katrina's* down for the evening. He had been away for two weeks and she is eager to talk to him about his trip.

"Come in, Brandy."

She pushes the door open and sees Skynyrd over by his washing bowl with his head and face lathered up with shaving soap. He is finishing up with his face and beginning to shave his head. The long-handled razor blade in his right hand is expertly gliding over his skin as he pulls his skin taut with his left hand. Brandy says nothing when she steps in. She always enjoys watching Skynyrd shave himself. He had gotten so good at it that during the day, before he opens *Katrina's*, he would do some barbering for some of the ship's officers who stayed at his inn.

He looks up with that twinkle in his eye that Brandy so loves. "You still like to watch your pathetic old uncle shave off all of his beautiful blond hair every morning, don't you, girl?"

Brandy giggles. "That I do, Uncle. But how do you know it's still blond? It's been so long since you've seen any amount. For all you know, you could be a gray-headed, decrepit old man and not even know it." Before she can react, a wadded up wet towel hits her in her face. She grabs it, hauls it back and gets ready to return it to him in like manner.

Skynyrd holds up a stalling hand. "Hold on there, Brandy. Wrap that around your neck and shoulders. I am seeing some red roots."

Brandy sighs and sits down on a stool. Skynyrd finishes up with his shaving and grabs a bowl of black dye from the shelf by his cleaning bowl. He brushes the dye into her scalp and then begins to knead it in with his fingers. "Are you going to ask me about my trip or not?" he says as he finishes up.

"I knew you'd get around to telling me. So, go ahead and tell me how another poor, pitiful crew member of *The Red Witch* came to an untimely end for shooting his mouth off," Brandy says with a sulk in her voice.

"Now, come on Brandy, that not be fair. The last time I had to do anything like that was almost eight years ago and that son of a whore tried to kill me first. This last one was just a scared little man who got drunk in a tavern in Barbados and was talking about how the Scarlet Mistress cursed him all those years back, and he would find a member of her family and get relieved of that curse. Most of them who heard him didn't believe a word, anyway. But when that mate on that merchant ship that stayed here last month mentioned it in the tavern, I knew I had to check it out. That braggart was still at that same inn when I got to Barbados. He and I just took a long walk and had a pirate's heart-to-heart conversation. He did not recognize me like the other did. I got him signed on with a merchant ship headed to the Far East. I told him that as long as he stays out of these waters, the curse could not affect him."

Brandy walks over to the mirror, looks for any black dye on her skin and wipes it off with the towel. She takes the towel and throws it in Skynyrd's fireplace, which he immediately sets to flame, and they both watch it burn. "So, no one got killed because of me, then?"

"No one, Brandy. I promise."

"I wish *The Red Witch's* crew would just desert that cursed ship and burn it into the sea. All it is anymore is a slaver. I've heard that more slaves die on *The Red Witch* than any other ship from Africa. If the crew is waiting for someone like me to come and claim her, then they'll all die of old age."

Skynyrd takes the bowl of black dye off his shelf and puts it in a secret compartment behind his mirror. He places both hands on his niece's shoulders. "Lomoche has grown powerful under Regional Governor Bennets. Those left of *The Red Witch's* crew have no loyalty for either man. I don't know if any rumors of you being alive have reached those black-hearted devils, but we must be careful. As for the crew that's left, we can only pray that they keep their oath to your mother. But like the sailor I caught up with in Barbados, every one of them has his limits of what he can endure. Lomoche be reminded every time he looks in the mirror what the daughter of Captain Erasmus did to him. I hear he takes that hook he wears for a hand and likes to torture young girls that have red hair with it. He takes his eye patch off and makes them stare at his empty right eye socket. He be as crazy as they come, Brandy, and he has all of Bennets's men and ships to back him up. If he thought for one moment that you were alive, he'd sack this whole port looking for you."

The old rage erupts in Brandy's core, as she thinks of what Lomoche is doing to young girls because of her. But she sees the fear and concern in Skynyrd's eyes. She reaches up, clasps his hands and brings them to her lips and kisses them. "He will never find out, Uncle Skynyrd. We have been hiding in plain sight right under his nose all these years. Thank you for taking care of the sailor in Barbados. Now, get ready—the port is full, and lots of sailors will want to indulge themselves with Skynyrd's famous stews tonight."

Brandy walks out, leaving Skynyrd to ready himself for the evening. He puts on his cooking trousers and shirt, wraps a scarf around his bald head, and heads down to the kitchen to see if the shrimp and crabs he smells boiling are ready for him.

Chapter 3

Someone New

Three Hours Later in *Katrina's* Main Dining Room

Brandy walks into the kitchen area and sees her Uncle Skynyrd talking to two of the governor's personal guards. Skynyrd catches Brandy out of the corner of his eye and quickly hands one guard a pouch of coins. They take it and leave out the back way. Brandy steps up and begins to say something, but Skynyrd holds up a hand to stop her. "Brandy, don't give your poor old uncle any more grief than he already has. The last thing you or I need is any attention from Governor Bennets or Lomoche. I'll pay their taxes, and we'll keep our heads down. That be the end of it."

Brandy gives a huff, grabs her serving apron, and heads to the dining room. As she predicted, the dining room is packed with sailors. In fact, it is so full that some are waiting outside for room to come in. Zhang Yong's music is now being backed up on the piano by an older, chubby-looking man with a peg leg and a sweaty face and neck, who is doing his best to keep up and in tune with the expertise of the Chinese minstrel he is endeavoring to accompany. To make up for the lack of harmony, Zhang breaks into a song he sings in Chinese. It has such a catchy rhyme to it that half of the patrons endeavor to sing along with him while clapping their hands and pounding their mugs on the tables. Brandy, Davonte, and two other girls are doing their best to keep up with the sailors' appetites and thirst. Skynyrd yells from the kitchen that he only has two more pots of stew left and then the patrons will just have to make do with bread, cheese, fruits, and drinks.

Brandy notices a new group of sailors making their way to a recently vacated table. She has always prided herself on being able to pick out a ship's captain in a crowd. In this group, it's easy. The man is about sixty years old with graying hair, piercing sharp but kind gray eyes, and a deeply tanned and sea-burned face accentuated by a grandfatherly smile. He carries himself with the decorum of a military officer that suggests he's been more than a merchant ship's captain. He and three others take their seats at the table. She is about to make her way over to ask them what they would like when she feels a hand on her shoulder and a deep, British-accented voice says in her ear, "Pardon me, miss, I just want to join my shipmates over there."

When she turns to see who it is, her pulse jumps a beat as she looks up into the purest blue eyes she has ever seen. He is about as tall as her father was and similarly built, with massive shoulders and strong arms and hands. He has nicely groomed dark hair, is clean-shaven, and has a ruggedly handsome face that is tanned and weathered, suggesting that he has also seen many a year on the open sea. The sailor slips by her, momentarily pressing his body against hers. They awkwardly smile at one another and when the man gets past her, he looks at her and says, "Oh, miss, just bring five ales and five bowls of whatever that intoxicating aroma belongs to that is coming from the kitchen. Thank you!"

Brandy acknowledges the order and heads over to the bar to prepare it.

The older man that Brandy guessed was a ship's captain looks up from his companions seated at the table with him and stands, smiling as he grasps the new arrival's hand. "John Edwards, I hoped you would join us tonight." He motions for the man to sit. "I've heard that the stews here are the best on the island, and the entertainment so unique that you, having served in His Majesty's Navy and travelled to the Far East, may be one of the few that have heard its like."

John returns the handshake and takes a seat. "Thank you, Captain Joshua. I took the liberty of placing our orders with that tall, dark-haired maid as I came in."

Captain Joshua leans back in his chair and takes a deep draw on his mahogany pipe filled with rich, dark, Cuban tobacco. He swirls the smoke around in his mouth and throat a little and then puffs it out. "That would be the one I hear is named Brandy. Your mates here tell me she's the niece to the owner and chef. I'm told she is the most beautiful barmaid on the island. Be careful, John. They say many a sailor has had his heart broken by that one."

To cover for the slight blush, he feels coming to his cheeks, John pulls out his own pipe. He takes the same dark tobacco, stuffs it in the bowl and uses the candle on the table to ignite it. "Please, Captain, I just passed the poor girl coming in. I assure you, flirting with her, I was not."

John sees that his captain and mates are all about to laugh at him. He is about to say something when he hears a voice from behind him.

"Five ales and five bowls of Skynyrd's stew. That will be ten schillings, three pence. The schillings are for the ale and stew, the three pence is what I charge all sea bachelors for flirting with me."

John's face is now as red as the fires of Hades. He turns and once again sees the tall, dark-haired maid. As he stands to help her pass out the bowls and cups, Captain Joshua and his mates burst out in hysterics.

This time he realizes what a true beauty she is. Her striking green eyes and full smile have a hypnotic effect on him that he can't remember ever experiencing before. Behind her is an equally beautiful, dark-skinned girl, helping to carry the order to the table. John pulls out his coin purse, counts out eleven schillings, and hands them to Brandy. "Please split the last between the two of you, and pardon my friends. They love to have a good laugh at my expense."

Brandy bobs a curtsy with a devious twinkle in her eye. "And who might you gentlemen be, and where have you sailed from?"

John takes off his cap, holds it to his chest and bows his head. "John Edwards, first mate of *The Morning Star*, at your service, most recently sailed from Miami, Florida. This is my captain, Arthur Joshua. These other rascals are the second and third mates, Tom Roberts and Jacob Hind. And this young man here is our midshipman, Ralphie Austin."

"Welcome to *Katrina's*, sailors. Enjoy yourselves. Zhang Yong is in rare form tonight and will probably play till past the stroke of midnight. To keep this table, you must keep your glasses or bowls filled. Once we're out of stew, we have plenty of bread, cheese, and fruits. Davonte or I will drop by from time to time to see if you need something."

All five men raise up halfway in their seats and thank her and Davonte.

Heading back to the bar, Brandy looks over at Davonte. "If there were more sailors with their manners in this world, it might tempt me to go back to that life myself."

"He is a dreamy-looking bloke, Missy Brandy. I didn't know you were a sailor!"

Brandy swallows down a choke. "My father was a ship's captain when I was a little girl. My mother and I sailed with him most of the time. Mother said it kept our family close. When they died at sea, my uncle brought me here."

Davonte's eyes go wide with concern. "I am so sorry, Missy Brandy! I didn't mean to pry and bring up bad memories. How did they die, if you don't mind my asking?"

Brandy turns her head and solemnly smiles. "Pirates," she replies, and goes back to serving other tables.

John Edwards can't decide what is more intoxicating—the stew he is eating or the beautiful and witty barmaid who just served it. He, like his captain, has spent a considerable time in Her Majesty's Royal Navy. John has seen thirty-eight summers, and seventeen of them were as an officer aboard a British warship. Having sailed on all seven seas, he has eaten many a fine dish in his day and known many beautiful women, but nothing matches the stew his taste buds are now devouring and the woman who just served it. Lost in his daydreaming, he barely hears Captain Joshua's question. "John, how are our passengers faring?"

He shakes the reverie from his mind and looks up. "Oh, fine, Captain. They are being fed as we speak, although our galley cannot produce a meal the likes of the one we are enjoying now. Half the crew are on shore leave and the other half are staying aboard *The Morning Star*, seeing to their needs. Our guests should bed down soon. I had extra blankets brought out for the mothers and babes in case a chill sets in from off the sea at night."

Captain Joshua takes his pipe from his mouth. "Thank our Lord God in Christ's name that they are safe from their wretched masters now." He looks around the table and bends in close. "These are slave-free waters, and we should have no trouble caring for them, but never doubt the hypocrisy or the greed of men. They will not truly be safe until we have delivered them to the Maroon they are destined for. Far too many English businessmen still profit from the selling of human beings for slavery. We must be circumspect and vigilant to make safe our guests until we can get them to their new homes."

The other four men lift their mugs and say in unison, "The faith of our Lord Jesus Christ give us strength. Amen."

When they set their mugs down, a gasp and a woman's screech are heard. John turns around and sees the dark-skinned barmaid who helped serve them earlier being harassed by a large sailor at another table. The man is pulling on her arm and she is crying as she pleads, "Please sir, I must get back to my duties."

He answers, "Ah, come over here, you black wench, and warm my lap like you were made to do. I've been out to sea for over a year and am in need of some caring for."

Zhang Yong and Brandy drop what they are doing and make their way to the altercation. To their amazement, the sailor whom Brandy met earlier gets there before them and confronts the obnoxious sailor harassing Davonte.

John walks up behind the man, grabs his shoulder, and spins him around in his chair to face him. In the spin, Davonte breaks away from his hold on her and retreats to Brandy and Zhang. John's blue eyes take on a dangerous steel as he points his finger in the man's face. "That was a lady you were manhandling there, lad. I don't allow the mistreatment of a lady in my presence. Apologize to her now and show respect."

The sailor, a blond-haired man with a full beard and mustache, pushes his chair back as he stands. He is almost half a head taller than John. He looks down at his companions, then points at John, guffaws, and says in an accent that suggests he is from the Louisiana Territory of the United States, "You should mind your own business, English. I'm just trying to give this litter nigger girl a chance to do what she was born to do—take care of a superior man like me!"

He throws his head back and laughs, but before he can let out a breath, a large hand shoves into his throat, and steely fingers wrap themselves around his neck. John leans forward and shoves the man up against the wall, and then with the hand that is wrapped around his throat, lifts the man off the floor and slides him up the wall almost a foot. With his other hand he sticks his index finger in the man's face. "Lad, if you do not apologize to the young lady, I'll break your worthless neck."

The sailor is holding on to John's arm with both hands, and his eyes look like they are about to explode out of his head. He can barely breathe but spurts out, "I am sorry, miss!" At that, John tosses the man sideways away from him, and he lands with a thud and rolls across the floor. By this time, the tavern is silent as all eyes are on John and the sailor he just threw to the floor.

Skynyrd heard the commotion from the kitchen and steps out just in time to see John pin the man to the wall and then throw him to the floor. He makes his way toward the altercation but is caught by Brandy, who tells him what just happened. He first looks over at Davonte to make sure she is all right and then proceeds over to the scene of the incident. He looks down at the blond-haired man and says, "If you and your mates here clear out right away, I won't call for the constables."

The blond-haired sailor stands up and motions for his mates to go with him. He then looks menacingly over at John. "I'll see you again, English!"

John stares back. "I sincerely hope so. I truly felt held back here in this gentle establishment. Another time and place with no restraints would serve my tastes famously." John then turns to Skynyrd. "Forgive me for my rashness. I can't abide a man treating another human being like a piece of property, and especially if that person is a lady. I will pay for any damage I caused to your establishment."

Skynyrd stands there for a moment and looks at this man with a bit of astonishment in his eyes, but then a huge grin manifests itself across his face. He walks over and puts his arm around John's shoulders. He then shouts to the whole crowd in the tavern, "Now here is a gentleman whose mum raised him the right way, and he is still remembering the lessons. Brandy!"

"Yes, Uncle Skynyrd?"

"See that our friend here … what's your name, boy?"

"Uh, John Edwards, sir."

Skynyrd laughs and pats him on the back. "John Edwards and his companions do not see the bottom of their bowls or their mugs as long as they stay at *Katrina's* this evening."

Brandy's green eyes sparkle with delight as she puts both fists on her hips and feigns indignation as she loudly exclaims, "Well, thank you very much, Uncle Skynyrd! You just went and took away the best tipper Davonte and I have had in as long as we both can remember." She reaches in her apron pocket, pulls out a coin and says, "He already gave us a whole schilling to split for a single round of ale and stew. We both would be as lucky as an Irish leprechaun if any of these other cheap, seagoing braggarts squeeze out over one or two pence the whole night." The entire tavern bursts out with laughter.

John reseats himself with his captain and shipmates. Captain Joshua leans toward him and says, "Nicely done, John. Standing up for a lady is always the right thing to do."

Before he can respond, a hand touches his shoulder, and he turns to see the barmaid, Davonte, standing behind him. "I just wanted to thank you for your kindness over there, sir." She reaches up and wipes a tear from her eye. "Before coming to work for Skynyrd and Missy Brandy, I did not know white folk could be so nice to my kind."

John places a hand on her shoulder and looks deeply into her eyes. "Oh, Davonte, I only stood up for your rights. It was the only moral choice to make."

Before she can respond, Captain Joshua stands up and says, "My first mate here knows that we are all equal in the eyes of the Almighty.

Someday, child, there will be a world where His will and love will be lived by all. Until that day, all we can do is speak His truth and stand for what is right."

Davonte smiles and curtsies and walks off, promising to return with more ale. John and his companions settle back into their evening and talk about one another's sea adventures over the years.

Skynyrd catches up with Brandy on his way back to the kitchen. He gets close to her, kiddingly rubs his shoulder against hers and in a hushed voice says, "Quite an impressive man you've found there, Brandy. I have not seen strength in a man's arm like that since your father. Thought those green eyes of yours would pop right out of your head when he hurled that ape to the floor."

Before Brandy can respond, Skynyrd chuckles and darts back into the kitchen. Brandy manages to hit him in the back of his head with a cloth she carries to wipe the tables down. She walks over to where Zhang Yong is getting ready to play another one of his instruments. She stares at him intently and then motions with her chin in the direction of John and his companions. Zhang nods. "That one is fast and strong, and there is no hesitation in his action. He has the soul of a warrior and gives himself to protect those weaker than himself. He made enemies tonight. He may need our help later."

"I agree. We should follow him back to his ship, just in case."

An hour after the incident with Davonte and the blond-haired sailor, *Katrina's* has settled back into its jolly atmosphere. Zhang Yong is now playing a long, bamboo pipe instrument that looks something like a flute, in that it rests under his lips as he blows down into it from a hole carved into the side end. There are also finger holes he rhythmically holds and releases as he blows, but the instrument is almost four feet long and has to be propped up on a chair in front of him. The sound is also much more diversified in range and volume than a simple flute; and with the full, rich, and exotic melodies are having a powerfully positive impact on the tavern patrons.

Brandy is bringing the last of Skynyrd's stew to the table where Captain Joshua, John Edwards, and their companions are all deeply infatuated with a story from their youngest member, Midshipman Ralphie Austin.

"No, I am telling the truth, Captain Joshua. 'Twas the scariest night of me young life. There I am, standing next to John Edwards at the helm. It was a stormy night but not the kind one panics from. Some of you chose not to even get up because it just wasn't that bad. But then out of nowhere it appeared right there beside us. The biggest wave these eyes have ever seen! Ten times taller than the masts of *The Morning Star*, it was. I thought it would take us to the bottom of the ocean that very moment. I look over to John Edwards here for guidance, or at least some comfort in me last moments breathing God's air. He just looks at me, grins, and then looks up at the wave and sees the very top of it crest and break. John Edwards looks up and yells at the wave at the top of his voice and says, 'Calm yourself down, my lady! You got your panties in a bunch and your undergarments are out in public for all to see. Not the kind of behavior one such as you should be displaying!' I swear on my faith in the Eternal Father, that is what he said. Then he takes the helm and turns it hard to starboard and orders us to pull the sails that way as well. The whole of *The Morning Star* then rides up sideways into the wave and follows through the hole as it funnels out and dissipates. Within a few minutes, we were riding on calm seas and Captain Joshua is up on deck in his sleepin' clothes, telling us to stop horsing around because he just fell out of bed on account of not reading the waters properly."

John reaches over and pats Ralphie on the back and smiles at the rest of them. "I think our young friend has had one too many of this fine ale. It was a big wave, yes, but nothing *The Morning Star* and its crew couldn't handle."

Captain Joshua raises his mug. "I will agree with you on that one, John. *The Morning Star* is the best cruiser I've ever commanded, and her crew the finest in the Caribbean Sea, but she needed the best navigator and helmsman on God's seven seas to handle her on that one, and that be you, John Edwards. I've spent fifty-some summers sailing the oceans and I've never seen your like. You feel and ride the oceans like a champion equestrian rides his favorite steed. With a good ship as your saddle and the helm as your reins, you can ride anything she cares to give, and that be my testimony, John Edwards, and I won't take it back." Captain Joshua raises his mug to John and so do the other three at the table. "To John Edwards, first mate of *The Morning Star* and betrothed to her majesty the sea!"

Brandy steps up behind John, carrying a large bowl with a serving spoon sticking up out of it. With a wicked grin she says, "Seeing how he is only betrothed and not yet married, that must mean there is still hope for all of us love-lost maids waiting by the sea, pining away for his blessed return. Oh, I don't know how we'll manage! In the meantime, does anyone want more stew? This is the last."

Two hands go up.

Captain Joshua stands, puts his hands to his stomach and rubs it as he says, "Four bowls is enough for this old sea captain. I'll be heading back to our ship. Any of you lads care to join me?" The other two men who didn't ask for a refill stand and nod that they would. He smiles and looks at John and Ralphie. "Don't keep my midshipman out too late, John. Every time we're at New York harbor, his mother makes me give a detailed report of all his activities whilst with us. Having to be bailed out of the drunk cell of the Kingston garrison is not a report I would ever care to give to her." He walks over and ruffles Ralphie's thick brown hair. "Don't know if I could survive the repercussion of that encounter."

All five laugh as Captain Joshua says his goodbyes to John and Ralphie and tells Brandy it was a pleasure to have been under her care this night.

Brandy fills the remaining two men's bowls and heads back to the kitchen to clean up for the evening. John and Ralphie finish their last bowl of Skynyrd's stew and have another half mug of ale while they talk about more of their sea adventures.

When Brandy is done in the kitchen, she comes out to see that John and Ralphie are the only two left. She looks over at Zhang and then at her uncle and they both nod their heads, which tells her it's time to clear everyone out. As she approaches the two, she catches the tail end of a story in which John and Ralphie dove into the sea, intending to touch a big sperm whale that popped up beside *The Morning Star* one evening. They are both in hysterics at the tongue-thrashing they got from Captain Joshua for their foolishness.

She can't help but be drawn to their enthusiasm and mirth. It intrigues her that someone could spin so many fond memories of life at sea. When she thinks about her own adventures aboard ship as a child, all she can recall is the harshness of life as a bloodthirsty pirate. She steps up to the table with a cleaning rag in her hand. "It is time for all good sailors to leave *Katrina's* pleasant berth and head home to their ship." She pauses and then remembers something. "John Edwards, your Captain Joshua left a deposit of a month's rent for one of our rooms when he entered this evening. Does he still plan to use it?"

"Thank you for the reminder, Brandy. Captain Joshua will be by tomorrow to begin his stay. These days, he can't sleep in another bed whilst his ship is still accessible. We have a delivery to Trinidad and Tobago that he will let us do without him. For over a year, he's refused to take any shore leave and we all finally talked him into it this time around." With that he smiles, tips his hat to her and Davonte on the other side of the room, says his thanks to Zhang Yong and Skynyrd, and leaves.

Brandy gets her towel ready and is picking up the bowls and mugs when she sees a small piece of paper with something written on it. When she picks it up, five schillings roll out, and she reads what the note says: ***To Brandy and Davonte, thanks for taking care of me and my mates. John Edwards.*** She looks up and says, "Davonte, come over here."

"Yes, Missy Brandy?"

"How much did you make in tips tonight?"

Davonte reaches in her skirt pocket and pulls out some change. "Including the half schilling from John Edwards, I have enough to make a whole schilling. This be the best night I've had at *Katrina's* yet."

Brandy takes three schillings and hands them to her. "This has been the best night for both of us, period!"

When Brandy is almost done with her duties, Zhang Yong walks over to her and says under his breath, "I watched them both leave toward the harbor. Five minutes after they left, several men followed them. We need to go now!"

Chapter 4

Night Watch

Harbor of Kingston, Jamaica

John and Ralphie are slowly climbing some steps that lead to the main dock where their ship is berthed. Both have been entertaining themselves with their favorite shipboard tunes. John scrutinizes the seventeen-year-old midshipman and decides that he and Captain Joshua probably should have cut his ale intake off a little earlier than they did. Ralphie almost falls backward and down the stairs, but John's strong hand reaches out and grabs him. "Easy there, lad. We're almost back. Just a little bit further from here, and your cot on *The Morning Star* will give you a warm welcome." He holds the boy by the shoulders and sees he can hardly focus as his head sways back and forth. "Although, I don't envy the whale of a headache you'll have when you wake up."

"At least he will wake up tomorrow, English. But you'll be fish food by then."

John looks up and sees the same large, blond-haired sailor he had encountered at *Katrina's*, now flanked by at least eleven others, all holding clubs and sticks of one form or another. It is illegal to walk through the streets of Kingston with a blade or musket these days, so many a sailor will have some kind of a club on them for self-defense. Unfortunately, neither John nor Ralphie have a weapon of any kind on them. John takes Ralphie and sits him down, leaning him up against a pole. He then turns to the blond sailor and says, "I don't believe I caught your name."

The man bows. "Well, pardon my lack of manners, English. Faustin Reece is my name. Pleased to meet you. John Edwards, is it?"

John moves a step closer, putting more distance between him and Ralphie and closer to his assailants. "That is my name. I thought you were of French descent. Louisiana Territory, if I had to guess."

Faustin sneers, brings up a big club and swings it at John, trying to crack his skull. John steps in and throws a forearm upward to block the club. He catches his attacker's wrist midswing. He crashes his forehead into Faustin's face, then reaches up, grabs the club with both hands and disarms him with a violent twist. He continues to twist around until he has made a full circle, using his momentum to thrust the club into Faustin's stomach. The Louisiana man falls over face first onto the dock and vomits. John, now armed, looks up and steps back to guard his now standing charge, Ralphie, who's still swaying.

"You'll not do this by yourself, John Edwards. I'll be fighting by your side," Ralphie manages to say.

John is no stranger to battle. Whether it be with cannon, steel blade, club, or fist, he's seen his share. Ralphie, on the other hand, has the heart of a lion and could hold his own in a fair fight; but John knows this will be anything but that. Eleven more men cautiously approach the two, weapons raised and bloodlust in their eyes. Two of them barrel into John. He sees the move coming and crashes the club down on both their backs at the same time. One rolls to the side, but the other lifts himself up and swings at his face with a small, black flexible club. It catches John across the cheek and causes him to see stars. He then gets hit on the back of his head and drops his club. He manages to keep himself upright and smashes the attacker in front of him square in the jaw with a powerful right cross. Then he turns to see another attacker swinging a club at him. He pushes himself into the man, gets behind him and wraps his arm around his neck. As he is choking the man, he feels another crash on the side of his skull, and that's when all the lights go out.

Ralphie is sure he will die after John falls flat on his face in front of him. The first of the four men whom John took out stirs and wobbles to his feet. Two men try to pick John up by his arms, and the man called Faustin says, "Take the boy too. We can't have any witnesses. If Lomoche hears we were down here, he'll have all of our heads."

Ralphie hears something zip through the air and one of the men trying to pick John up falls over; then another zip and the other falls as well. He hears a metal chinking sound and looks down to see two metal balls like those loaded into a musket, only twice as big, rolling away. Two more attackers, including Faustin, are hit by the strange balls and fall to the ground, unconscious.

What he sees next is something right out of the storybooks his mother used to read to him when he was little. Two figures dressed all in black vault over the railing next to the stairs. One appears to be female. She pulls out two sticks roughly the size of a small rapier and attacks the nearest man to her. The man tries to fend her off with his club, but her two sticks are swinging and arcing at him so fast that he can't even put his guard up. She catches his club in a downward X formed from her sticks, twists it up and sideways, and then pushes down with a hard jerk. The club falls harmlessly to the ground. She then strikes the man with downward, and upward slashes across his body so fast that Ralphie has a hard time keeping up with her movements. As the man is sinking to the ground, she continues to beat him down. Stealthily, another sneaks up behind her with a similar club. Before he can reach her, the other dark-clad figure dashes forward, lifts his leg up in a sideward arc and hooks the man in the face with the heel of his foot. The man instantly falls to the ground.

In the meantime, Ralphie tries to intervene and fend off the two that attacked John from behind. He engages one and smashes him in the face with his fist; but just as the man stumbles back from the blow, lightning bolts go off in the back of Ralphie's head and he almost falls over. He regains his balance and sees the last two men still standing.

Both men look at the two figures clad in black like they are demons from hell. They throw down their weapons and start to flee. The black-clad individuals reach over to their wrists and pull up something that looks like the slingshot Ralphie used to play with as a boy, but they are somehow fastened to their wrists. They pull out some metal balls from their pockets, put the balls in the leather pockets that are fastened between two flexible cords, pull back and aim at the two running away, and let the balls fly. The two men drop to the wooden dock with a dull thud.

The two clad in black look at one another and nod, then calmly walk over to Ralphie and John. The one who is female bends down and checks John's head for serious damage, then looks over at Ralphie and says in a muffled voice, "He will need medical attention. Do you have a physician on your ship?"

Ralphie shakes his head no.

The female responds. "We need to get him to *Katrina's*." She looks at her companion. "Should I stay here while you go get help?"

The man nods, turns and runs toward the ship. The woman then goes over to John and rolls him sideways in case he vomits from concussion, and then braces his head on her lap. She then looks back at Ralphie. "He will tell your shipmates where to find us."

Ralphie is so dazed by what has just happened that he can hardly think straight. He reaches back, touches the back of his head and pulls his hand forward. His fingers have blood on them. He feels dizzy. He sits and tries to concentrate on the rescuers, trying to figure out why these two seem so familiar—and then it hits him. The female has the most piercing green eyes. After that thought, he falls over, unconscious.

Next Day, Office of Kingston's Harbor Master

Captain Arthur Joshua steps into the Kingston harbor master's office just after the chief administrator, Mr. Sam Dohan, opens his door. Sam is a short, pudgy, balding man in his mid-fifties. As he looks up from his paperwork, a huge grin manifests itself across his face as he recognizes his old friend. "Captain Joshua, what brings you out so bright and early this beautiful June day? I thought you would lounge in your luxury room over at *Katrina's* while those beautiful maids there waited on you hand and foot."

"I had to cut my holiday short, Sam. Have you heard of the incident last night? Someone attacked my second-in-command, John Edwards, and our midshipman, Ralphie Austin."

"I heard of an incident on the dock from a constable as I came into the office this morning, but I didn't understand that it was John Edwards and Ralphie. Are they all right?"

"Dr. Johansson says that Ralphie will be fine. But John Edwards—he tried to take on the whole gang and single-handedly thrashed four before they beat him down with clubs. Now he's in my room at *Katrina's* and they are hopeful he will recover, but the head wound is nothing to take chances with. I left John and Ralphie there, and I'll take *The Morning Star* on her next run."

"Well, I'm sorry to hear that, Captain. How may I be of service?"

Captain Joshua takes a canvas satchel with a royal seal stamped on the side of it and hands it to Sam. "I want you to give this to the next royal message carrier on the first British naval ship bound for London.

King William himself gave me this seal when I served under him in the navy. His niece, Queen Victoria, will respect the seal and receive it. Those men who attacked John and Ralphie last night work for Governor Bennets's man, Don Lomoche. They are slavers, and I think it's high time we stop tolerating a man who owns a company that transports slaves to the United States being our regional governor."

Sam cautiously receives the satchel and places it on the table in front of him. "There is a frigate set to sail this morning, berthed at the other end of the port. I will deliver it immediately."

Captain Joshua smiles gently, places a hand on the forearm of the man, shakes it lightly, then turns and leaves.

Sam puts the satchel under his arm, hurriedly locks up his office and heads out toward that frigate. Sam has only seen a seal like that once before in his long career working at Kingston Harbor. Forty-five years ago, the harbor master gave him a similar satchel containing the news that the King's cousin and regional governor had been murdered at the hands of a servant girl. He can still remember the man telling him that to lose or tamper with a seal of that nature is a crime against the British royal crown, and thus punishable by death. Even now, being much older and fatter, he swears he runs just as fast to deliver this satchel as he did the first one.

Two Days Later, Room at *Katrina's*

John Edwards opens his eyes to a beautiful Caribbean sunrise coming through a strange window. He endeavors to sit up but feels dizzy and lays his head back down on a very comfortable feather pillow. He reaches up to feel the cloth bandage around his head, and then it hits him—*the fight…Ralphie!* He shoots up straight in his bed and, though the motion almost makes him vomit, he yells to no one in particular, "Ralphie… is he okay?"

"I'm right here, John Edwards. Now lie back down before you get sick again and Brandy comes and scolds me about it."

John turns and looks over to see Ralphie sitting up in another bed with his head bandaged, looking at a book. "Ralphie, what happened? Where are we?" John asks. The nausea from his concussion becomes almost too much to bear and he lays his head back down.

Ralphie lays his book down. "Well, this is about the tenth time you have asked me that and the doctor told us you should be getting better by now, so I'm hoping you'll remember this time. We're at *Katrina's* in the room Captain Joshua was supposed to stay in. After you choked out the fourth man, a couple more came up behind you and used your head for batting practice. Apparently, one got me as well, but I don't remember. You got knocked out cold, but I stayed awake long enough to see those who rescued us."

"Who was that?"

Ralphie smiles. "Well, I have my suspicions, but I don't want to bring them up right now. Just know that it was like the stories my mom used to read to me about Robin Hood and the Black Knight. 'Twas two of them and they came out of nowhere, using strange weapons and even stranger fighting methods to take down the remaining cutthroats. Then one stayed with us and one went to our ship to get help. Luckily, two constables showed up and as soon as they saw all the men lying around unconscious from fighting, they blew their whistles. Next thing you know, there were about twenty of them, and then some wagons showed up and collected everyone and took us to the local garrison. That's when I woke up."

John holds up a hand. "Wait a minute, Ralphie. How do you know about the constables at the dock if you were passed out like me?"

"Because when I woke up, Miss Brandy and her Uncle Skynyrd were there with Captain Joshua and some of our mates. They explained to the captain of the garrison what had happened earlier at *Katrina's* with the one we now know is Faustin Reece. The garrison captain said he talked with one of those black-clad people he calls 'The Night Watch,' and they explained how we were attacked and that when they got there, Faustin's men were trying to kill you. Later, Dr. Johansson showed up and examined both of us. He said I would recover quickly, but that you needed to stay in bed for at least a week before he can tell what kind of damage all those blows to the head did to you. Captain Joshua decided that I should stay with you, and he didn't want you or me to have to stay in some overcrowded hospital, so he asked Miss Brandy and Skynyrd to look after us until he gets back in three months."

John sits straight up in his bed. "Three months! We were only supposed to drop off the passengers at Trinidad and Tobago and then head right back here. That's three weeks at sea, one month at best!"

Ralphie sheepishly stands, walks over to John's bed, picks up a bucket beside it and holds it out to him, expecting that John will upchuck any second. "I'm sorry, John. Captain Joshua decided that he would sail down the South American coastline and look for another Maroon site to take on more of our future passengers. Plus, you know how bad the captain wants to find his wife and daughter. I think he's given up hope that they are here on the island and wants to look in other Maroons. That's what the extra two months are for."

John grabs the bucket and heaves, but to his astonishment hardly anything comes up.

Brandy steps into the room with fresh towels. "It's not surprising your stomach is so empty, John Edwards," she says. "You've been here going on two days and haven't eaten a thing,"

Davonte is behind her with a fresh bucket of water. Both women go over to John and help him get settled down and lay him back on his pillow. Brandy looks over at Ralphie. "Since you're the one who got him all worked up, take that bucket out back and clean it up and get me more of that elixir of his to settle his stomach down. Dr. Johansson said he needed to get some fluids back in his body and that once he wakes up, we can use the elixir to keep him from throwing up again."

As he leaves, both girls can hear Ralphie say, "I took a good crack on the head too, you know. Don't see the two most beautiful women in Jamaica fawning all over me. No. Everywhere *The Morning Star* berths, it's always John Edwards they have their hairs in a hissy over."

Brandy smiles at Davonte. "Did he just call us the two most beautiful women in Jamaica?" They both giggle. Brandy looks down at John and sees he has already dozed off again. She takes the elixir, props his head back and uses her fingers to squeeze both sides of his cheeks so that his lips part a little, then she lets half a dozen drops of the thick liquid fall on his tongue. She puts her hand around his chin and turns his head back and forth, acting like she is inspecting his face. "He really is a very handsome man, I'll give him that. How old do you think he is?"

"I heard them talking at the table the other night, Missy Brandy. I believe they said he is near forty."

Brandy reaches down and feels his arm. "Well, he's as strong a man as I have met in a long time, and well preserved for his advancing age. I guess I can understand why girls could fuss over him."

Davonte holds her fist to her mouth and bites on her knuckles to keep from laughing out loud. "Missy Brandy, you be thirty years yourself. He's not that much older than you." She then shyly looks out the door and then back at Brandy. "Mr. Ralphie is eighteen and closer to my age. I don't know why he is fussing so much about John Edwards. If you ask me, he is just as easy on the eyes."

Courtyard Behind *Katrina's*

Ralphie knows that his own injury is nothing compared to his friend's, and frankly he's been pretty worried about John for the last two days.

He's glad that Captain Joshua ordered him to stay with him. John Edwards seems to make a habit of keeping him out of trouble and saving his life. The way he took down four cutthroats the other night was something he will never forget. Then those two black-clad individuals that the Kingston garrison commander called "The Night Watch" showed up with their fancy wrist-mounted slingshots and fighting sticks and took out the remaining eight. He remembers now when he got clocked on the head. While John was fighting the second two who attacked him, Ralphie tried to intervene with the two behind John. Both had clubs, and he smashed one in the face with his fist; but the other hit him in the head with his club. He doesn't remember much after that.

While Ralphie is busy behind *Katrina's* thinking about all of this and using the well pump to clean out the bucket, he doesn't notice Zhang Yong come into the backyard. When he turns to head back inside, he sees him standing behind him, staring at him with the slightest smile across his yellowish-bronze face. Ralphie had heard that Zhang had taken off to the interior of the island the morning after he and John were attacked, to look for herbs that might help with their recovery. Zhang reaches up toward Ralphie's bandage, looks the boy in the eyes and says, "May I?"

Ralphie nods and Zhang lifts the bandage to look at the wound on the back of his head. He presses his fingers around the outside perimeter of the gash left by the assailant's club and examines the stitches that Dr. Johansson sewed, then brings his face close to the wound and smells it. He replaces the bandage and reaches in the large pouch he carries on his side and gives Ralphie a small clay jar with some paper on top and a string holding it on like a lid. "When you feel it get itchy up there, apply this ointment. There is a plant that grows on this island that has some good healing properties to it. I made this from the plant. Your wound is mending nicely and there is no sign of infection. The doctor has done a good job with you. How is John Edwards doing?"

Ralphie smiles big. "He woke up a little while ago and it's the most alert we've seen him. He emptied his stomach again when he tried to sit up too many times, but Brandy gave him more of the elixir Dr. Johansson left to settle his stomach. I think he's sleeping again."

Zhang shakes his head and sighs. "Aye, western doctors concern themselves too much with symptoms and not enough with cause." Zhang slaps his forehead with his palm. "When a man takes a blow to his head, his brain sometimes can be jarred and then swell. That causes him to lose his balance." He then places both hands on Ralphie's ears and lightly cuffs them. "There is something here that causes our body to balance. When the brain is swollen, these can become impaired. We must help his brain heal, and then what is behind John Edwards' ears will do what they are supposed to do and keep him balanced. Then no emptying of the stomach and he can eat and regain strength."

"Are you some kind of Chinese doctor, Zhang? How do you know these things?"

Zhang shakes his head vigorously. "No, not a doctor. In English you would call me a priest. In China, I am Shaolin. Now, I go see John Edwards. Come with me."

Ralphie takes a little of the ointment that Zhang gave him, puts it on his head wound and then follows him to John's room. When he gets there, Zhang is already looking at John's head injury. John is unconscious at the moment, and Brandy and Davonte have left the room. Zhang reaches inside his pouch and pulls out a vial of clear liquid. He pours two drops in each of John's ears and massages them by gently rubbing each ear simultaneously. He then places John's head on the pillow so that he is facing straight up, and motions for Ralphie to come over. "Hold his head steady but do not force him to stay that way if he tries to move it."

Ralphie gently braces John's head. Zhang reaches inside his pouch and pulls out several two-inch-long, thin, steel needles and inserts them in different spots on John's neck and head. Curiosity getting the best of him, Ralphie asks, "What are you doing, Zhang? I've never seen a doctor or a priest use those on a sick person before."

"*Zhen ci.* In your language it means accurately poke or puncture. John needs to realign his balance. What I put in his ears will help the swelling, and these pins will help the thing in his ears to bring his body back into alignment and harmony. Hopefully, no more sickness when he wakes up and then John can eat and get strong again."

Ralphie doesn't understand what Zhang is doing, but he trusts him because he thinks he's figured out that Zhang and Brandy are the ones who rescued them the other night at the docks. John Edwards has told him stories of the exotic and ancient sciences that exist in the Far East and how effective they can be.

Zhang waits roughly ten minutes and then pulls the pins out and puts them back in a cloth pouch. He hands the bottle of clear liquid to Ralphie. "Do to his ears three times a day what I did with this. Let Brandy administer the elixir from Dr. Johansson to calm John's stomach as she sees fit. I will be back tomorrow to see if more *zhen ci* is needed."

Chapter 5

Lessons in Life

One Hour Later, Courtyard Behind the Showers and Toilets

One of the kitchen staff told Brandy that Zhang Yong had returned from his trip to the interior of the island and was waiting for her in their training place. Zhang had always been a bit of an enigma to everyone at *Katrina's*.

Five years ago, he showed up fresh off a boat from the Far East and came in to ask for a job as a minstrel. After Skynyrd heard him play three different instruments and listened to his vibrant and exotic singing voice, he hired him. Zhang did not even ask how much they would pay him, just where his quarters would be and if there was someplace private where he could practice his arts. Skynyrd and Brandy had been planning to use the small field behind the shower and toilet facilities to make a garden where patrons could enjoy the plants and flowers. But, wanting to please the new addition to their staff, they helped Zhang build a tall, gated fence and told him he could use that area at his leisure.

Brandy sees that the gate is slightly open, which means that Zhang is inside and is inviting her to come in.

When she walks in, she sees him sitting cross-legged on the ground in the middle of the now cobblestone floor. She walks up to him and stands up straight with her feet and knees touching each other. Her back is straight with perfect posture. She bows her head, puts her right fist in her left open palm and joins them under her chin. She bows and says "Sifu."

Zhang rises from his meditative pose, moves to one side, and exposes two sets of weapons. Brandy gasps with astonishment and excitement when she sees them. One set is the two sticks she used the other night when they rescued John and Ralphie, and the other is a set that Brandy has wanted to own since she and Zhang first started training together over five years ago. Both weapons are the same length and width as the sticks, but they are identical, single-edged swords with exotic ivory handles with Chinese symbols etched into them. Brandy can barely control her excitement as she stares at the master's weapons. "Sifu, is it time? Are you really going to teach me how to use them now?"

Zhang looks at Brandy with paternal pity in his soft brown eyes. "No."

"But why not? Why do you have them lying out here like some kind of ritual?"

Zhang motions for Brandy to sit and then regains his own cross-legged position. "Tell me, Brandy, if you would have had the master's swords in your hands the other evening on the dock, what would have happened to the one man out of the twelve that you engaged in personal combat?"

Brandy's eyes get hard and glassy, the reference to her only fighting with one man not lost on her awareness as she stares right into Zhang's gentle gaze. "He would be dead, like he deserved."

Zhang looks down at the cobblestones and shakes his head. "Brandy, he would not only be dead, but he would have been flayed enough that one could have used his parts as scraps to feed the stray dogs that roam the streets of Kingston."

Brandy squirms a little in her seated position as she wrestles with her anger. "What was I supposed to do? Tap him on the shoulder and say, 'Pardon me, sir, but could you throw that club down and give up like a good old chum?'"

Zhang gently raises an eyebrow. "Oh, Brandy, with all that I have taught you and all that you have come to master since I have come here, you could have easily subdued him with your hands and your feet. Instead, you let rage guide your hands as you wielded the sticks. This is the old training from your mother coming to the surface again. Destroy what is in front of you and move on to the next. You had that man completely at your mercy when you took his club away. But instead of a quick stroke to render him unconscious, you beat him to the ground and kept going."

"I took out a threat efficiently and permanently," Brandy barks back.

"What of the threat behind you that I dealt with? You did not even know he was there, and so you were not even aware when I saved you from getting your head bashed in," Zhang calmly replies.

"That is what we do out there together, Zhang. We watch each other's backs. I don't see the problem," Brandy replies a little less forcefully.

Zhang stands up and walks over to the gate and opens it, but turns before he leaves. "Ralphie is a fine young man. He has much promise and shows a good balance in his life. He is worthy of protecting. John Edwards knows this. Protecting the boy kept John Edwards on his feet and fighting far longer than he should have been able to. When you were being attacked from behind, another was attacking the boy. We could deal with him only after I saved you. Ralphie received a good blow to his head because of my choice to help you first. A balanced warrior will be aware of who and what they are protecting as much as who they are fighting. A desire to defend and protect those around you will help you see and do more than you ever thought you could. Rage only helps you destroy the one in front of you. Decide before you enter combat what will guide your actions. Will it be rage, or love for those you are fighting with and for? We can only find balance in the second choice, Brandy. The first leads to destruction and misery." Zhang walks out and closes the gate behind him, leaving Brandy with her thoughts.

Stunned by his words, Brandy walks over to the two sets of weapons. She looks at the sticks and then the identical swords. She takes both sets and brings them to the little storage shed that contains all the training equipment and special weapons that belong to Zhang Yong's personal arsenal. She puts both sets back in, and as she is closing the door, she notices that the Chinese fan that Zhang has been training her with lately is sitting out and not in its regular place. Zhang told her that the purpose of the fan was to teach her to move with more grace and delicacy in her steps. In order for that flimsy fan to be an effective weapon, one had to learn to be quick, graceful, and more than anything else, precise. The concentration it took to just go through the most basic form with a fan was up to this point more than she could stand, but she knows Zhang left it out for a reason.

So she swallows her pride, grabs the fan, and spends the next three hours forcing herself to execute all those exasperating moves as she goes over and over in her head what Zhang said when he first started to train her with the fan—*"A butterfly can defeat a water buffalo with the graceful beauty of its flapping wings."*

Kingston Garrison Infirmary, Same Day

Captain Arnold Walters is a British soldier, with dark, curly hair, graying at the temples. He sports a clean-shaven face and thick, bushy eyebrows that augment his steely, gray-green eyes. He sits at his desk at the Kingston garrison going over the endless mountains of paperwork that seem to pile up on his desk every day.

Arnold joined His Majesty King George's Royal Marines as a boy of only twelve and spent the first ten years of his life attached to a British man-of-war that patrolled the Caribbean Sea. Most of the time they were simply protecting British interests and colonies in and around the area, but then the War of 1812 broke out, and he spent the following two years fighting the newly formed United States of America. Mainly because of the help the United States received from the pirate John Lafitte and his friends, the Yanks won that war on land and at sea. The British king then decided to put more resources into taking care of what the empire had and not trying to get back what it lost, so they left the Yanks to their lands and went back to managing the rest of the Caribbean.

Life did not settle down after that. Not by a long shot. The constant slave uprisings all over the British-controlled Caribbean Islands guaranteed that he saw much more action after. Though a commoner who never expected to rise above the rank of sergeant in the Royal Service, he distinguished himself in many of those squabbles and received several field promotions. When he was twenty-two, he returned to England as a full lieutenant, and met and married a young woman who was considered above his class. She had family in the British Parliament. He stayed only long enough to marry and impregnate his wife with what he later found out to be a son.

Because of his wife's family connections, he quickly received an official promotion to captain, quite an accomplishment for a man of his lowly birth, but that is the last promotion he has seen to this date. Now at three years shy of fifty, he has not seen his homeland of England for a quarter century , and then it was only a quick two-week stay with his wife and then five-year-old son. His wife refuses to come and visit him and he can never get permission to go back to England and visit her or his now fully-grown son, whom they tell him is now a member of the House of Commons and rising quickly in British political circles.

While lost in his daily musing over these matters, he fails to notice the entrance of probably his least favorite person alive. He looks up and leans back, surveying the man from head to foot. Don Lomoche looks and smells more like a French brothel owner than the infamous, back-stabbing Spanish pirate who betrayed and killed Captain Eric Erasmus, the Plague, all those years ago. One would think an eyepatch and a hook for a hand would make him look more formidable, but with his black mustache and beard groomed and waxed, along with his expensively cut British admiral's vest, a red sash with gold embroidery, fluffy white shirt, white leggings, an auburn set of trousers, and a chest full of medals he would have no idea how to earn; he just looks ridiculous.

"I see you have been rummaging through Governor Bennets's old wardrobe again, Lomoche. Why don't you go down to the docks and see if you can impress some of your old friends with that getup?"

Lomoche scans the room, making sure no one is listening, and then leans in very close to be sure Captain Walters is the only one who can hear him. "I don't go to the docks in Kingston. Too many men down there remember Captain Erasmus, his whore of a wife, and their Satan's spawn of a daughter. Some have gotten it in their foolish brains that if I were to die, the Scarlet Mistress's curse would be lifted off *The Red Witch* and her crew. That is why she is sent on very long voyages to Africa to pick up Governor Bennets's cargo and deliver it to the Carolinas and Louisianan territories. She hardly ever docks at British-controlled ports anymore. What if some of them were to escape from the cargo hold? It would force a military officer like yourself to give them asylum, and our good governor would be out all that profit."

Captain Walters has to force himself to understand that the man is sincere and looks to him like he is some kind of ally. "Lomoche, don't you ever tire of looking over your back all the time? Eventually one of your old comrades will get close enough to put a knife in it like you did to the Plague."

Lomoche stands back, holds out his hook and waves it at the captain in an almost dainty fashion. "Not to worry. Soon, Don Lomoche will be feared and admired. The governor has given me Port Royal, and I have been rebuilding it. I'll bring it back to its former glory, and all the pirates of the Caribbean will look to me as their leader. Then we shall launch out to new territories and new treasures. Governor Bennets says there is much bounty and slave trade to be had in the Pacific Ocean and its exotic islands. It will be a new era of pirate-controlled waters, and we will be a nation unto ourselves."

Captain Walters looks into the half-crazed eyes of Don Lomoche. True, two centuries ago, Port Royal was a pirate's haven—some say the seat of a true, pirate-controlled kingdom in the Caribbean—but that was before the great earthquake that destroyed the entire fortress. Most in the Caribbean took it to be a sign of heavenly justice against the sins and depravity of the place. There has always been talk of rebuilding, but no one has ever accomplished it.

Since being appointed the regional governor over all the Caribbean, Bennets enjoys a great deal of power. After having hanged the infamous Scarlet Mistress, the one responsible for slitting the throat of the king's first cousin and former governor, King George IV knighted Admiral Bennets himself and then promoted him to governor. Bennets took the Spanish peacock Lomoche under his wing and has continued to give the man much power and prestige, both politically and professionally, as a high-ranking official in the governor's court and one of the main administrators of the governor's East Indies Trading Company. Lomoche oversees all of Bennets's dealings as a slave broker and supplier for the southern United States. Although England has outlawed all slavery in its empire, it still allows companies like Bennets's to profit from its commerce.

Walters, becoming irritated with having to think about all of this, sighs. "Don Lomoche, what can the Kingston garrison do for His Lordship, the governor's right-hand man?"

Lomoche reaches up, twists his waxed mustache and smiles, beaming with self-esteem at the mention of his elevated status. He reaches in his jacket and pulls out an official letter from the governor that has His Lordship's seal stamped at the top. "Governor Bennets orders you to release all the men listed on this notice over to my custody immediately."

Walters takes the official document and looks at it for a moment, and then places it on his desk. "Don Lomoche, you understand we arrested these men for public drunkenness and attempted murder. All twelve of them are in the infirmary right now. One is so badly beaten the doctor doesn't think he will survive." He picks up the paper and looks at it again. "Governor Bennets has the authority to release them, but his is not the only authority I answer to. I have to send a monthly report to the Admiralty in London of all the actions that the governor orders the garrison to take. As you well know, the queen may not read every report, but I am told that Parliament takes special interest in them, and that these reports sent in by garrison commanders can cause some heated debates that will likely gain her attention."

Lomoche steps back and holds up his good left hand and points his index finger at Walters, shaking it. "His Lordship thought you might have a hard time parting with the likes of these men. It is interesting that you bring up Parliament, Captain Walters. Your son, William Walters, has gained a lot of power and influence in the House of Commons in such a short time, being the son of the stoic and steadfast Captain Arnold Walters, Garrison Commander at Kingston, Jamaica. The man who rose from the common rabble of the streets of London to such a prominent position because of his military prowess is a great boon to his blossoming career. Why, His Lordship just the other day told me he received a private communication from the boy's mother, your wife, requesting that you be given a more active role at sea, where your military abilities can be put to better use and aid in her son's rapid ascension in Parliament. She promises all kinds of special benefits to His Lordship if he complies. It would seem that she wants her husband to become even more of a hero than he already is."

The sickly-sweet sarcasm in Lomoche's voice makes Walters want to vomit, but he sees the true threat behind the man's words. "More like have me martyred so they can play off the sympathy of their constituents and peers. Take the men in the infirmary. My report will be vague enough that no one in London will give it a second glance." He starts to write out the release order but then stops. "I will not be responsible for the one who is dying. If he dies, it's on you and Governor Bennets. Understood, Lomoche?"

Don Lomoche grabs the signed release from Captain Walters, then turns and walks away. "If he lives, he'll wish he hadn't."

Kingston Garrison, Prison Infirmary

Don Lomoche strolls into the infirmary of the Kingston prison and orders the first person he sees to take him to Faustin Reece immediately. The orderly is well acquainted with the man who is telling him what to do. Don Lomoche sends all the young, red-haired girls he tortures to the prison infirmary, whether they live or die. The ones who die are disposed of quietly. The ones who live are sold into indentured servitude to rich and powerful families that Lomoche knows around the Caribbean. The orderly leads Lomoche to a section of beds at the far end of the long hall of a room where Faustin and his men are being cared for. When Lomoche sees Faustin, he dismisses the orderly and walks up to the bed.

Faustin has been in and out of consciousness all day. The blow he took to his gut from that Englishman John Edwards broke two ribs and bruised him up good on the inside. As he opens his eyes, he sees the one person he has been dreading to talk to since being arrested.

"Don Lomoche, I can explain. We were just down at the docks looking for some whores who ply their trade down there when we were jumped by these two demons dressed in black. They took us by surprise and—"

Smack!

Lomoche hits Faustin across the jaw with his hook and then leans in, puts his left elbow on the man's neck, and inserts the hook down at his crotch. "Faustin, you should never lie to me. I know everything. Your little skirmish with the first mate of that ship *The Morning Star*. How he embarrassed you at Katrina's tavern. That you waited for him to leave and then followed him to the docks. The little demons you're referring to are being called 'The Night Watch' by the city garrison commander. Apparently, they help the local constables out on the streets at night from time to time. Captain Walters refuses to do anything about them because he feels so undermanned. His Excellency, the governor, will not allow us to take any retribution on them because he values Captain Walters."

Lomoche releases his hook from Faustin's groin and stands up. Faustin, now fully engaged, says, "What of the Englishman? Can I still have him?"

Lomoche takes his left hand, twists the pointy end of his beard and holds his hook up, waving it daintily. "Oh, my dear Faustin, he is the only reason the governor and I are not having the lot of you hanged. It would seem that your John Edwards and his Captain Joshua are both former officers of the British Royal Navy. They were highly decorated and retired with royal gratitude. When Captain Joshua retired, His Majesty King William IV awarded him with one of those new Baltimore clipper-style sailing ships. He named it *The Morning Star*. Apparently, Joshua served under 'the Sailor King' for a good deal of his career. They both held the same sentiments about slavery, and Joshua was a huge supporter of King William when he abolished the practice. Now, it appears that Joshua and Edwards are part of the abolitionists' movement. They run with a fleet of ships that pick up and transport runaway slaves from the United States and relocate them to Maroons around the Caribbean."

Faustin is sitting up in his bed now, crinkling his brow and trying to suppress the panic that is going through him. "Am I in danger of being hanged for assaulting a former high-ranking English officer?"

Lomoche can't help but grin. "Why yes, Faustin, you are. You see, First Lieutenant John Edwards was second-in-command of a four-decker man-of-war that served in an armada protecting British interests in the Far East. They even offered him his own command when he announced his retirement. I understand that he was considered somewhat of a genius when it came to navigating a ship. Also, they say he is quite good at boosting the morale of a ships crew."

Faustin, sitting nervously on the side of his bed, pleads with his eyes for Lomoche to throw him a bone of mercy. Lomoche laughs and continues. "All is not lost yet, my dear friend," he says. He grabs and shakes Faustin's shoulder. "Governor Bennets does not want to prosecute you, and no official complaints have been filed against you or your crew. But we need to get you out of here quickly. Your vacation, I'm afraid, is over, and you'll have to return to *The Red Witch* immediately."

Faustin shakes his head. "Please, Lomoche, I can't stand that ship or its crew. The thought of another year of sailing to Africa and picking up all those black devils and bringing them to the United States sickens me. The stench alone is enough to drive a man insane. Then you have all their crying and carrying on down there in those pits we put them in. Can't we do something else? Besides, that crew doesn't respect me as a captain. I feel like they're always looking to put a knife in my back. If it weren't for that curse, they would."

Lomoche stands up and walks to the foot of Faustin's bed. "Faustin, you will take command of *The Red Witch* and her crew, but you'll not be going back to Africa to pick up cargo. Instead, you'll hijack *The Red Witch* and return it back to a pirate ship. Then you'll prey on abolitionists' ships and return the runaway slaves back to their rightful owners in the United States. The governor has already worked out a deal with their owners to pay a hefty finder's fee for their return. Since the governor has control of all British vessels in these waters, even though you will officially be an outlaw, unofficially no ship of ours will pursue you."

"What of any other spoils—like the crew, cargo, and non-slave passengers?"

"Yours, minus my cut of twenty-five percent, which will go to our rebuilding of Port Royal."

The tentacles of greed assuage Faustin's previous fears and his mind races to see if there are any holes in the plan. "What if word gets back to England? Won't they force the governor to send the fleet after us? It was the Sailor King himself who freed all the slaves in the colonies. The whole of the Royal Navy laud him to the sky and they'd take great pleasure in drawing and quartering someone like me just to honor his name."

Lomoche snickers. "King William has been dead for almost seven years now. His niece, Queen Victoria, takes a much more passive role in ruling. Albert, her husband, wants to develop good relations with the southern states. Governor Bennets informs me that there is a schism developing between the North and the South up there. Her Majesty's husband, the true power behind the throne, wants to support the southern states in the coming conflict." Lomoche leans in closer to Faustin and says in a hushed whisper, "If a war were to break out between the North and the South, and England supports the South, it will be just enough so that they win, but both sides will be crippled. Then Albert can send in the full strength of Her Majesty's forces and reclaim the colonies. So, you see, Faustin, our little contribution of returning these pesky runaway slaves to their rightful owners will be seen as a small but contributing factor in restoring a part of the British Empire back to where it belongs."

Faustin is now so excited that he forgets about his injuries, hops out of bed and holds out his hand to shake Lomoche's. "Don Lomoche, I am your man! Just tell me what to do."

Lomoche extends his right arm and uses the hook to lock onto Faustin's wrist. As he painfully presses the locked hand he says, "Faustin Reece, you have always been my man. Forget it again, and I will remove this hand from your body and have you fitted with a hook like mine." He lets go, turns, and walks out of the infirmary, then stops and turns back at Faustin. "The governor's guards will be here within the hour to collect you and your men. *The Red Witch* will be at Port Royal in three days. I have a man in the guard who will explain to you how we plan to get you to the ship to take command. Don't let me down, Faustin!"

Lomoche strolls out of the infirmary to his private carriage, which takes him back to the governor's mansion.

Chapter 6

Friends and Allies

Three Days Later at *Katrina's Tavern*

John Edwards, Ralphie, Brandy, and Davonte are seated around a small table in the middle of the men's room. When Dr. Johansson steps into the room, he is a little astonished but happy to see his patient sitting up and playing cards. Dr. Avery Johansson has been on the island for a little under seven years. At fifty-four years of age, he keeps himself very busy and periodically hikes to different settlements on the island to offer his medical expertise to the more remote regions.

The atmosphere is jovial in the room and the doctor surmises they are all in a heated card game. It appears to be boys against girls, and the girls are winning.

John looks across the table at Ralphie. "That is the third hand in a row that these ladies have stomped both of us into the ground. If I didn't know any better, I'd think they were cheating."

"Cheating! Tell me, Davonte, why is it that when a man is bested by a woman in any category, he assumes that there must be something unnatural or unfair going on?!" Brandy exclaims with a wicked grin.

"Well, Missy Brandy, it might just be as my second momma told me when I was a little girl. She would say, 'Child, you always have to protect the way a man sees himself, as he tends to see himself in how he thinks us women see him.'" Davonte giggles shyly and looks in Ralphie's direction. Brandy notices that both John and Ralphie's cheeks are showing some red blushes.

"Pardon me," Dr. Johansson says, coming into the room. "I hope I'm not intruding. I just returned from the other side of the island and thought I would check in on our patients."

Dr. Johansson makes his way over to John and Ralphie. All four get up to acknowledge the good doctor. The doctor stops John and puts a hand on his shoulder. "Good lord, man, I did not expect to see you up and about this early." He extends his other hand toward the bed. "Please sit and let me have a look at you."

John sits down on his bed, and Dr. Johansson takes off his bandage and examines the wounds. "Well, there are no infections, and it appears to have mended at a very encouraging rate." He tilts John's head back and looks into his eyes, feels his glands around his neck, checks his heartbeat, and listens to his breathing. "John Edwards, I believe we can safely say you received no permanent damage. It would seem that your concussion is gone, and by the way you jumped up to greet me, you're not experiencing any more dizziness or disorientation. Quite remarkable, to say the least."

"Well, it helps to have our own Shaolin priest who knows all about ancient Chinese healing potions and ointments right here at *Katrina's*," Ralphie exclaims as he sits on his bed, ready for his turn.

Dr. Johansson looks over at Ralphie. "Yes, Zhang Yong spoke to me before he left for the interior and said he knew of some ointment he could make to pour into the ear that might help with the swelling and disorientation. He also mentioned a treatment involving small needles. Did he use that as well?"

Ralphie laughs. "Yes. He called it *zhen ci*, or accurate needle insertion. Said it was to align his balance and help his brain heal from bruising. I've seen him do it to John Edwards three times now, and every time he does, he seems a little better."

Dr. Johansson looks over at Brandy. "May I see the bottle of ointment Zhang put in his ears?"

Brandy goes over to the table with the washtub on it, grabs the bottle and hands it to Dr. Johansson. He takes the bottle, removes the top and smells it, then places his finger on the top of the bottle and shakes it once; then he puts that finger to his tongue and tastes it. "Hmm, I believe this has an antihistamine and an analgesic, probably something that has anti-inflammatory properties to it as well. Putting it right into the ear is a bit odd; but now that I think about it, it would get it to the source much faster."

He takes the bottle and holds it up to the sunlight coming through the window, rotating it back and forth in front of his eyes. "This is why I left England in the first place, to discover things like this. The fellowship of physicians ruling council at Oxford University can be so close-minded to new ideas." He brings the bottle over to John. "Well, I spoke with Zhang before coming up here. He said you are due for another dose of this and invited me to administer it for him." He places his hand on John's forehead and tilts it to one side, administers it to one ear and then to the other.

When he is done, Ralphie asks, "Are you going to do the needle thing now, too?"

Dr. Johansson looks over his spectacles at Ralphie. "Good heavens, young man, no! I don't even pretend to understand the science behind that practice. I'll leave it to our learned Chinese friend. Now, Ralphie,

I don't see any need to examine you. Zhang told me you have made a complete recovery. Why don't you go get some fresh air and do some work? It'll be the best thing for you."

Davonte perks up and rushes over to Ralphie. "Skynyrd wanted me to go to the docks and get more crabs and mussels for his stew tonight. I could use some help with carrying it all back. Would you like to come, Ralphie?"

Ralphie's cheeks flush as he cautiously looks over to John as if to ask permission. "I'm a big boy, Ralphie. I am sure I can manage without you for a while, if it's okay with Davonte's manager over here?" John glances slyly at Brandy.

"Oh, so you're all going to put this on me. Well, seeing as how these two have been dying to spend some time together, and I am never one to turn down free help with *Katrina's*—especially the kind that is already paying to be here. Okay, off with the two of you. Oh, and Davonte ..."

"Yes, Missy Brandy?"

"Make sure you stop by the kitchen and get some money from my Uncle Skynyrd to pay for the crabs and mussels. Our friend Ralphie is so enamored by you that if you both show up and you don't have payment, I fear he would pay it himself just to impress you."

Ralphie stares at the floor, trying to hide his embarrassment. "I would not," he mumbles. Then he looks up at Davonte's soft gray eyes and says, "Well, maybe I would."

Davonte flashes Brandy a knowing grin and then turns back to Ralphie. "You are such a gentleman." She grabs his hand. "Let's go."

Both rush out the door together.

Brandy watches the two leave and then turns to John. "It looks like we may have a budding romance on our hands, John Edwards. What will Ralphie's family think of him being so infatuated with a dark-skinned girl?"

John does not hesitate to answer. "Probably that they would like to meet her. You see, Ralphie's mother and father are staunch abolitionists. His father is a member of the New York City council and an outspoken supporter of the abolitionist cause, and his mother is an organizer in the movement. They, like Captain Joshua and myself, believe the Lord God made us all equal and that no man may own another as property or look down on them for the color of their skin."

Dr. Johansson steps up. "I knew there was a lot about you and your captain that I would like, John Edwards. Well, I must be off. John, you need to get out of this room and get some fresh air and a little exercise. Brandy, is there anywhere close that he can go to just stretch his legs a little? Nothing too strenuous, mind you, just a bit to get his blood moving."

Brandy thinks for a moment. "Well, there is a little courtyard behind the showers and toilets that Zhang Yong uses to practice his oriental arts. I think it would be okay for me to take him down there for a while."

"Excellent. Then I am off to the garrison prison infirmary. I'll be back in a day or two to see how you are doing, John. In the meantime, just let Brandy or Zhang Yong administer whatever treatment you may require."

Dr. Johansson briskly exits the room and John sits down to put his boots on. Brandy fidgets impatiently as she waits for him to lace up the standard-issue English naval footwear. When she can't stand waiting a second longer, she kneels down next to him and starts lacing up the other one. "Good Lord, John Edwards. We'll be in our graves by the time you get these things on. I'll do it."

John's pulse skips a couple of beats as Brandy kneels and leans forward to work on his other boot. With his face down, he suddenly finds it within inches of Brandy's partially exposed and rather full breasts. Remembering himself to be an officer and a gentleman, he immediately drops the laces, sits straight up and looks across the room.

Brandy finishes up the boot she was working on and looks up at him. "Are you all right?"

"Uh, I'm fine, thank you. I just felt a little dizzy, bending over like that."

Brandy finishes up the second boot and looks straight into John's eyes. "If you're not feeling up to the exercise right now, you can try a little later. I have a lot of work to get done before we open *Katrina's* tonight. Ralphie will be back in a couple of hours and he can take you down to the courtyard then."

John takes both of Brandy's hands and stands gently. *Those green eyes could steal a sailor's soul from the sea,* he muses, and then says out loud, "No. I appreciate the concern, Brandy, but I really want to get out of this room." He wipes the cold sweat from his forehead with his hand. "It's getting a little hot in here and I need some fresh air."

Brandy gives John an innocent smile. Her mother taught her to pay very close attention to how a man reacts to all of a woman's alluring qualities. She knows exactly why he is so uncomfortable and can't help but acknowledge that this very interesting man has just jumped up another notch on her respect scale. "You are quite the gentleman, John Edwards," she says as she turns and heads for the door.

"Uh, thank you. Why do you say that, Brandy?"

"Never mind. Follow me," Brandy says.

John, quick to respond, stays on her heels all the way to the courtyard.

Brandy opens the unlocked gate to the courtyard and they both step in to see Zhang Yong in the middle, doing some kind of exercise involving slow and then fast hand and feet strikes, sweeps, and brushing movements. He seems to be unaware of the two as he takes his right hand and lifts and cups his right foot in it. He pulls the foot so that the leg is sticking straight up in the air with the calf next to his ear, while maintaining perfect balance on the left foot. He then releases the foot and, with perfect balance and posture, he does foot and knee striking movements, starting high and ending low to the ground. When his right foot is on the ground again, he repeats the same exercise with his left foot and leg.

John gets a gleam in his eye as he watches the Chinese man's astounding control and skill. He leans over to Brandy. "I have seen this before. It's called kung fu, and is one of the most formidable of eastern martial arts. When I was in Hong Kong, we visited a school where mainland monks trained young students in these forms. One of those instructors later signed on to my ship as a cook. He showed me some forms that promoted calmness and tranquility."

"May I see what someone taught you, John Edwards?"

John and Brandy look up to see Zhang standing calmly in front of them with his hands clasped behind him.

"Sure," John says. He steps over to the middle of the courtyard. "What would you like me to show you?"

"Show me the first thing he taught you and then the last."

John steps away from Zhang and places himself in a stance where his feet and knees are touching each other, his hips and legs are straight but relaxed, his hands are held together in prayer posture in front of his face, his shoulders are squarely over his hips, and the crown of his head is pointing straight up. He lifts his arms over his head in a wide arc while breathing in through his nose. As he brings his hands down to about shoulder height, he gently exhales through his mouth and extends his palms forward with his fingers pointed toward the sky. Once they are fully extended, he takes his right hand and pulls it back as far as his shoulder. At the same time, he pushes his left hand to the right and down. While he is doing this with his hands, he is taking his right foot and arcing it back and to the right twelve inches until the distance between his feet from front-to-back and side-to-side is shoulder width. He holds that stance for a moment, then while breathing out through his mouth, brings his feet and hands back together the way they were at the beginning and then starts the whole process over again, this time emphasizing his left side. When he returns to the original stance, he exhales a long, slow breath and bows his head slightly.

The next form starts out the same way but lasts five times longer and involves a series of strong but gentle movements, low kicks, hand sweeps, strikes, brushes, and flowing arcs and twists. When done, he is back to almost the same spot he started from. Brandy is standing next to Zhang while boring into John's face with her fiery green eyes, not knowing whether to be astonished or angry at how much this man continues to surprise her.

Zhang rushes up to John and grabs his arm and pats his back. "How did that make you feel, John Edwards? Your tai chi is superb. The instructor took you through all the pong movements. Very impressive."

John takes another long, slow breath in, then out, and shakes his head. "I feel better than I did a few minutes ago. I had forgotten how invigorating that can be. The man who taught me was named Lee Tong. He was a monk who instructed at the school in Hong Kong. He signed aboard our ship as a cook to gain passage to Borneo and was with us for about a year. The reason he taught me those forms was that I was always complaining about backaches from the constant combat drills we did aboard the ship. The forms really helped with them. I am sorry I left off doing them after we departed from the Indian Ocean."

"You should do that every day, John Edwards. Better for you than *zhen ci* now. If I had known you did tai chi, I would have started you doing it two, maybe three days ago. Tell me, did the monk ever tell you the meaning of the movements?"

John shakes his head. "Why, no, Zhang. He said it was ancient forbidden knowledge, only available to Chinese monks and priests. He asked me to never teach the forms to anyone else either."

Zhang smiles from ear to ear and nods his head vigorously. "That is very good. Now Zhang Yong doesn't have to go to Borneo and scold stupid monk. I can stay here and complete my pilgrimage. Come, I'll show you what movements mean and how to use them in combat."

"Wait a minute. I just heard John say that the monk told him it was forbidden knowledge to anyone but monks and priests," Brandy says, her green eyes boring into Zhang and John.

"Ha! Forbidden to stupid monk but not me," Zhang fires back with some vehemence in his voice but with an equal amount of mirth in his eyes. "Zhang Yong is Shaolin, high priest in my order. I can teach whatever I want to whomever I want. No one forbids me! John Edwards has good balance. I trust him."

"Just what do you expect me to do while you and John dance around the courtyard together?" Brandy says with a little more vehemence than she intended.

"Brandy can do what she always does—whatever she wants. But if she wants Zhang Yong's opinion, the fan is over in the cabinet and needs a dance partner."

Brandy stands there for a second and tries to stare Zhang Yong down. When that fails, she reaches around to her back and undoes the latch to her long skirt, takes it off, and throws it to the side. She takes her blouse and her shoes off. Her undergarments are short silk briefs that barely cover her thighs and a silk top that is cut as low as her blouse was but fits tight around her midsection. The whole outfit has a definite oriental look to it.

She picks up her clothes and takes them over to the storage cabinet, where she finds some slippers. She initially grabs the fan but then sets it down on a shelf of the cabinet. "I will warm up first." She then goes over to the side of the cabinet where some poles and crossbars have been constructed. The first thing she does is get down in a plank position and do push-ups. By this time, she has John's complete attention. She does fifty perfectly executed pushups, then jumps up and grabs the extended pole above her head and does twenty perfect pullups. When done, she remains on the pole and extends her feet and legs in a perfect arc, raising her feet to her hands another twenty times. She hops down to the ground, walks over to the cabinet, and grabs a towel and wipes her face.

John has not moved an inch since she started.

"What are you gawking at? Better get to your ancient forbidden Chinese secret training before Zhang changes his mind."

"Uh, yes, that's a good idea," John says as he tries to get a hold of his pounding heart. *She is the most remarkable and beautiful woman I have ever seen in my life,* John mumbles to himself. He walks over to the other end of the courtyard, where Zhang is waiting for him. He turns to see that Brandy is now waving a fan around while dancing, kicking, jumping, and twirling.

John feels a hand on his shoulder and turns to see Zhang softly laughing at him. Zhang holds his hand to his mouth, nods in Brandy's direction and in a hushed voice says, "She is my student since I live here." He looks to make sure Brandy isn't looking and whispers, "Best student Zhang Yong ever train. But some imbecile before me make her think she has to be strong as a man to fight. The fan will teach her this is not so."

"That imbecile was my mother, and the only man I ever knew that did not fear her as a warrior was my father," Brandy says while still maintaining perfect form and posture in executing her moves. "If she saw me now, dancing around with this silly fan, she would tan my rump with the flat side of her sword."

"I mean no disrespect to your mother's training, only to her skewed perspective. To try only to strengthen one's weakness and ignore an individual's innate strengths is the folly. Men have more strength and power; but women have more agility, flexibility, and speed. For one to attain the state of mastery over any discipline, they must balance the focus not only on what is hard for them, but also what comes easiest. That is all I am saying, Brandy. You have strengths you have not fully explored yet, and the fan will help you see them."

Brandy smiles and nods to Zhang, then continues to finish her forms.

Zhang leads John over to the corner and has him get into the first form position. Zhang steps up close, places his hands on John's throat and says, "Begin." John's hands then come to prayer position and shoot up and out, causing Zhang to release his grip on John's throat. Then when John brings his hands down and pushes forward, his palms meet Zhang's shoulders with one palm on each side, and he pushes Zhang back. When John turns and steps back with his right foot, he finds that his right hand is in a perfect position to grab Zhang's left arm, and that his left hand naturally goes to Zhang's upper arm by the shoulder.

As John steps back and twists, Zhang is brought off balance and is pulled forward, and he trips over John's right leg. Zhang performs a graceful, diving somersault to the ground, which brings him to a standing position facing John. John grins from ear to ear as he stands there looking at his hands and then at Zhang. He is rendered speechless because he was able to execute such a graceful throw using a technique that was originally taught to him to help with his backaches from combat training.

"You see, John Edwards, that is the secret behind step one of tai chi that the monk Lee Tong taught you," Zhang says.

"This is incredible! Tai chi is a common practice all over China, Zhang. Why is it that your priests keep its secret meaning so guarded?"

Zhang squints his eyes, holds up a finger and shakes it in John's direction. "That is a good question, John Edwards. First reason is that when new student comes to a monk or priest for special martial arts training, they already know way more than they think they do. Many times, students are afraid of combat. The fear and frustration that comes with learning something that could get them killed or make them kill another causes much stress in a mind. Sometimes they think they can't do it. When we show them what they are already knowing through tai chi, it makes monk and priest job of teaching much easier. Second reason is that when student come to us, we have them do tai chi and we watch. Those who do it well, we accept as a student. Those who don't, we send home, tell them the warrior's life is not for them." Zhang grabs John's shoulder and vigorously shakes it. "You do good tai chi, John Edwards. Zhang Yong knew other night when you confront man in tavern that you have no fear of combat. You are good student. Zhang proud to teach. Come, I show you more."

Brandy finishes up her set of routines with the fan, grabs her stuff, and tells both men that she will see them later, then heads off to her quarters to get ready for the evening's opening of the tavern. John and Zhang spend the next couple of hours going over the practical application of the tai chi pong movements John knows.

Docks Market of Kingston

Davonte and Ralphie walk up to a stand where a large, bushy-haired man with his back turned to the duo is standing in front of several big, cast iron, square metal boxes that have wood-fueled fires ignited inside. The pleasant aroma of smoked crabs and mussels permeates the entire area. Davonte steps up to the counter. "Hello, Mr. Stine! Do you have Skynyrd's order ready?"

The large man wipes his hands on the apron tied around his midriff and claps them together. "Davonte, I love it when Mr. Skynyrd sends you. Whenever he sends that green-eyed bully of a niece down here, she always gets me for the lowest price. But you are a nice girl and will pay Mr. Stine what his product is worth. Won't you, girly?"

Davonte turns to Ralphie and giggles, then turns back to Mr. Stine. "Mr. Stine, this is Ralphie Austin. He is a midshipman aboard *The Morning Star,* captained by—"

"Captain Arthur Joshua. Yes, yes, I know him well. Served under him when he was with Sir Charles Napier when we rousted that usurper, King Dom Miguel of Portugal, back in thirty-three. Joshua was one of the finest captains in the Royal Navy. They lost a good one when he retired. You know, he was close friends with the Sailor King himself. 'Twas His Majesty who gave him *The Morning Star* eight years ago when he retired. Fastest damn ship in the Caribbean. We are all strong supporters of the work you lads are doing under Captain Joshua, son. Pleased to meet you." The burly old sailor grabs Ralphie's hand and shakes it heartily.

"The pleasure is mine, Mr. Stine. When the captain returns, I'll let him know I met you," Ralphie says.

Stine fills up some baskets with Skynyrd's order. "Yes, Captain Joshua stopped by before he sailed the other day. He always makes sure he comes by old Stine's and gets some of me smoked crabs. Told me he has a new lead on his wife and daughter and will sail down to Trinidad and Tobago to talk to a fella who used to be a pirate on *The Red Witch* back when the Plague was her captain. Don't know what that has to do with Captain Joshua's wife and child, but he sure seemed excited about the whole thing. He's then heading down to Argentina to visit a new settlement down there near Mar Del Plata that may take in some of those poor souls you folks keep rescuing from the United States."

"That's interesting. My poppa and momma left for that settlement in Argentina about nine months ago," Davonte says. "Poppa is a carpenter, and they needed a lot of help to build down there. He'll be paid well.

When they're done, they're coming back, and we'll all live in a much nicer house. That's why I'm living and working at *Katrina's* now."

Stine sets the two big baskets on the table between him and the teenagers. "Well, I think five schillings should cover this order. What do you say, girly?" he says with a twinkle of greed shining in his old, blue eyes.

Davonte pulls out the money she got from Skynyrd and hands it to Stine. "Three schillings, eleven pence is all Mr. Skynyrd gave me to pay you. I'm sorry, Mr. Stine."

The smile drops from his face as he reaches out and receives the coins from Davonte. He starts to say something, but Davonte's soft, gray eyes and bright smile leave him disarmed with nothing to complain about.

He shakes his head, and his jovial smile returns to his face. "At least with Skynyrd or Brandy, I get to have a good arguing negotiation with them before I accept rock-bottom prices for my product. Oh well, off with the both of you. Old Stine's got to whip up another batch before all these hungry sailors head to town." As he waves goodbye to them, it occurs to the old sailor that there was another he recently sold some product to that has those same disarming, soft, gray eyes that could always take the argument right out of him.

At first, Ralphie insists on carrying both baskets of smoked crabs and mussels back to *Katrina's*, but after going about three blocks with the bulky load, he begrudgingly allows Davonte to take the basket that he is convinced is the lighter of the two. As they leave the docks and make the hike up the hill to *Katrina's*, Ralphie pauses for a second to catch his breath. Davonte also stops and sets down her basket.

"Davonte, you said earlier at the card game that your second momma told you how men see themselves in a way they think girls see them. She sounds like my mother—you know, someone smarter than everyone around her. What did you mean 'second momma'?"

"Me and my first momma got to Jamaica fifteen years ago when I was two years old. That was one year before the Sailor King freed all the slaves in the Caribbean. I remember little about the trip over, but they tell me that when we got here, we were sold to a sugar plantation owner. I was told later that my momma was sickly, and she died after a year of working in the fields. The couple who took me in are the ones who raised me. When I called the woman 'momma,' she would remind me that I had a momma and that I should call her my second momma. They said my first momma was very kind and very smart, and that she taught a lot of the slaves on the plantation how to read and write. That's how my poppa does so well as a carpenter now. He can read the posts at the market and respond to jobs like the rest of the craftsmen."

"You don't remember your first momma at all, Davonte?"

She picks up her basket again and walks off. "Ralphie, can we change the subject? I don't want to talk about this stuff anymore, if you don't mind."

Ralphie catches up to the girl. "I apologize, Davonte. I don't mean to provoke painful memories; just trying to get to know you."

Davonte stops and turns. "That's okay, Ralphie. Why don't you tell me about your mother? She sounds interesting."

Ralphie chuckles and rolls his eyes. "My mother—oh man, where do I start? Well, the Good Book says that the man is the head of the house, but sometimes I wonder if my mom ever read that part."

As the two teenagers stroll down the lane laughing, two figures come out of a side alley. They have been following the two since they left *Katrina's* and did their best to overhear what they were talking about with the old sailor who sells smoked seafood at the dock. They are still trying to hear what they are talking about now that they are by themselves. The bigger one looks at the kids, then back at his partner. "So, *The Morning Star* is sailing down to Trinidad and Tobago to drop off those runaways they are carrying, and then heading down to Mar Del Plata in Argentina to look for more Maroon sites. She's too fast for *The Red Witch* to catch her, but I bet Captain Reece can get down there in time to catch her on their next visit."

"What about that stuff old Stine said—that an old pirate who used to sail on *The Red Witch* was in Trinidad and Tobago and had some information for Captain Joshua about his family? What was that all about?" the smaller guy asks.

"Probably nothing we need to concern ourselves with," the bigger one replies. "Stine was probably talking about old Clover, who jumped ship last year. He was one of the original crew from the Plague's days. Those boys are all half crazy for fear of the curse the Scarlet Mistress put on them all those years back. Clover finally got up the nerve to leave, and he must have heard that some heartbroken old sea captain will pay for info about his long-lost family. I bet you he's got himself a nice little story all cooked up and ready to sell for Captain Joshua's consolation. He'll probably believe him too. You know, back in the day, the Plague sank more ships and sold more refugees than anyone else on the Caribbean."

"Yes, until Lomoche put his blade right through the big man's back and took his ship, that is!" the little one says with a cackle.

The big one pats him on the back and they both turn toward the dock where they meet up with a small sloop ready to take them down to Port Royal so they can join up with Captain Reece on *The Red Witch,* which he has just hijacked.

Next Morning, *Katrina's* Courtyard, Zhang Yong's Training Area

Upon waking, Ralphie takes a deep breath and stretches his arms to yawn away the morning fog. His thoughts return to the day before, when he and Davonte spent most of the day and evening together. He is so enamored with the young woman that he volunteered to help in the dining room as a busboy and focused his efforts on helping her keep her tables clean and ready for the next set of patrons to occupy them. He sees that John Edwards is already up and gone. He surmised that he would be down training with Zhang Yong.

As he approaches the gated entrance to the area, he sees John and Brandy emerge with towels in their hands, wiping the sweat away after the morning exercises Zhang had just put them through.

"Ralphie, good to see you up, lad. I've been wanting to talk to you." John smirks, then looks at Brandy. "I think it is high time I resume training my midshipman. Would not want him to lose what little discipline Captain Joshua and I have been able to get through that thick skull of his. Ralphie, go grab your rapier and meet me down here in ten minutes."

Ralphie lets out a gasp of air. "Geez, John, I just woke up. Can't I at least get some breakfast?"

"Maybe if you had gotten out of bed at a decent hour. But daylight is burning, and you'll just have to double up at the noon meal," John says as he turns and heads back into the training area.

Ralphie lowers his head and turns back toward *Katrina's*. Brandy looks back to make sure he is out of sight. She then briskly steps up, grabs Ralphie's arm and whispers, "Drop by the kitchen on the way down and I'll have something you can eat quickly."

Ten minutes later, Ralphie walks into the training area with his rapier and scabbard strapped to his side. He takes the last of the muffin Brandy gave him and pops it in his mouth as he walks up to John. "Midshipman Austin reporting for training."

John Edwards' face is unreadable, save for the bright twinkle of mirth in his blue eyes. He too is carrying his own rapier and steps back in a classic dueling stance and bellows out, "Draw your weapon, Mr. Austin. Basic dueling form one. Begin!"

Ralphie engages in a modified training speed and begins to throw a slash that is met by a block from John, then a thrust that is also met by a block from John. When finished with the two attacks, they reverse and John attacks while Ralphie defends. They continue this for about ten minutes until John steps back and places his left palm on his head as he starts to sway back and forth a little. "Hold on, Ralphie, I got a little dizzy ..."

"Not surprising, John Edwards. For one hour you have been down here with me doing tai chi. And now you want to train? I think you are overdoing it for man who just spent almost a week in bed for a head injury!"

Ralphie and John turn around and see Zhang Yong standing to one side. He walks over and puts a hand on John's shoulder. "You should go rest. With your permission, I will train boy on use of blade." John nods, sheaths his blade, takes off his scabbard and hands it to Zhang.

Zhang straps the scabbard on and unsheathes the blade, smiles, and steps over to Ralphie. "When Zhang agree to teach student, student must commit to Zhang's teachings. Brandy and John Edwards come here every morning one hour after dawn to train. You come at dawn and Zhang promise to teach you Chinese sword combat called Dao. It is basic single-edge combat sword fighting and can be learned quickly. Zhang promise that if young man do as I say, he will become much better sword fighter and make John Edwards and Captain Joshua very proud. Do you agree to this commitment?"

Ralphie eagerly nods, and he can't help but remember the vision of Zhang and Brandy in their black-clad "Night Watch" attire, taking on their attackers so proficiently the other night on the docks.

Zhang says, "This is good. Draw sword and we shall begin."

CHAPTER 7

SECRETS REVEALED, PLANS MADE

Two Weeks Later on the Deck of *The Red Witch*
Near Miami, Florida

Briskett has been serving as one of the first mates aboard *The Red Witch* since Captain Eric Erasmus was murdered. Lomoche only stayed on as captain for the first couple of years. His fear of assassination became an obsession, and he soon begged then-Admiral Bennets to relieve him of the position and give him another responsibility. *The Red Witch* has since gone through a half dozen captains who, for the most part, took the ship and her crew on runs to Africa and back with a new load of slaves bound for the southern United States.

Just a week ago, while anchored out beyond Port Royal awaiting orders from Lomoche, a small sloop showed up and one of the more recent captains boarded *The Red Witch* and told everyone that the ship and her crew were going back to being a pirate ship, He also told them that their first stop would be Miami, Florida, where they were are to meet up with a representative of the plantation coalition in the southern states to discuss a deal.

Briskett walks up to Captain Reece. "Captain, since we are not picking up slaves and transporting them for months at sea anymore, will we be reconverting the lower gun deck back to cannon? Fifteen 32-pounders would make all of us feel a bit more comfortable if we had to deal with any well-outfitted abolitionist ships."

Faustin Reece stares at the scarecrow of a man standing before him. "Who will man those guns, Briskett? One third of the original *Red Witch* crew is dead or has deserted, and the rest of you are like the walking dead. To get a man to sign on to this hellhole of a ship, we have to pay him three times more than any other ship on the seas. These bastards we are meeting with will not offer over a third of the standard price for a slave or for any returned runaways. No, we won't be out as long, but we will have to pack them in to make this profitable."

Briskett shakes his head. "Not all the abolitionists on these waters are of the pacifist Quaker persuasion. I believe you ran into one over in Kingston who put you and your mates in the garrison infirmary. They say that one is a wizard on the waters, and his captain is one of the finest battle commanders the English ever produced. Men like that don't sink easily and they rarely lose a fight. Just sayin', Captain Reece."

A cold chill goes up and down Faustin Reece's spine as he considers what Briskett said. He really does not understand who John Edwards is or even what ship he sails. "Wait a minute, Briskett. How do you know this John Edwards and his Captain—what is it, Joshua—are abolitionists?"

Briskett turns and sneers. "It's called know who your potential enemies are, Captain. Captain Arthur Joshua served under and was good friends with the Sailor King. It was the king himself who gifted him with *The Morning Star* in order to find his lost wife and daughter. It was the same Captain Joshua who led the armada under Sir Charles Napier when they took down the usurper, King Dom Miguel of Portugal, back in '33. His first officer, John Edwards, has a legendary reputation from the Indian Ocean and Hong Kong for being one of the greatest navigators and helmsmen on the seven seas. He too has seen his fair share of sea battle. Now those two battle-hardened abolitionists are sailing together on the fastest ship in the Caribbean, and both of them will probably hunt us soon enough."

"Why do you say that, Briskett?"

"Because, Captain Reece, Captain Eric Erasmus, the Plague, used *The Red Witch* to send the ship Joshua's wife and child were on to the bottom of the sea fifteen years ago. There is a former crewman of *The Red Witch* waiting in Trinidad and Tobago right now to sell that information to him. He was supposed to ship out on a frigate headed for the Orient three weeks ago, but he found out about the money Joshua was offering for the information and stayed to capitalize on the situation. You see, Captain Reece, not only is Captain Joshua one of the best British sea captains alive, but he is also stinking rich. He and his older brother own one of the biggest docks and ship-building houses in London."

Reece steps in close. "What if Joshua's family did not die? You always took prisoners back then. Maybe they were in your hold when Bennets boarded. They processed all those people at Kingston. I could ask Lomoche to find them and bring them to Joshua."

Briskett almost feels sorry for the idiot when he says, "Captain, there was only a handful of people who survived from that ship—an elderly, wealthy merchant and his wife, a couple of young Englishmen, a Scottish farmer and his son, and a half dozen slaves with their children."

"What about this former crewman down in Trinidad and Tobago? Can't we send someone down there to kill him before he meets up with Joshua?" Reece says, his eyes boring into Briskett's.

"That would have been a good plan a couple of weeks ago, Captain, but by my reckoning, they should already be meeting right about now."

Same Evening, Tavern at a Small Port in Trinidad and Tobago

Arthur Joshua can barely contain his excitement as he steps into the tavern to meet up with the man named Clover who guaranteed him, through a messenger, that he knew the fate of his lost wife and daughter. After he and the crew of *The Morning Star* off-loaded their passengers at the Maroon fifteen miles south of their present port, they sailed up here so he could make this appointment.

The tavern is sparsely occupied, it still being only late afternoon, and most of the ships in the little dock are conducting their loading and unloading of passengers and goods. Joshua spots a little mouse of a man sitting in the far corner table. With his face hidden in the shadows, the man's silhouette is all he can make out. He confidently walks over and lets his eyes adjust to the dim light in the corner so that he can finally see the man's features. He can't be over five and a half feet tall, with a narrow chin and pointed nose, a mustache and beard, a red scarf for a hat, and one gold earring in his left ear. Before Joshua can speak, the man gets an ear-to-ear grin on his face that, much to the captain's dismay, exposes a mouthful of rotting teeth.

"You must be Captain Joshua. Pleased to meet you, sir! Me name's Clover. At your service, sir," the man says as he stands to offer his hand to him.

"I thought you were the man I was looking for. Please, let's sit and talk," Joshua says as he shakes the man's hand and sits in the chair across the table from him.

"Don't mind if I do, your Lordship. Care to order some ale? It's not bad."

"I am not a lord, Clover, just a retired British naval sea captain who wants to find out what happened to my wife and daughter."

"Well, you see, Captain, that's just it. I mean, have you ever heard the phrase 'Don't shoot the messenger'? Because what I have to tell you, you probably not goin' to like much."

Captain Joshua's usual kind gray eyes take on a glassy hardness as he leans forward in his chair and bores into Clover's face. "Don't toy with me, pirate. I have been looking for answers in these waters for almost eight years now. What do you know?"

Clover fidgets in his seat as beads of sweat form on his brow. "'Twas *The Marigold* frigate that sailed from London in 1829 that was supposed to drop off its passengers right here in Trinidad and Tobago that you are enquiring about, am I right, Captain Joshua"

"Yes!"

"That frigate was sent to the bottom of the sea fifty mile east of here by Captain Eric Erasmus, the Plague, and his crew of *The Red Witch*." Clover can barely squeak out the information under Joshua's gaze.

"Were there any survivors?" Joshua asks in a very low and harsh tone.

"Yes, there were, Captain, but no fine lady and her daughter were among them. Just a father and a son, an older couple, two young men, and some slaves—two men and four women, three or four little boys, and one little girl. All just little tykes barely out of diapers. No one else."

"What happened to those people, Clover?"

"Well, soon after that is when Don Lomoche stabbed Captain Erasmus in the back and double-crossed us all by leading us straight into the English armada led by Admiral Bennets. The admiral had that whole group taken to Kingston to be processed. They sold the slaves to a local sugar plantation owner. For all the good it did, the next year the Sailor King freed all the slaves in the Caribbean."

Captain Joshua sits there and glares at Clover for just long enough to make the man think that he has breathed his last breath, but then an almost imperceptible smile creases the old sea captain's face and he reaches inside his jacket pocket and pulls out a small cloth pouch full of coins and tosses it at the little man. "One pound's worth in gold coin, as promised." He rises from his chair but fixes Clover with another hard stare and says, "I suggest you get on a ship and get out of these waters as fast as possible. Any cutthroats who had a hand in sinking the ship that my wife and daughter were on are not safe men for as long as I draw breath."

Without giving the little man another second of attention, he turns and walks to the front of the tavern where his second mate, Tom Roberts, is waiting for him. He walks up to the man and smiles in his normal, grandfatherly way. "I do not lose hope, my boy. When we get back to Kingston, I will know the truth. There are people there who know the fate of my beloved Cassandra and Daphne, and I know where and who to look for now."

Tom looks at his captain quizzically. "Are you really going to hunt down all those responsible for sinking that ship, Captain?"

Captain Joshua puts his hand on his second mate's shoulder and walks to the door with him. "As tempting of a prospect as that is, Tom, that is not who I am anymore. The Good Book says, 'Vengeance is mine; I will repay, saith the Lord.' I just want that little weasel far enough away from here that he won't cause anyone else to interfere with my investigation by trying to capitalize on my generosities. Any of the wretched crew from that demon spawn of a ship who are left and breathing need not fear me unless they threaten us directly. The truth is, Tom, that if the Good Lord allows us to have might, it is for defense and building, not offense and taking. Now, let's be on our way. After we visit the new Maroon site in Argentina, we will get you back to New York harbor and your wife and newborn son."

Captain Joshua walks out with his second mate and muses that he will be sorry to see such a confident and reliable officer as Tom Roberts leave the sea to raise his family. But he is also a little excited about the prospect of promoting his midshipman, Ralphie Austin, to third mate and then looking for another young whippersnapper that he can throw at John Edwards to whip into a fine young ship's officer like he did with Ralphie.

Two Weeks Later, Port of La Plata, Argentina

After sailing all the way to Mar Del Plata, Captain Joshua finds out that his intelligence on where there was an emerging Maroon that would give sanctuary to runaway slaves was slightly off. The actual settlement was farther north, toward the capital. He and his crew sail up the coast and find the settlement to be located about ten miles inland from La Plata.

As his custom was when setting up contacts in new Maroons, Captain Joshua would come to the camp with only one of his officers and a representative from another Maroon close by to speak on his behalf. This time, he takes Tom Roberts and an older African man, James Cromwell, the head of the Maroon in Trinidad and Tobago that Joshua just visited and brought his passengers to.

As the three make their way into the clearing where the settlement is located, they can see that the main area is almost complete, and they have already set up several huts and living structures. James Cromwell walks ahead of the two sailors and asks one worker who the head man is. They talk for a few moments and then the workers turn and run toward the main part of the settlement. James waves Captain Joshua and Tom to him.

"How did it go, James? Is the one in charge willing to talk with us?" Joshua asks as he steps up to his friend.

"Captain Joshua, not only will he talk to you, but I think you know him. The one I just talked to says that a lot of the people here are runaways that you settled in different Maroons over the years. We try to take care of our people all over this part of the world. When starting a new settlement, we send word to other Maroons for help with the building.

The man in charge here is a runaway that you settled in Barbados three years ago. His name is Neseem, and he is this way."

Captain Joshua laughs and pats Tom Roberts on the back. "Neseem. Of course, who could forget that rascal? He was a runaway that we picked up off Florida. Had only been a slave for five years when he escaped. Came from one of the more warlike tribes in Africa. You remember him, don't you, Tom? He was the one who had everyone so organized on the ship. By the time we got to Barbados, he had the whole Maroon planned out for them to build. Makes sense that he is here helping more of his people. This should go very well."

"Yes, Captain, I do remember him. He refused to take a slave name while in captivity and kept his African one. The man has a steel spine."

James leads the men in the direction of the workers. When they get to the center of the compound, they find a bamboo structure with a grass roof and four large poles sunk into the ground, but no walls. In the center is a large table with big pieces of canvas laid out on it and hand-drawn schematics of the village they are constructing.

Standing behind the table and using an ink pen to draw on them is the man Captain Joshua remembers as Neseem. The large, muscular African is now looking in the trio's direction and smiling from ear to ear, exposing his mouthful of shiny, white teeth. He steps out from behind the table and walks over to the group, throws both arms out, and embraces Captain Joshua. "Arthur Joshua, my old friend! It is so good to see you again." Neseem pats Joshua on the back and gives him a big bear hug. He steps back and looks over at Tom. "Here is Tom Roberts but where is John Edwards? This will not be a proper reunion without him. Where is that big ape of a man?"

"I am afraid we had to leave John back in Kingston. He got into a little scuffle and took some blows to the head. He should be okay by the time we return."

"Blows to the head, huh? How many men did it take to bring him down? Next to me, John Edwards is best warrior Neseem knows."

"Well, it was John and Ralphie who confronted twelve of them. But after John took down four and I believe Ralphie got one, they got some help from a couple of strangers all dressed in black with their faces covered. They put all twelve men in the garrison infirmary after that. John is recuperating at a tavern called *Katrina's* under Dr. Johansson's care. Ralphie stayed behind to help."

"Four is good. Little Ralphie got his warrior spear bloodied. That is good too. Oh well, I will pray that John Edwards makes a quick recovery and comes to see his old friend Neseem soon! Now, why does Neseem's old friend, Arthur Joshua, come to see him?"

Joshua takes a seat next to the table that Neseem was working on. "We would like to know if you can handle any more people here. Some of our Maroons are getting too full and we need to expand."

"That is what I thought. Yes! We can take one hundred men or thirty-five families." He holds up his finger and shakes it at Joshua. "But if you bring me the men, you have to promise to have an equal number of women here within one year. No way Neseem is warrior enough to watch over one hundred men who have no women."

Joshua shakes his head and muses at what a leader this man is. "Neseem, will you be seeking to rule Argentina soon? I don't see how the challenge of organizing this community will take you more than that year you're talking about."

Both men have a good laugh. Neseem sits next to Captain Joshua and pours him some water from a pot on the table.

Captain Joshua and Neseem spend the better part of the day going over logistics on how they can incorporate new slave runaways into the newly formed community. Tom Roberts takes a self-guided tour around the village with James Cromwell.

When Tom and James get to the main structure in the center of the village, they see that it is almost complete and that it is made completely out of wood; but unlike most of the structures in the area, it has a shingled roof. It looks similar to a church building but without a steeple. As they are about to enter, a middle-age man and his wife come from around the side of the structure and wave to get Tom's and James's attention.

"Excuse me, are you here with Captain Joshua from *The Morning Star?*" the woman asks.

"Yes, I am Tom Roberts, second mate on *The Morning Star,* and this is James Cromwell, a leader of the Trinidad and Tobago Maroon. How can we be of service?"

The woman puts her hand on her husband's shoulder, looks him in the eye, and says, "It will be okay." She turns to Tom and says, "Is *The Morning Star* going back to Kingston anytime soon?"

"After we leave here, we sail back to Trinidad and Tobago and then on to New York City; and then yes, it's off to Kingston. Why do you ask?"

This time the man speaks. "Pardon me. My name is Ben, and this is my wife, Elisa. We are both from Kingston. I came here to help build this new Maroon settlement. I am finished with my part of the job. The next scheduled ship that is to leave from La Plata and go to Kingston is not for another three months, and that will be during the big storm season, during which neither my wife nor I care to travel. The only other thing to do is wait another three months and go then. That is unless Captain Joshua will give us passage. We will pay, of course."

"I don't think that would be a problem at all. We just dropped off all our passengers at Trinidad and Tobago. You must talk to Captain Joshua about payment, though. He rarely charges for passage. Most of our passengers are usually runaway slaves from the United States and we never charge them."

"We are free English subjects and have not been slaves for a long time. We may not be rich and wealthy British sea captains, but we can pay our own way and prefer to, sir."

The vehemence in the carpenter Ben's reply takes Tom a little aback, but he recovers quickly. "I did not mean to offend you. I am sure Captain Joshua will let you pay whatever you were going to pay the other ship. I will speak to him if you like. We'll be heading back to La Plata in the morning, so you must be ready to leave by then."

Ben shakes his head and looks at the ground, trying to get under control whatever is bothering him. His wife, Elisa, says, "Thank you, Tom Roberts. If you could speak to the captain for us, we would appreciate it. We will be ready tomorrow morning to join you."

As the couple walks away, Ben says to his wife in a hushed tone, "How am I supposed to be on the same ship with that man? If Davonte knew the whole truth about that hypocrite, she would never speak to us again for asking for his help."

"Darling, it will only be a three-to-four-week journey. I am sure you can keep yourself busy enough not to have to associate with him. I want to get back to our daughter. We finally have enough to buy that house we wanted. And now that you finally got some training in ship mending, the work in Kingston will be plentiful."

Early the next morning, Captain Joshua, Tom Roberts, James Cromwell, Neseem, Ben, and Elisa are all out at the edge of the compound. Neseem is his usual jovial self as he is saying his goodbyes to the party. He places his hand on Captain Joshua's shoulder. "You tell those people that if they want to be a part of this community, they will have to work very hard. We are building a world for our children and their children as well. Neseem will not tolerate lazy men with lots of pride."

"Free men always work harder when they know that the fruits of that labor mean something and are theirs to appreciate and enjoy, Neseem. No one knows that better than you."

"That is the truth you speak, my friend. I look forward to our next encounter. Hopefully, it will be before the stormy season?"

"If the sea is calm and the wind is fair, we should be back with a full load of eager people wanting to join your little community within two to three months. Good day to you, my friend." Captain Joshua shakes Neseem's hand and looks over at the rest of the group. "Let's be off."

Once all the passengers and cargo are loaded onto *The Morning Star*, they launch from La Plata and head out along the coast northwest toward Jamaica.

"Tom, Jacob, watch the waves as they crash against those rocks and then recede," Captain Joshua says as he points to some high cliffs along the coastline. "The waves will at times go completely over the top of the cliffs, and once they recede for a brief instant, some very sharp rocks that extend some hundred meters out past the cliffs are exposed."

Jacob Hind shakes his head in amazement. "Those are some treacherous waters there, Captain Joshua. One would never know how shallow and close that reef is there until it is too late."

"Neseem told me about those cliffs. The local fishermen named them 'The Devil's Curve.' Many good men have lost their lives sailing too close to that wretched area. You remember that place well, Jacob. After we reach New York harbor you're going to be second mate. It will be your job to keep John Edwards from trying to ride *The Morning Star* up over those cliffs at high tide."

"An order easier given than carried out with John Edwards, Captain Joshua, but I will do my best," Jacob says with a chuckle.

It takes *The Morning Star* three weeks to make it to New York harbor. There, Captain Joshua, third mate Jacob Hind, and most of the other crew have a farewell dinner for Tom Roberts at a local tavern. Tom is joined by his wife, Melissa, and their newborn son, Tom Jr. Mainly because Ben and Elisa came to be very close with *The Morning Star's* second mate, they agreed to join the group. Ben and his wife made it a point to socialize with Captain Joshua as little as possible during the voyage to New York. Tom did his best to make the couple feel welcome aboard ship and tried at times to figure out what the couple had against the captain, but to no avail.

Ralphie's parents, city councilman Robert Austin and his wife, Rebekah, also attend. It was the councilman who procured the tavern for the going-away party. As grace would have it, the Austins are seated next to Ben and Elisa for the festivities. During the meal, Elisa and Rebekah begin to talk. "Our son is the midshipman aboard *The Morning Star*. Have you and your husband met him yet? His name is Ralphie."

"No, Mrs. Austin, we have not had the pleasure. We heard how the first mate stood up for our daughter at *Katrina's Tavern* and was later attacked while walking back to the ship that night with your son. I hope they are both okay by now."

Rebekah takes a big, deep breath, reaches over and squeezes her husband's hand as she fans herself with the other. "Yes, yes, we know all about it. We received Ralphie's first letter three weeks after it happened. Then another came a week later. It seems that he is okay. But poor, dear John Edwards. They said it was touch and go for a while but that it looks like he is recovering nicely."

Ben leans forward. "That John Edwards sounds like quite a man. I owe him a huge debt of gratitude. Few white men will stand up for a former slave girl like he did."

"There are a lot more of us than you might think, Ben," Robert Austin says. "My wife and I are staunch supporters of complete emancipation of all slaves in our country, and Rebekah here is the New York head of the abolitionist movement and Captain Joshua's main contact for this region. Everyone knows he has moved more runaways to freedom in the Caribbean than anyone in that part of the world."

At the mention of Captain Joshua's work, Ben and his wife stiffen, and Elisa's eyes dart back and forth to her husband and then to Captain Joshua at the head table. She leans in and sternly says, "I don't understand what a rich and powerful man like Arthur Joshua is doing all this abolitionist work for, anyway. Isn't he part owner of the biggest dock in London? You would think that after retirement from the Royal Navy he would have stayed there to help his older brother run the family business."

Rebekah Austin is quick to answer. "Elisa, it sounds like you know some things about Captain Joshua. But what you may not know is that his wife and two-year-old daughter were lost at sea fifteen years ago while they were traveling from England to the Caribbean to settle and wait for him to join them. Word did not even reach him until years later that the ship they were on never reached its first stop. Before he had sent for them, he knew that the Sailor King would take the crown and free all the slaves in the British Empire. You see, Captain Joshua's wife was a dark-skinned woman whom he had rescued from a derelict slave ship off the west coast of Africa. They fell in love on the voyage back to England. Even though he knew he could never live in London with a former slave for a wife, he married her. Before he took the crown, it was the Sailor King himself who performed the wedding at sea.

"His Majesty planned to assign Captain Joshua to the Caribbean, where he could be with his wife and daughter for the rest of his service. But then war broke out in the north seas, and the usurper had to be dealt with in Portugal. It took Captain Joshua another seven years of fighting England's battles at sea before they released him from service. It was then that they told him the frigate his family was on was never heard from again. He went to King William in his last year as king and demanded an explanation. His Majesty was very remorseful for his lack of communication with his favorite captain, and he gifted him with his fastest ship and told him to take it and find out what had happened to his family.

"Arthur Joshua enlisted the help of John Edwards, whose father worked for Joshua, and they set out to find what had happened to his beloved family. While searching every Maroon settlement in the Caribbean, he contacted us in the abolitionist movement to see if we could find out if his family was somehow brought here to the United States and sold as slaves. It was almost immediately after seeing the horrid things that are done to slaves that Captain Joshua and John Edwards offered the services of *The Morning Star* to help in our cause. Since coming here, he has refused to take any money from anyone for his help, and he has never given up hope that he will know the truth about what happened to his wife and daughter."

Stunned to the core and with a quiver in her voice, Elisa asks, "So, you say that Captain Joshua did not even know that his family went missing until seven years after they did? How could anyone keep that from a man?"

"The Sailor King was better than most, but he was not perfect. He himself had to leave his first wife and ten children when he took the crown. High English society would not tolerate his marriage to a common actress; so, he divorced her, labeling his children as bastards, and then he married his cousin to legitimize his royal inauguration. Captain Joshua was one of the finest commanders in the Royal Navy and the king needed victories to win over parliament and the people. Throughout his seven-year reign, William, the Sailor King, kept the captain very busy fighting his wars. Before he died, he repented for what he had done and tried to make amends by giving Arthur Joshua a means to find out what had happened to his family. God be thanked that he did, for Captain Joshua and the crew of *The Morning Star* have since proven to be true champions in the abolitionist cause in the new world."

Ben and Elisa look into each other's eyes and nod their heads, then they politely excuse themselves from the table and exit the inn to walk back to the harbor where *The Morning Star* is docked. The next day after they launch, the couple spends the whole day in their cabin, only leaving to get food or use the facilities. Three days at sea go by and the couple finally ask to have a private meeting with Captain Joshua, and he agrees to meet with them after supper that night.

Ben and Elisa go up to the captain's cabin and rap on the door. He invites them in and asks them to have a seat. Ten minutes later, a frantic, pale-faced Captain Joshua rushes out of his cabin and hurriedly makes his way to the helm, where newly promoted second mate Jacob Hind is at the wheel. Joshua grabs the man by his shoulders and says, "Jacob, at best speed, how fast can we make Kingston?"

Jacob, stunned by the sudden and out of character interruption from his captain, grabs his wits and responds. "With fair winds and calm seas, three weeks, Captain. Why the rush?"

Joshua releases the man and leans heavily on the wheel, looks down at the deck, and shakes his head as he wipes a tear from his eye. "My God in heaven. Everything I sought was right there in front of me. and I could not see it. I need to get back. I need to tell her everything …" Captain Joshua's kind, gray eyes go glassy and unfocused as he clutches his chest with both hands and collapses. Jacob catches his arm and eases him down to the deck as he orders some men to come and help. Before Joshua loses consciousness, he looks up at Jacob and says, "Get me to her, Jacob. Promise me you'll get me to my daughter as fast as possible."

CHAPTER 8

All the Evil that Men Do

Three Weeks Later, Office of Regional Governor Bennets

Governor Christopher Bennets sits behind his eighteenth-century French Kingwood Ormolu Bureau Plat Desk, drinking his evening cherry and talking to Don Lomoche and Admiral Robert Thompson, commander of the British naval forces in the Caribbean.

Thompson shows a slight bulge at his waist and two bright red cheeks that show he has spent the last fifteen years since Bennets promoted him from ship's captain to admiral dulling his senses with brandy and other spirits. When he helped Admiral Bennets hunt down *The Red Witch* and hang the Scarlet Mistress, he has since enjoyed Bennets's gratitude. The price of staying in the governor's inner circle was to turn a blind eye to all his business dealings in the slave trade that still illegally goes on in British-controlled Caribbean waters. But now Bennets is suggesting nothing less than treason should the plan being discussed ever come to light.

"Governor Bennets, giving Lomoche control of Port Royal and having him build a pirate network of slave ships to help supply the southern United States with fresh slaves and runaways is bad enough. But now he wants to use the fort as a staging ground to branch out and extend into the Pacific. This is not only preposterous but will most likely get us all hanged. We cannot keep a secret like this from the crown. And now you both want to have that wretched, diseased ship, *The Red Witch*; hunt down and sink Captain Arthur Joshua's ship that was gifted to him by the Sailor King himself? The Queen will have us brought back to England to be drawn and quartered. If Joshua had stayed in the navy, he would be sitting on the panel of grand admirals by now." Thompson stands up and points a shaky hand at Bennets. "Governor, as ranking admiral of the British naval fleet in the Caribbean, I cannot turn a blind eye to this insane plan."

In his hysteria, Thompson does not notice Lomoche get out of his own chair and come up behind him until he feels the cold steel of a pistol barrel press against the back of his head. The last thing Thompson hears is the click of Lomoche pulling back the striker and trigger that sparks the flint that ignites the black gun powder, propelling the lead ball into the back of his skull and exiting out his forehead, taking a quarter of his face with it. Blood from Thompson sprays on Bennets's face as chunks of his gray matter stain his fancy desk.

Bennets wipes his face off with his handkerchief. "Dammit! Lomoche, couldn't you just have stabbed him in the back like you did that pirate, Erasmus?"

"I had two hands then, governor. Not to worry. My servants will clean this mess up and dispose of the body," Lomoche drags Thompson's corpse to a large rug in the center of the room. He turns toward the door and gives a loud whistle. Two bare-chested, brown-skinned men in colorful ornate skirts and sandals come in and roll the corpse up in the rug and carry him out. Two brown-skinned females come in and clean up everything else.

Lomoche walks over to a small table on the side of the office that has a pitcher of water and a ceramic bowl next to it. He pours the water in the bowl and uses it and a towel to clean himself with his one good hand. One of the female natives helps the governor clean himself up. As they finish, Lomoche turns to the governor. "I really don't want to sacrifice *The Red Witch* or Reece if I don't have to. He and that ship will be very useful when we expand to the Pacific. The islands around Hawaii are countless and full of natives such as these. There are markets all over the world for a good new stock of slaves. As you have already seen, governor, their females are exquisite."

Bennets's eyes are devouring the female who is cleaning Thompson's blood off his face. He pats her on the bottom and then looks back at Lomoche. "If we can save your precious ship, we will. All will depend on how fast we can encourage war in the United States. The queen's husband will not come out and openly support us unless we can guarantee that war. Killing Captain Joshua of *The Morning Star* will go a long way toward bringing that to pass. We can use his abolitionist passions to cover our having anything to do with his death. But his friends in the northern states will be that much more emboldened to force Washington to abolish slavery, thus igniting a war between the north and the south. Then when these colonials are done slaughtering one another, Great Britain will step in under my command and mop up the mess and bring her wayward child back into the fold."

An evil smile creases Lomoche's face. "You're a madman, Bennets," he says. "I want to bring back the glory of the Caribbean pirate. You want to change the world into something that will hail you as one of its shapers and molders. I'll play your game for now, but the world is big, governor. If this blows up in your face, I will take *The Red Witch* and seek my fortune where no one has ever heard of you or your plans."

He sees the women are done cleaning up the blood and gore on Bennets's desk and begins to motion for them to leave, but Bennets waves his hand. "Leave these two with me tonight. I have not yet sampled this new product of yours, Lomoche."

Lomoche grins. "By all means, governor. But please try to send them back to me in working condition. I plan to bring them to Louisiana before the storm season and sell them to the New Orleans brothels there. As for your Captain Joshua, I have it on good intelligence that he will be back in Kingston within the week. His next pick up of runaways should be within a month after that. He has contacted a Maroon in Argentina near Buenos Aires. That will be his next drop-off of the runaways. I plan to meet him there with a full armada. There we will either sink him with our cannon or run him into Devil's Curve. Either way, he'll be dead before winter."

CHAPTER 9

LOVE UNFOLDS

Kingston, Jamaica, Beach Close to the Main Harbor

Ralphie and Davonte frolic hip-deep in crystal clear, wavy beach water while John Edwards and Brandy sit in beach chairs and talk under an umbrella staked in the sand. It was Skynyrd who insisted that if Ralphie and Davonte continued to develop a romantic attachment for one another, they should be properly chaperoned while out together. He said to Brandy that Ben and Elisa had entrusted their daughter to his care while they were away and he wanted no shenanigans to report upon their return.

John offers to go out and take a swim with Brandy, but she refuses, saying that she spent the first half of her life living on the sea and found saltwater distasteful. The truth of the matter is that she loves to swim but knows that fifteen minutes in saltwater and all the black dye in her hair would start to wash out.

John is now fully recovered from all his injuries and has spent a good deal of time with Zhang Yong working on the practical applications of all the tai chi forms. After about a week into the lessons, Brandy joined in and helped John acclimate to Zhang's unique teaching style. He and

Ralphie also figured out that it was Zhang and Brandy who rescued them that night on the docks when Faustin Reece and his men attacked them.

"Brandy, do you and Zhang do this 'night watch' exercise often?" John asks.

Brandy grabs her tea and takes a sip. "In Zhang's country, his order of Shaolin are self-appointed protectors of the common people. They will intervene when robbers and thugs prey on the innocent, and sometimes will even stand up to unjust government officials abusing their power. When Zhang came to *Katrina's* five years ago, Uncle Skynyrd asked him to help me with the anger that I had held onto over losing my parents at sea. My mother and father were exceptional fighters and had trained me from my youth to be the same. It was my mother who taught me to use my rage and channel it at my enemy. Apparently back in Ireland, my family on her side were well known for their horrific tempers. She taught me that it was a gift to be cultivated." She sips her tea and sees that John is captivated by the discourse and continues, "Zhang has since shown me that it can be a prison. The answer to your question, John, is that Zhang invited me to go along with him when he wanted to keep with the mandates of his order and help the common people wherever he could. He takes me out only when he has a specific lesson that he wants to teach me. He feels that the real-life training will help me implement his teachings of calmness, control, and stillness on the inside while in combat. It all still feels like a big, bloody contradiction to me. But I have never known a fighter who can do the things Zhang can, and I want to learn."

John puts his drink down and turns in his seat. "Brandy, Zhang is right. You have to learn how to stay calm when in combat. When I served in the Indian Ocean, we had many battles with the pirates in those waters. What I learned then is that when confronting an enemy, especially multiple ones, you have to be able to think and choose when and where to apply aggression so that you can achieve maximum success. I used to pretend that I had jumped into the ice-cold waters of the Northern Sea before going into the battle. That way I could think clearly …"

While John is speaking, Brandy suddenly bolts out of her chair, puts both hands around her mouth and yells, "Ralphie Austin and Davonte, you two stop that right now! We are in public and I will not have the entire port gossiping about you two out here acting like a couple of love-sick kittens."

John turns and looks in their direction. He sees Ralphie and Davonte in a passionate kissing embrace.

"You two come here right now!" Brandy yells.

John stands up. "I don't know about Davonte— women have always been a mystery to me—but a tongue-lashing from you will do that boy no good. Right now, he needs to work off his raging hormones." He reaches up and unlaces the strings on his pullover shirt neckline, takes it off, then takes off his footwear. He then runs out to Ralphie and Davonte. As he gets close to them, he says, "Mr. Austin, with me to the reef and back. If you keep up, then you won't have to work off any demerits."

"Demerits!" Ralphie exclaims. "We're not at sea."

John stops and stares the boy in the eye for a few seconds. "This isn't dry ground slapping up against my chest, midshipman. Now swim!"

Ralphie's shoulders slouch and he sighs. "Aye, aye, sir."

John smiles and turns to dive into the first wave coming his way. When he surfaces, he swims in smooth, even strokes toward the reef, which lies half a mile out past the beach. Davonte looks back at Brandy, but she cannot tell if she is using those intense, green eyes to bore into her and Ralphie, or John Edwards. She then turns back to Ralphie and laughs. "Well, you better hurry before he's too far ahead of you, Ralphie. I wouldn't want you to have to work off any of those demerits John

Edwards was talking about." She giggles, gives Ralphie a peck on the cheek, then turns to make her way back to Brandy.

Ralphie battles down the impulse to grab Davonte and kiss her again, then shakes his head and looks down at the water. "There are many things that John Edwards can do better than me, but swimming is not one of them. It'll be a cold day in hell before that English gentleman will ever beat this Yank to that reef and back, head start or not." Ralphie then dives through a wave and smoothly strokes his way toward John. Within fifteen strokes he catches John; but much to his amazement, he can barely maintain a half-body-length lead on the man for the entire swim.

Davonte strolls up to Brandy with a sly smile on her face and mischief in her eyes. "I am sorry, Missy Brandy, but Ralphie is such a darling boy, and he treats me like a princess. I fear that we might be falling in love. What do you think Momma and Poppa will think of him?"

Brandy tries to maintain a scolding stare as she holds Davonte's gaze, but a smile creases her face and she lets out a giggle. "I think that if Ben and Elisa hear about you smooching some sailor on the beach here, they will skin both of us alive then make you quit *Katrina's* to stay at home and help them with the house and the animals. Come over here and sit down. You can have some of John's tea while we wait for those two to finish showing off."

Forty minutes later, John and Ralphie emerge from their swim. Ralphie barely beats John to the shore and declares himself the winner. As they walk to the girls at the umbrella, Brandy and Davonte can't help but notice what fine physical specimens of men they are. Davonte looks over at Brandy and winks. "Easy on the eyes, huh, Missy Brandy?"

Brandy abruptly stands, folds up the chairs and takes down the umbrella. Davonte almost falls out of her chair when Brandy grabs it, and she hears her say under her breath, "Why does that man have to look like some kind of Greek god?"

Ralphie sees the commotion and says with exasperation, "Do you girls really want to leave now? John and I just finished a mile swim. We'd like to rest a second."

Brandy hands a chair to John and the umbrella to Ralphie, grabs the other chair and walks back to the dock. "We need to keep all the raging hormones going on around here in check. Besides, Davonte and I have lots of work to do before we open tonight."

"But Missy Brandy, that's why we got up so early today," Davonte exclaims as she runs after Brandy. "We got all that work done so we could go to the beach with Ralphie and John Edwards."

"Well, I just thought of more we need to get done. Let's go."

John and Ralphie stand there looking at the backs of Brandy and Davonte as they make their way off the beach, both men annoyed by the turn of events. Ralphie turns to John. "You know, if you would take a little initiative with her, I think she'd respond. Davonte is sure that she likes you a lot more than she's willing to admit, even to herself."

John drops the chair, thumps his chest with his palms. "Likes me? She sure has a funny way of showing it. The only thing she will ever talk to me about is the combat training we do with Zhang Yong. Every time I ask her about something personal or invite her to do something together, she just brushes me off. She wouldn't even go swimming with me earlier."

Ralphie laughs. "You know, John, Davonte told me Zhang never taught Brandy any tai chi. So, you wonder why she's even interested in it? She said that the only thing Brandy really likes about Zhang's lessons is when he shows her more about those 'sticks' she uses. She says Zhang has a special set of swords that Brandy will get if she masters all the lessons he's giving her, which includes none of the tai chi he is teaching you. So why do you think she sticks around and helps him with you?"

"I don't know, Ralphie. Maybe she finds it amusing to watch that old Chinese man make me look like a crippled baby," John says with a little more force than he feels.

Ralphie lets out a roar of laughter that almost causes him to lose his breath.

"What's so funny, Ralphie?"

"You are, John Edwards. In the three years I've sailed on *The Morning Star*, I've never seen a man best you, or a woman's heart you could not win with just a smile. Yet, Zhang can toss you around like a rag doll and this Brandy girl has got you so turned around you can't even think straight."

John grabs his folded chair from the sand and looks up at Ralphie with a devious grin. "You may be a faster swimmer than me, but I'll wager I can thrash you with this chair even if you do have that umbrella to defend yourself with, boy."

Ralphie puts the folded umbrella over his shoulder and bolts off toward the girls, who are now climbing the stairs to the docks. Once he knows he has a safe lead he yells back, "I am also a faster runner than you are, John Edwards. It would appear that I have won the day! Ha ha!"

Late that evening, Brandy and Davonte and the crew clean up the front of the tavern, and Skynyrd and Zhang do the same in the kitchen in the back. As Brandy is taking some cups and bowls to the wash area, John Edwards and Ralphie, as has been their habit for the last month, come into the kitchen, grab some towels and aprons, and help. Brandy is now feeling a little embarrassed about why she stormed off the beach earlier. She hates the fact that she is so attracted to the man, who is definitely committed to life at sea. John, however, has been a perfect gentleman for the whole two months that he and Ralphie have been guests at *Katrina's*, which does little to assuage her annoyance. If anything, it empowers it, because she can't even use bad behavior for an excuse to dislike him.

She comes into the kitchen with Davonte in tow, both carrying a load of dishes, and sets them next to the wash basin John and Ralphie are working at. "Why do you two insist on helping us close every night?" Brandy says with a little more fervor than she intends. "You're paying guests of one of the higher-priced inns in Kingston. We're supposed to be taking care of you two, not the other way around."

John smiles as he finishes towel drying a large stew pot. "Brandy, Ralphie and I are sailors. Aboard ship, everyone pitches in and helps with the chores. I can't let this young officer-in-training lose that discipline while we lounge around here in the luxury of your and Skynyrd's fine establishment. Yes, we're paying customers. I do try to let you and your staff take care of us, but I'll not have a midshipman under my watch spoiled of all discipline."

Brandy rolls her eyes. "Suit yourselves. It's not like we don't need the help." She turns and heads back to the dining room, catching Davonte's quizzical gaze aimed in her direction. Brandy shakes her head, points back to the kitchen and exclaims, "What, did that man fall from heaven tied to a balloon or something?" Davonte giggles. Brandy shakes her fist. "Oh, he's just so good and sweet and thoughtful. I wish I could ring his burly neck and knock him into tomorrow with my foot."

"Oh, Missy Brandy, why don't you just tell him you like him and want to spend some nice time with him? We both know that's what you're really saying," Davonte replies as she finishes locking down the windows and doors to the dining room.

"I have no such desire, Davonte! He's a sailor, and first mate on a very important ship. His life is at sea, a place I want nothing to do with." As she is telling this to Davonte, she sees that the girl is trying to motion with her eyes that someone is behind her. When she turns, she sees John Edwards standing there.

"Brandy, I have been feeling antsy at night of late. Probably some herbs Dr. Johansson is making me take before I turn in. Would you care to join me for a midnight stroll to the dock and back to help me sleep better tonight?"

Before she can answer, Davonte says, "I think that is a wonderful idea, John Edwards. I know Missy Brandy loves to take midnight strolls before bed, and I always have been nervous about her going out alone. I would sleep better knowing she was with you to mind her safety."

Brandy glares at Davonte with her best *you have got to be kidding* look and turns back to John to tell him no, when John says, "Oh, Davonte, we both know that it is Brandy who has protected me while out at night roaming the dangerous streets of Kingston. I only wish her company for that same purpose as well."

Brandy's eyes dart back and forth between John and Davonte and she utters a big *ARGH* and says, "Oh, give me a break, both of you. John, come on. I'll walk your poor, helpless self to the dock and back, so you can have your good night's sleep, and Davonte can have a nice laugh at my expense."

John grins from ear to ear and runs back into the kitchen to put away his apron. He sees that Ralphie is helping Skynyrd take some big pots of stew broth to the cool room in the cellar and tells him he'll be back in an hour or so. He stops at a handwashing pot and uses it to freshen up. He combs back his hair with his fingers, cuffs his hand over his mouth and blows out to check the smell of his breath. Not liking what he smells, he looks for something to freshen his breath. A voice behind him says, "John Edwards." He turns to see Zhang standing behind him with one of his little alabaster vials in his hand, which he tosses to John. "Put three drops of this on your tongue and your breath will smell like a fresh mountain lake in springtime."

John catches the vial and without a second thought twists off the top and does exactly what Zhang said. "Thanks," he says as he rushes out to the dining room. He scans the room for Brandy and sees her at a wash-basin at the back of the room, primping herself. He goes to the door and makes sure she did not see him. "Are you here, Brandy? I'm ready."

"I'm right here, John." He turns around and sees Brandy's beautiful green eyes staring up at him. He offers her his arm and opens the door.

Brandy takes his arm and turns to Davonte. "You can lock the door, Davonte. I have my key. That will be all for the night. If Skynyrd needs nothing else, you can turn in. Goodnight."

"Okay, Missy Brandy," Davonte replies. "You have a nice time pro-tecting each other out there tonight." She giggles and locks the door behind the couple.

It is still warm in the late August night as the couple begin their trek to the docks, a thirty-minute walk from *Katrina's*. John looks up and scans the clear, starlit sky. The moon is large and bright. He points to a spot in the sky to the right and under the moon. "That one there is 'The Bright and Morning Star' that represents our Lord Jesus Christ. Captain Joshua named his ship after that one."

"My father and Uncle Skynyrd taught me to navigate by the stars when I was a child," Brandy says. "So I am familiar with their names and the many meanings people have put on the different stars in the sky. I also remember from your Bible that the devil was once the bright and morning star."

"You say my Bible, Brandy. Don't you believe the Holy Scriptures?"

"Oh, I suppose that I do. My parents were not very religious and did not teach me much when we lived at sea. But after moving to Kingston and opening up *Katrina's*, I've read it several times. I have to admit that what I have read and what I have seen among many so-called Christians don't always match."

"Sadly, that is more often than not the case. We are weak in our flesh. Fortunately, we have a powerful savior who is always there to offer forgiveness and strength if we accept it."

"I'll not doubt you on that one. If what I have read is true, there never has lived a man more kind, loving, and forgiving than Jesus. His purity and gentleness could soften the hardest of stone hearts, yet he manifested unimaginable power. Dead people raised, blind made to see. He could even calm that raging mistress of yours, the sea herself," Brandy says as she looks up at John's face with a teasing twinkle in her eyes.

John swallows nervously. "I am not engaged to the sea, Brandy. It's just that when I was a boy I worked on the docks where my father managed for Captain Joshua's brother. I saw hundreds of ships come and go every day. I worked sixteen hours a day loading and unloading those ships, hearing all the tales of the exotic places the sailors had just come from or were going to. It was more than my young, eager mind could tolerate. I couldn't wait to sail away on one of them, but my mother would not let me go until I was the proper age. It was Captain Joshua who got me a commission as midshipman aboard a British naval frigate when I was thirteen years old. In three years, I finished all my studies and passed all the requirements and was awarded my commission to lieutenant. Since that time, I've sailed on all seven seas in this big, old world and seen a big chunk of its lands. It's because of the sea that I got to do all that; and yes, I do love life aboard a ship, traveling to different places and meeting new people."

Brandy smiles softly. "Oh, John, don't get so defensive. We all were sure you weren't truly romantically involved with the sea." She takes her free hand, reaches across to his shoulder and shakes it. "But now I know why you are so freakishly strong. Working the docks as a young boy forced your body to develop some tough muscles and bones." As she retracts her hand, she lets it lightly brush across his chest, and when it comes to his neckline, she feels some metal beneath his shirt. "What is this?"

John reaches inside his shirt and pulls out a silver medallion in the shape of a heart and shows it to her. "I had this made on my first trip to Spain. It is made from the best northern Spanish silver. I gave it to my mother when we got back to port in London later that year."

Brandy takes the medallion in her hands to examine it. Still being around John's neck, it forces her to stand very close, almost pressing into him as she looks at it. It is a pure silver, heart-shaped piece with the image of a young man around thirteen wearing a three-pointed English naval officer's hat. On the other side, the inscription says *John of My Heart.*

"I was her only child and she used to call me that. The first time I sailed out, she was there to see me off, along with my father. There I was, a brand-new midshipman trying to board my first ship, with my captain and all his officers staring at me as my mother had me in a bear hug as she kept saying, 'John of my heart, don't leave, don't leave.' My father finally made her release me and let me board. When we got to Spain nine months later, I was experiencing so much homesickness and guilt that I went and spent almost my whole pay to have this made for her."

Brandy looks up into John's eyes, with the beginning of a tear forming in her own. "John, if you had this made for your mother, why do you wear it? How is it that I've not seen this before? I took care of you, clothed and bathed you for the first couple of days you were with us."

John reaches down and clasps Brandy's hand as she holds the medallion. "My mother passed the last time I was in England. As she laid there in her last moments of life, she took this from around her neck and placed it in my hand and told me to keep it and give it to the woman I would marry. I rarely wear it, but today I just found myself thinking about her."

Brandy releases her hold on the medallion, then brushes away the tear that is running down her face. She presses up on her tiptoes to kiss John on the cheek, lays her head on his chest and embraces him. "You are a unique man, John Edwards. I've met no one like you."

By this time, the couple is standing on the dock almost at the exact place John and Ralphie were the night someone attacked them.

"Thought I might find you two here." John and Brandy release from their embrace and turn to see Captain Arnold Walters, Kingston's garrison commander, standing behind them. "I am sorry. I did not mean to startle you. I was just over at *Katrina's* looking for John Edwards and they told me I could find the two of you here."

"That's quite all right, Captain. How can I be of service to Her Majesty's garrison commander?"

"Well, for starters, you can tell me when *The Morning Star* is due back to the Kingston port."

"I imagine that she left New York Harbor three weeks ago. So any day now, I would think."

"Is Captain Joshua picking up any runaways or making any stops at Maroons along the way?" Walters presses.

"Why, no. The last dispatch I received said they are heading straight here. Our next scheduled pickup of runaways is in early September. We want to get them picked up and delivered to a new Maroon that Captain Joshua visited in Argentina a month ago. Why? What is this all about, Captain?"

"I'm sorry John, it's that scum Faustin Reece you had that scuffle with a few months ago. He used to work for Governor Bennets's man, Don Lomoche. He has even captained that wretched slaver ship, *The Red Witch,* for him a few times. Two days after the incident, that Spanish peacock Lomoche showed up at the garrison with signed orders from the governor to have Reece and his men transferred to the governor's private guard. Two weeks later, Reece escaped and hijacked *The Red Witch* off Port Royal. I just got word earlier today that *The Red Witch* was the same ship that attacked *The Fisher of Men* a week ago, confiscated all her runaway slave passengers, and sunk her off the coast of Cuba. Reece has declared himself the new buccaneer captain of *The Red Witch* and has some commission from a United States southern plantation guild to round up all the runaways they can and bring them back to their owners. That's why I'm worried about Captain Joshua."

Brandy stiffens at the mention of her father's ship and of his murderer. The old rage builds in her gut as the past comes barreling into her conscience. Before she can stop herself, she says, "I wouldn't put it past that egg-sucking governor of ours to have set this whole charade up through Lomoche. Everyone knows his company still deals in slave trade and that Lomoche runs that end of his business."

John raises an eyebrow and looks quizzically at Brandy. "I did not know you were so keen on local politics." He then directs his attention back to Captain Walters. "If Reece is hunting abolitionist ships, he would be a fool to take on *The Morning Star* at high seas in *The Red Witch*. That thing is too heavy and too slow to ever be a threat to a naval battle commander like Captain Joshua. He'd send that ship to the bottom of the ocean in five passes. Besides, if he chooses not to fight, they could never catch him. Howbeit, once he hears of the fate of *The Fisher of Men* and the death of its captain and crew, I would not give two pence for how long Reece will last out there. It destines them to a rude introduction to one of England's greatest warriors at sea. I'll be right there with him, sending those black-hearted bastards to the abyss."

Captain Walters's eyes dart back and forth between John and Brandy. He inhales deeply. "When I was ordered to put down the slave rebellions, I did my duty, albeit with a heavy heart. When the Sailor King William freed the slaves, I felt a great weight lifted off my soul. Men like Lomoche and Reece belong at the bottom of the sea. But it is our wretched Governor Bennets who should take the lead. I can't prove it, but I know in my heart that he is behind everything. I've shown so much in many a report sent back to Parliament since taking command of the garrison in Kingston. Maybe someday someone will listen."

Brandy turns to John. "What are you going to do now? Captain Joshua will be here soon unless he ran into some foul weather, but that would only delay him a few more days."

"Ralphie and I will have to get the word out to the Maroons around the island. There is one forty miles northeast of Kingston. They all have a special network to communicate with one another. It should not take more than a week before they all know what is going on. Once warned, they'll be hard to raid, even if Lomoche and Reece have an army to do it with."

Captain Walters nods. "I have to agree with you on that, John Edwards. Once those camps know you're coming, it's like storming a castle to get through their defenses. The governor will get as little help from my garrison as I can manage. But one thing I do know—he'll make no open moves against Captain Joshua or the crew of *The Morning Star*. If he does, the Royal Navy in these waters will string him up by his ears; and once Her Majesty hears of it, she will give her blessings. But that won't keep a snake like Bennets from having his minions sneaking around doing his dirty work for him. Well, I must get back to the garrison command. If you need my help, you need only ask." Captain Walters reaches out and grabs John's hand and shakes it.

John and Brandy walk back to *Katrina's* in silence, both lost in their own thoughts. Brandy takes her key out and opens the door. As they step in, she remembers the medallion and the story of John's mother. Halfway through the entrance, she turns toward John and places her hands on either side of his face, pulling him down just enough to give him a gentle kiss on his lips. She steps back with a soft smile in her eyes. "I enjoyed being with you tonight, John. You are a courageous gentleman." Then she turns and walks to the stairs that lead to her room. Once on the fourth floor, she unlatches the door to her apartment, plops down in front of the vanity, stares at her reflection in the mirror and sighs. "I can't believe you did that," she says.

John Edwards has a very hard time sleeping that night.

Early the Next Morning, *Katrina's*

John Edwards and Ralphie get up before sunrise to assemble some gear for their trip. The forty-mile trek will have to be on foot because John does not want to alert anyone's suspicions by chartering a boat. When they go downstairs, they hear a noise in the kitchen and figure Skynyrd is already up. "Good morning, Mr. Skynyrd. Ralphie and I are taking a trip today and we would be deeply grateful if you could help us with some traveling supplies," John says as he walks into the dining room.

Not only is Skynyrd up, but Brandy, Davonte, and Zhang Yong are with him, and they are all filling traveling bags with food and equipment. "Aye, John. Brandy woke me up before the first rooster crowed and told me what the garrison captain said about *The Red Witch* being hijacked by that scoundrel Reece and preying on your friends out there doing all that good work. She insisted that we outfit both of you for your trip to the Maroon. Much like her mother before her, Brandy is not an easy person to say no to. So here I am."

John scans the table with all the gear. "But Skynyrd, there are enough supplies here to outfit a small company. It's just Ralphie and me."

"Well, that is where you are wrong, because Davonte, Zhang, and I are joining you," Brandy declares. "Now, before you make a fuss, know that Davonte spent five years in that Maroon before moving to Kingston with her parents. And because you want no one in the governor's and

Lomoche's circle surprising us on this adventure, Zhang wants to come as well. I hardly think anyone will get within a quarter of a mile of us on the trail without him knowing about it."

Before John can respond, Zhang looks at him and says, "John Edwards, your cause is just, and your strategy is sound. If the governor's men are attacking your ships that are carrying runaway slaves, then they will soon raid the Maroons as well. It is important that they be warned quickly. You and Ralphie are brave and strong, but if you two are seen leaving alone, one of Lomoche's men will quickly figure out what you are up to. If Davonte, Brandy, and I leave together in that direction, no one will care. Zhang talked to a friend at dock earlier. He will meet you and Ralphie on the opposite end of Kingston at the small port, wait until evening, and then take you to port halfway between here and Maroon where Zhang, Brandy, and Davonte will meet you. Boat travel much faster and be there at the same time as us."

The room is silent for a few seconds as John thinks about Zhang's proposal. Being a military man, he can't deny the soundness of Zhang's strategy. "Zhang, what if Lomoche's men follow us to that smaller port north of Kingston and then overtake us at sea after we launch?"

"Good point, but Lomoche has no ships at that port. It's just a small fishing port and they would have to run back to Kingston, get to ship, and launch to follow you. I told my friend to head straight out to sea with you and once out of eyeshot, to turn and head south to the port where Zhang and friends will be. Once Lomoche's men get back to Kingston, they will go on, as you say, 'a wild goose chase' looking for you."

"Geez, I'm glad Zhang's on our side. He thinks like Captain Joshua!" Ralphie says.

"I think you're right, Ralphie. We'll go with Zhang's plan."

John and Ralphie assist Skynyrd in preparing the supplies for their departure. An hour later, Zhang, Brandy, and Davonte leave *Katrina's* and head south for the hike.

Brandy walks beside Zhang, carrying her pack in silence. She is a little disappointed that John and Ralphie are not with them because she was hoping for an opportunity to explain to John why she kissed him last night. Albeit, when she got honest with herself, she really had no logical explanation, let alone what she would say to him. But she wants to nip this in the bud as fast as possible. She has never been one to lead a man on and give him any false hope. She thinks of what a kind gentleman he is and how he is not like any other she has known, which she tells herself is why it is important that he knows right away that it was just a friendly kiss and did not mean much at all. Or did it? *Brandy, stop it! He is a sailor and more committed to the sea than anyone you have ever known, including your father,* she chides herself.

While Brandy is entertaining herself with her internal struggles over John, Zhang Yong stops her and Davonte and calls their attention to an altercation going on between a mother cat and three dogs on the side of the street. Brandy shakes the reverie from her mind and focuses on the situation. Three large dogs have surrounded a mother cat that is protecting her five kittens. Stray dogs on the streets of Kingston are not an uncommon sight and they will usually eat just about anything, including kittens, if they can get their jaws on them. Brandy instinctively steps forward to shoo the dogs off when Zhang grabs and holds her shoulder. "Brandy, this is good lesson for you. Look and see what mother cat does to protect her young."

Brandy knows that when Zhang wants to teach a lesson, no amount of annoyance on her part will dissuade him. She focuses on the situation and sees that the three dogs have the mother cat surrounded and pinned up against a wall at a corner on the side of the road. The dogs are growling and barking as the mother cat covers her young with her body and is hissing back. The mother will not leave the young and uses her paws and fangs to strike out at a dog if it gets too close. As she looks closer, she sees that all three dogs are bleeding around the eyes and nose from scratch marks inflicted by the cat. The momma cat seems to be equally focused on all three dogs and will strike back at each one only as long as it takes to make the dog back off.

One dog gets brave and rushes in. The momma waits until the dog is close and then she springs onto its face. The dog is so close that the other two can't get around their friend to get at the kittens, and the momma cat bites and scratches its eyes until the dog lets out a loud yelp. When the mother cat jumps off, she covers her young with her body again. The dog that she just counter-attacked, which looks to be blinded in one eye, jumps up and hangs back from the attack. The other two sense that they are in a bigger fight than they originally thought, but are still determined to get to their prey. Both press their attack when, from behind the wall that they have the mother cat pinned against, three more cats jump over and attack the dogs. Seeing that they are now outnumbered and have already taken a thrashing from the mother, the dogs turn with their tails between their legs and run off. The momma herds her kittens to safety.

Zhang watches the animals disperse, then looks to Brandy. "What did you learn from that encounter, Brandy?"

Brandy stares at the area where the conflict occurred. "The mother cat's main priority was protecting her young. She could not afford to spend too much time focusing on any one of the attackers. She had to keep them all away until help arrived."

"How did mother cat know that help would arrive?"

"How am I supposed to know, Zhang? I can't read the cat's mind."

"By strategy employed by mother. Why stay at the wall? Why not head for alley and safety? Maybe sacrifice one or two kittens if she runs, but the others are safe. Instead, she stays at the wall and fights. She loves all her kittens. She knows she has allies close by and is not willing to sacrifice any of her young. She therefore goes to wall at corner and protects. Then her allies come and help. Mother knows where her friends are. Mother knows what dogs want, what they will do. She fights to protect, and she wins with her friends. She does not think only of destroying an enemy. She has rage and uses it on the most aggressive dog by blinding him. But she controls rage and jumps back to her young. She thinks of protecting kittens. Nothing else is as important to her. She sees everything and knows what best to do to protect. She wins because she did it with her friends."

He stops for a moment and takes a deep breath. "You see, Brandy, to care, to love, to protect, and to rely on friends is more powerful than rage. Rage only sees an enemy in front of its face. Love sees everything!" He winks at Brandy and Davonte. "Come. Now we go to help John Edwards protect friends."

Northern Kingston Harbor

John and Ralphie wait another hour at *Katrina's* after the first group has departed, and head north toward the fishing dock on the outskirts of Kingston to meet up with Zhang's friend. Zhang told John that the name of his contact is Thomas, who owns a large fishing schooner there. It takes two hours to walk to the small dock. When they get there, Thomas is easy enough to spot. Sitting on a bench on the dock next to his schooner, Thomas is eating some smoked crab and drinking fresh lemon tea. He is a large native man with a potbelly, and he's missing all but one front tooth. John walks up to him. "My name is John Edwards, and this is my shipmate, Ralphie Austin. Zhang Yong said you could help us."

"You are from *The Morning Star*. All of us know Captain Joshua and you too, John Edwards, first mate of that great ship. Come, we can leave right now."

In thirty minutes, they launch and sail out to sea.

Two members of Governor Bennets's personal guard stand on the beach a quarter mile south of that same dock and watch the schooner disappear over the Caribbean horizon. The higher ranking of the two says, "You ride to Kingston and tell Lomoche's man to follow and find out where that ship is headed. We need to know what Joshua's man is up to. Tell them to make sure they're not spotted. The governor wants none of us to openly confront Joshua or his men. He says that if this is not handled delicately, the queen will have us all hanged. Reece and *The Red Witch* are the only way to take care of *The Morning Star* and her crew without Governor Bennets or us being blamed."

"So, what will happen to Reece once he's sunk *The Morning Star*, sir?" the guard asks.

"Probably a royal warrant will be issued for the man and his crew for killing one of England's most celebrated sea captains. They will be hunted and hanged or sent to the bottom of the sea. Who cares? Reece is a rat and will get what he deserves. The governor and Lomoche will be above suspicion, and their business will quietly move forward unhindered by the abolitionist's biggest champions in the Caribbean."

The officer and his man get on their mounts and head in different directions.

Later that Evening, Small Fishing Dock Just North of Port Royal

Zhang Yong sits on the wooden dock in the lotus position, comfortably smoking his pipe and staring out at the Caribbean horizon, scanning for sails in the twilight. Brandy and Davonte are at the end of the same dock, hands saluted over their brows and searching the same horizon.

Zhang finds it humorous that both women are in love with a member of that duo they are waiting for. But unlike Davonte, who has open feelings for Ralphie, Brandy has not admitted her feelings for John Edwards to herself. Consequently, Brandy is the one out of the three who is expressing the most annoyance at having not yet seen any sign of the men's arrival.

"You would think that the greatest sailor of the seven seas could get a schooner here by now. It's only a six-hour trek from Kingston, and we started walking here fourteen hours ago. What is taking that man so long?" Brandy paces the dock and continues to scan.

Davonte pats Brandy's shoulder. "Missy Brandy, we knew that they had to be careful not to be seen coming this way. John Edwards must have had Thomas sail in the opposite direction for a while just to throw off any observers."

Another hour passes and Brandy feels like she wants to jump out of her skin, but as she turns to say something to Zhang, she finds that he is standing right behind her. He points the end of his pipe out toward the right. "They are here."

Brandy jerks her head around and squints her eyes. Just past a protruding section of the shoreline, she sees the beginnings of a ship's silhouette on the horizon. "They're hugging the shoreline a bit close for a schooner of that size. No wonder they're so late," Brandy exclaims as Thomas's fishing boat becomes more manifest to everyone's eyes.

"Makes sense. John Edwards is a crafty one. A boat is much harder to see hugging the shore at sunset." Zhang points in the direction of the setting sun, that has now almost disappeared behind the island. "He hid in the island's shadow as they sailed."

Brandy glares at Zhang for a moment, certain that her sifu is having a good laugh on the inside at her expense. She turns to Davonte. "Don't make a big fuss when you see Ralphie. We have another three hour's hike to the campsite by the waterfall and need to get moving."

"Yes, Missy Brandy. You try not to think of a reason to scold John Edwards for making you wait for so long too." Brandy tries to glare at Davonte with her intense green eyes, but the girl's mirth is so infectious that she bursts out laughing with her.

Thomas's schooner takes another thirty minutes to make it to the little dock. Once there, Brandy and Davonte help secure the ship to the dock as John and Ralphie grab their things to join their companions. Thomas waves to Zhang and points to John Edwards. "That one is a wizard on the sea, Zhang. He spotted the cutter that launched from Kingston's main dock to follow us almost immediately. We sailed straight out to sea like we were headed to Cuba. Once we were out of their sight, he brought us around and headed back to Jamaica behind them. I thought for sure they would see us in the setting sun's glare coming back, but he knew their speed and line of sight and kept us out of it the whole way. Once back, we followed the shoreline, and he used the shadow of the island to hide us. He can read the flow of the sea like a learned man reads a book. Many of my people have heard of Captain Joshua's great navigator, but Thomas is the first to sail with him. This was a great honor for me."

John Edwards finishes handing his gear over to Ralphie, who is now on the dock collecting it with Davonte. He turns back to hold out a hand to Thomas. "The honor was all mine, Thomas. You have a fine ship there. May your catches be abundant, your seas calm, and the winds bring you home safe to your loved ones." The two seamen share a hearty handshake, then John turns and nimbly hoists himself over the side of the schooner and onto the dock, coincidently next to where Brandy is standing. The two stand and look at each other for a moment. John can't help but be grinning from ear to ear at seeing her. After last night's brief kiss in the doorway of *Katrina's*, he has found it difficult to think of anything else. The day's maneuvers at sea were a distraction, albeit brief.

Brandy is frantically trying to calm down her fluttering heart before John notices anything odd in her demeanor. She tries to swallow, but her throat is so dry that all she manages to do is cough. She covers her mouth, turns sideways and looks down. "I am glad to see you're finally here," she says as she walks off the dock. "We should get moving. It's a lot darker in the jungle and we still have about another three-hour hike to the campsite."

John gently reaches forward, grabs her shoulder, turns her around and kisses her on the cheek. "I am glad to see you as well, Brandy. I trust your trip was as pleasant as Ralphie's and mine."

Brandy's shoulders slouch and she relaxes. "Well, let me see. It started out with Zhang making us watch a ferocious battle between a mother cat who was protecting her kittens from some ravenous dogs. Not to worry, though. The mother's love won the day, and those dogs got a thrashing they will not soon forget. Then some feline friends joined in, and Zhang showed me the importance of relying on one's allies in a pinch. I believe the moral is that love is more powerful than rage." She looks at Zhang. "Do I have that right, Zhang?"

Zhang nods his head slightly and takes another puff of his pipe.

Brandy then motions over to Davonte with her chin and continues. "I spent the rest of the day listening to Davonte tell me what a wonderfully fabulous young man Ralphie is and how she knows that destiny brought the two of them together."

When John looks over at Davonte, he can tell that she is about to burst from embarrassment, but Ralphie comes up to her, grabs her hand, and kisses it. "I feel the same way, Davonte. God in heaven Himself brought us together, and I will believe nothing less." He then takes her in his arms and kisses her impetuously.

Brandy rolls her eyes and grabs her gear. "Good lord, you two, knock that off. Let's get moving before we have to find a minister and get you married right here."

Without looking back, Brandy walks off the dock and heads for the trail that will take them through the jungle and eventually to the Maroon. John goes to catch up with her, but Zhang stays him with his hand and says, "Let her be for now. Come, I will tell you about lesson of the mother cat Zhang taught to Brandy this morning." Zhang and John take up the rear, Ralphie and Davonte catch up with Brandy, and the group settles into a steady hike to the campsite.

Two and a half hours later, the five travelers hear water crashing over rocks as they make their way around a hill covered with thick, green jungle foliage. Fortunately, they are under a full moon on a clear night, so the freshwater lagoon they come upon is easily navigated in the bright, moonlit night. Brandy sets her things down and takes charge of setting up the evening camp. As she is helping Davonte get her things in order and her bedding laid out next to her own, the sound of laughter catches both girls' attention, and they turn to see John, Ralphie, and Zhang strip down to their undergarments, run over to the rocks at the bottom of the waterfall, and dive into the lagoon together. John and Ralphie have a friendly contest of seeing who can pull the other down under the surface first. Zhang gently swims to the other side of the waterfall, props himself up on a rock, takes out a blade from his pouch along with some soap, and shaves and cleans himself.

Davonte giggles and undoes her outer garments to get ready to join the boys when Brandy says, "You will have your bath when the children are done playing, Davonte. Right now, see if you can find some dry wood for a fire, and I'll get our meal together." Davonte sighs and rebuttons her top, then helps Brandy. John and Ralphie finish their games and climb out of the lagoon to help the girls set up camp.

Once the fire is set, Brandy walks over to Davonte and points to the other side of the waterfall. "The lagoon extends around the hill over there. You can bathe in private. I will take mine after supper." Davonte grabs a towel and some soap and then heads to the rocks by the waterfall. She turns to Ralphie and gives him an alluring smile, seductively raising her shoulder to her chin and winks, then heads around the corner to take her bath. Ralphie jumps up and follows her. Brandy bolts over to him and places herself between Ralphie and the lagoon. "Hold on there, you victim of cupid's arrow. You take one more step in that direction and I will show you what that momma cat did to those dogs."

Ralphie's face turns beet red. "Brandy, I would only go over there to talk. It's not like she will bathe nude or anything."

Before Brandy can respond, John Edwards steps up and says, "Midshipman, we are on a mission. Police this camp and help Brandy get our meal together. You will have first watch, and I'll take the second."

Ralphie comes to attention and throws a smart salute. "Yes sir, First Mate Edwards."

John leans in close to Ralphie. "Don't make me have you run all the way to that dock and back just to work off those raging hormones. Because I will."

Ralphie goes to help and says under his breath, but loud enough for Brandy, John, and Zhang to hear, "Geez, you'd think these old people would recognize true love when they see it. Someday, when I'm a first mate and my midshipman falls in love, I'll stick up for the poor boy, not make him exercise or work every time he wants to be with the woman he loves."

Brandy turns in Ralphie's direction, indignant. "Who does he think he's calling old?"

John holds up his hands to stay her. "He'll be fine. We'll let them have some time together before we all turn in."

"Well, okay. But if he calls me old again, I'll knock his block off."

After supper, Brandy and John let the two lovebirds take a short stroll around the lagoon together. When they get back, everyone but Ralphie turns in. He takes the first watch and stays up until an hour past midnight. When he gets back to the campfire area, he finds John Edwards already up and waiting for him. "Everything is quiet tonight, John. I saw Zhang up and about earlier, but there's nothing else to report."

John thanks the young man and sends him off to bed. He is on watch for less than a half hour when he notices Zhang making his way to him with a couple of tobacco pipes in his hand. John smiles as the Shaolin priest hands him one and offers to light it with a stick he brought from the fire. They stand in silence for a few moments while John enjoys the exquisite taste and aroma of the Cuban tobacco Zhang gifted to him.

Zhang blows a couple of smoke rings. "Funny that Brandy never took a bath after Davonte finished. Makes Zhang wonder if she plans to wear the same sweaty clothes tomorrow. Zhang heard a noise over in the lagoon where Davonte took her bath. Thought that since John Edwards is on watch, he should check out to make sure all is safe."

John stares quizzically at Zhang, trying to figure out what one thing has to do with the other, and why Zhang felt the need to have him check it out when Zhang was obviously the most skilled fighter of their group. Then it dawns on him, and he gets an eager glint in his eye.

Zhang laughs lightly and pats John on the shoulder. "You go, John Edwards. Zhang Yong can never sleep over three hours at a time. I will be up all night, anyway. Do not tell Brandy that Zhang sent you. I don't want to have that wrath on my head."

John hurries back to camp and finds that Ralphie and Davonte are sound asleep on opposite sides of the camp, but Brandy's bedding is empty and her outer garments look to be freshly rinsed and hanging over the fire. He strips down to the undergarments that he swam in earlier and makes his way over to the other side of the waterfall, where he hears light splashing. When he gets to the edge of the rock around the corner, he sees Brandy silhouetted in the moonlight, standing thigh deep in the water, using a cloth to wash her chest and arms. All she is wearing is a small piece of cloth that barely covers her very ample breasts, and skintight high-cut panties. The way the moonlight gleams off her bronze, shapely body and silky, black hair is the most intoxicating sight he's ever seen. He cannot fathom that in all the world there is any woman with such beauty as hers. He quietly steps into the water and makes his way to her. When close enough to be noticed, he says, "Brandy."

She continues to wash herself as she looks down into the moonlit water. "I saw you as soon as you came around the rocks, John."

He moves a step closer. "And you did not tell me to turn around and leave?" he says with a bit of hope in his voice.

"Oh, John, if you are anything, you are a gentleman. A woman can always feel that her honor is safe with you." John steps up in front of her, gently takes the cloth she is using and wipes her arms and neck with it. She then turns around and he washes her back. "Did you check on Ralphie and Davonte to make sure they are in separate beds and asleep?" Brandy asks with a huskiness in her voice.

"Of course."

"What of Zhang Yong?" she asks as she turns around, leans in close, puts her arms around John's neck, and pulls him in to kiss him hungrily.

When she finally lets John pull back for a breath, he says, "Zhang came to my lookout spot earlier with some of his tobacco and shared it with me, then he told me that he could not sleep. We talked for a while and I said I would take a trip around the camp to check things out. That is when I noticed you were gone and your clothing was drying. So, I assumed you were ..."

"You assumed I was here bathing and decided to join me. I am glad you did," Brandy says as she pulls John in and kisses him again. John's heart pounds as the blood rushes through his veins. He pulls her in closer and braces his palm against the back of her head and kisses her back with more intensity than he thought himself capable of. He takes his other hand and places it on the small of her back and pulls her in tight and lifts her off the ground, kissing her neck and shoulders. Brandy tilts her head back, sighing and moaning as the passion permeates her being. "Oh, John Edwards, what are you doing to my heart?"

John stops for a moment and looks deeply into Brandy's luscious green eyes. "The same thing you are doing to mine—opening it."

Brandy loses all that is left of her control and reaches back to undo the light cloth covering her breasts. John first stares lustfully, anticipating seeing her beautiful, full breasts in the sparkling, moonlit night. But somehow he calms himself down, and he gently reaches up and takes her hands in his, leans in, and kisses her tenderly. "If ever I am to have you like that, my love, it will be with a promise of forever. What you are to me is too precious for temporary passion. I am a man of the sea, and to this day, I have never considered leaving that life for anyone or anything. But you have the power to take me from that life. And because of that, I will not disrespect the promise of what could be for a mere taste of it now. Do you understand?"

Brandy takes John's face in both her hands and presses her lips to his again, kissing him with an emotion she did not know she had. A shudder goes through her body as she realizes how genuine John's plea to her is, and she pulls back from the embrace. "Who are you, and from what reality did you come, John Edwards? I know that you want me the same way that I want you. I can feel it in every part of your body. Are you saying you won't make love to me unless we promise ourselves to one another? I have never met a man like you."

John takes Brandy's hands and gently kisses her palms. "Brandy, I've sailed all over this great big world of ours and have known many women. But I have known no one like you. When I look into your eyes, I see the promise of a life beyond anything I ever thought possible." John closes his eyes and shakes his head. "My mother told me this would happen someday." He bows his head and walks over to some rocks and sits.

"Told you what, John?" Brandy asks as she follows him over and sits next to him, taking his hand in hers and leaning forward to look into his eyes.

John smiles and kisses her again. "When she gave me back that locket, she asked if I had met a girl that I wanted to marry yet. When I told her I hadn't, she said that I was just like my father. 'You Edwards men,' she said. 'You like to fool around and see how many hearts you can turn inside out, but one day one of them will do it to you and there is no turning back. It will happen, John, and when it does, you will belong to her, body and soul.'"

"So, you won't make love to me now because you are in love with me? John, that makes no sense."

"Why do women think that it's only okay for them to have feelings that make no sense? I won't make love to you now because I love you and refuse to hurt you. I have a commitment to Captain Joshua and his cause. We do good work out there on the sea, better than we ever did in the military." John then stops for a moment as he gets an idea, and a huge smile runs across his face. "You could be a part of that work, Brandy! *The Morning Star* is not a military vessel. Captain Joshua has told his mates that if they ever wanted to bring their wives with them, he would allow it. You said you grew up on a ship with your parents. How about coming back with me? Captain Joshua will retire in the next few years, and he has hinted that he wants me to captain *The Morning Star*. You could come with me and we'll sail her together."

"What are you saying, John? You want me to come with you and be your first mate or something?" Brandy shyly asks.

"Yes, Brandy, that would be like a dream come true. You, there with me on *The Morning Star*, sailing the Caribbean and helping men and women find their freedom from bondage. It would be paradise!"

For a moment Brandy sees how wonderful that could be, and in the depth of her heart thinks there is nothing she could want more. But then a dark cloud eases in over her conscience and she looks at John. "John, you really don't know who you are asking to join you in such a noble and beautiful life. I am not just some Kingston barmaid who spent half her life at sea with her merchant ship captain father and my mother. There is a much darker story."

John puts his arm around Brandy. "What do you mean, girl? What could be so bad that it brings this dark mood on you?"

"Do you remember when I said that pirates were the reason I lost my parents when I was fifteen years old?"

"Yes, I believe you said that Captain Eric Erasmus, the Plague, and his wife, the Scarlet Mistress, are the reason your parents are dead."

"Captain Eric Erasmus, the Plague, and his wife, the Scarlet Mistress, *were* my parents, John. I spent the first part of my life being raised to be a bloodthirsty, marauding pirate like my parents."

Much to Brandy's relief, John does not take his arm from around her but holds her closer and reaches to brush the hair away from her face. "But the Plague's daughter got her throat slit and then she was thrown overboard after she took Don Lomoche's hand and blinded his right eye. Besides, they say her hair was as blood red as her mother's."

Brandy reaches down and holds up a handful of her hair. "I have been dyeing it black for nigh on fifteen years now. That's why I would not go swimming in the ocean with you. Seawater will take the dye out."

John's expression on his face is unreadable, which makes Brandy very nervous. But then to her astonishment, he throws his head back and lets out a thunderous laugh.

His mirth is so overpowering that Brandy bolts out of his embrace and stands up, grabs both of his shoulders, and shakes him. "What is so funny? That I used to be a cold-blooded killer, or that my hair color is fake?"

John takes a deep breath and wipes the tears from his eyes and says, "No, Brandy, none of that. It's that if what you are saying is true, then I've fallen in love with a pirate princess."

"Pirate princess? What is that supposed to mean?"

John takes both of Brandy's hands and continues. "Brandy, when my father met my mother, she was a notorious pickpocket who worked the docks of London where he was employed. He caught her trying to pick his pocket one day and almost had her arrested. But she talked him into having an ale with her that night. They fell in love and got married within a month after meeting. I am sure your mother and mine would have gotten along famously."

Brandy stands there for a few moments, processing what John had just said. The emotions going through her are so contrary and powerful that she feels dizzy. John sees her disorientation and gently pulls her onto his lap, then places her head on his shoulder as he strokes her hair.

"You see, that is what I love/hate about you, John Edwards. You always see the bright side of everything. It is maddening!" She pulls her head up, looks into his big, blue eyes for a moment and then places her lips on his and fervently kisses him again. When she comes up for air, she lowers her head back down to his shoulder. "No one has ever called me a pirate princess before. I'm not sure if I like it or not."

The couple spends about another hour kissing and talking and enjoying each other's company. They tell each other their stories of how they grew up. John finds it especially interesting that Brandy was born at sea while her father's ship entered the eye of a hurricane. "You are a gift from the sea, Brandy. It makes sense. You have all her qualities. Veracity, stubborn self-will, passion, power, and you are almost completely unpredictable."

Brandy looks up at John as he holds her, and she giggles. "Is that why I am resting in the arms of the master sailor himself, the great John Edwards?" John's cheeks flush, but before the embarrassment gets the best of him, she presses up and kisses him again.

John eventually decides that it's time to head back and relieve Zhang, so he gets up, cups Brandy's face in his palms, and says, "You are the most remarkable woman I have ever met, Brandy." He leans down and kisses her once more, then turns and leaves. Brandy gathers her things and follows.

On top of the waterfall, sitting behind a boulder just above where John and Brandy were, Zhang Yong listens as the couple vacates the area. The slightest crease of a smile manifests itself on his face and he says to himself, "Brandy, you are finally learning balance. Zhang's work with you is almost done."

The next morning, Ralphie and Davonte are up early policing the camp. Zhang Yong told them he would scout ahead a little and would be back before they broke camp and were ready to leave. The young couple is a little perplexed that Brandy and John have not woken up yet, but they leave them be so that they can take a little morning stroll of their own.

An hour later, Ralphie and Davonte come back into the camp to find John and Brandy sitting by the fire, having a cold breakfast. At first, nothing looks out of the ordinary, but as the young couple approaches, they notice subtle and not-so-subtle changes in both of them. Brandy is seated right next to John on a log and they are so caught up in laughing and talking with one another that they don't notice Ralphie and Davonte approaching.

"John Edwards, Zhang is scouting ahead and should be back shortly. We should be ready to leave on your orders, sir," Ralphie says as he and Davonte enter the camp.

"Thank you, Third Mate Austin. We will leave as soon as Zhang comes back." John says this with a twinkle in his eye and a huge grin on his face.

Ralphie stops dead in his tracks and stares at John Edwards, bewildered by what he just heard. "John Edwards, did you just call me Third Mate Austin?"

"Yes, I did, Ralphie. By now you know that Second Mate Tom Roberts has left *The Morning Star* to be with his wife and new child in New York. Captain Joshua and I decided before we made port in Kingston three months ago that Jacob Hind would move up to second mate and you would become a full officer as third mate when that happened. I would wait for Captain Joshua to tell you himself, but seeing how it is against ship policy for a midshipman to be engaged, I thought it best to make it official now so that I don't have to penalize you for how you have been carrying on with Davonte. You are engaged, aren't you?" John asks with a humorous twinkle in his eyes.

Ralphie and Davonte nervously look at each other for several very uncomfortable moments before Ralphie lets out a huge sigh and reaches in his pocket. He pulls out a little gold ring, kneels down on one knee, and takes Davonte's hand. "Davonte, I love you more than life itself. Upon my faith in the Holy Father in heaven and His Son, my Lord Jesus Christ, I swear that I am yours for as long as I can draw breath. Will you marry me? Please?!"

Davonte looks down at the little gold band and cries as she answers with a quivery voice. "Yes, Ralphie, I will marry you." Ralphie stands up, takes Davonte in his arms and kisses her with devotion.

John and Brandy are standing up now and as Brandy reaches up to wipe a tear from her eye, she notices one running down John's cheek and she wipes that one as well. Ralphie and Davonte are caught up in their own bliss and walk off to the lagoon together to enjoy the moment. Once they are out of earshot, Brandy turns and says to John, "Pretty hypocritical of us being so judgmental of how those two have been acting, especially after how we behaved last night."

John laughs lightly and shakes his head then motions toward Ralphie with his chin. "I took him to a jeweler almost three weeks ago to buy that ring. He spent every penny he had on it. He's been carrying it around in his pocket waiting for Captain Joshua to return to see if he would get that promotion or not. The captain gave me the privilege of telling him whenever I wanted to. I guess now was as good a time as any. I am sure Davonte appreciates my help."

Brandy smirks at John and punches him lightly on the arm, then reaches up and pulls his face to her lips and kisses his cheek. She says, "You are a unique man, John Edwards. Ralphie is a very blessed boy to have you in his life."

Brandy holds John's hand, lays her head on his shoulder, and looks over at the young couple standing by the water. Davonte is holding her ring hand out in front of her, swaying back and forth in Ralphie's arms as they both admire the ring on her finger.

"Zhang is now ready to go warn the Maroon of Governor Bennets's and Don Lomoche's evil plans. As soon as all you lovebirds are finished flapping emotional wings, we'll go?"

Both couples turn to see Zhang at the entrance of the camp, backpack on and ready to leave. The four quickly get their things together and get back on the trail.

Eight Hours Later, Maroon Twenty-five Miles Northeast of Port Royal

John chose this Maroon because even though it was not easily accessible by the sea, it was the seat of the Maroon network of Jamaica. Two centuries earlier, runaway slaves in Jamaica sought refuge with natives of the island. Maroons began to develop around the island where the two oppressed peoples joined forces to protect one another. After the Sailor King freed the slaves in the British Empire, the Maroons began to flourish independently of the main settlements in Jamaica. This one became the unofficial capital of the different settlements and therefore the logical choice to begin the warning.

John is leading the five travelers through the jungle as they approach the first signs of the settlement. He holds up his hand to halt the other members and looks back to Ralphie. "Do you have the signal ready, Mr. Austin?"

"I have it right here, sir." Ralphie reaches inside his pack and pulls out a bow and arrow set, then puts the pack down, and strings the bow. John puts the arrow to the string and pulls it back, aiming at a tree just inside the camp about twenty-five yards in front of him. The arrow lodges into the tree about five feet off the ground.

Brandy walks forward. "Now what? And what kind of signal did you send them?"

"Now we wait." He motions for Ralphie to give him another arrow and shows Brandy the markings on the shaft. On the side are little carved figures of fish, and next to them is the figure of a star. "The fish symbols are the ancient signs that Christians used in the Roman Empire to signal to one another who they were. All of the abolitionist ships in the Caribbean use that symbol to let Maroons know who we are. The star is the symbol saying we are from our ship, *The Morning Star*."

As John is explaining these details to Brandy, an elderly, dark-skinned man and a young girl walk up. The man is holding the arrow that John shot. John immediately recognizes the two and breaks out a big smile. "Chief Desomond and Jada. I was hoping you would be the ones to see my arrow," he says.

Chief Desomond ignores John's outstretched hand and embraces him in a hearty hug. "John Edwards, so good to see you again!" He stops and looks at the rest of the group and to Brandy's surprise, seems to know everyone in it but her. First, he greets Ralphie. "Ralphie, the last time I saw you was when you were newly signed on with Captain Joshua as his cabin boy, all bright-eyed and ready to become a midshipman someday. Did you ever make it that far under that tough old sea captain?"

Ralphie grins. "Desomond, Captain Joshua made me midshipman three months after that, but now I am third mate on *The Morning Star*."

The old chief's eyes get big and round as he lets out a whistle. "Well, that is wonderful news! From what Captain Joshua has told me about your mother, I am sure she will bust her buttons with pride for you." He then looks over at Davonte and whistles again. "My, my, girl, but don't you become prettier every time I see you. Have you come to visit your old home, young lady?"

Davonte runs up and gives Desomond a hug and a kiss on the cheek. "John Edwards and Ralphie here have been staying at *Katrina's*. When I heard they were coming here, I so wanted to be with them to see you again."

"Well, I am glad you came, girl. We will have to talk later so you can tell me all about what those industrious parents of yours are up to these days."

Desomond then looks over to Zhang Yong. "Zhang, I told you the last time you were here that those herbs you wanted will not be ready for harvest for another month."

Zhang slightly bows his head. "Not to worry, honorable chief. Zhang not here for herbs. Zhang here to make sure John Edwards and friends are safe to deliver an important message to Maroon."

Desomond throws his head back and gives a big laugh as he looks over at John Edwards. "The stakes must be huge if Zhang thinks you need protecting, John Edwards. What is going on?"

Brandy steps up and says, "Chief Desomond, Governor Bennets and his chief administrator, Don Lomoche, have secretly commissioned a force of pirate ships to seek out, capture, and return runaway slaves to the United States. They have already captured some from an abolitionist ship and sunk it near Cuba. It won't be long until they raid the coastal Maroons."

Desomond stares at Brandy for a moment, then looks over at John Edwards with a bewildered look. "Who might this very passionate young woman be?"

John smiles. "This is Brandy. She and her Uncle Skynyrd own *Katrina's*, where Davonte works and Ralphie and I have been staying these past three months. It's a long story, but she and Zhang here saved Ralphie's and my life a few months ago and then she helped nurse me back to health. She is very trustworthy, Desomond. She volunteered to come with us to give you this warning." John pauses for a moment and looks at Brandy for permission to proceed. She seems to understand what he is asking and nods. He looks back to the chief. "She knows Lomoche—in some ways better than anyone. Her insights will prove invaluable."

Desomond nods to Brandy and John, then takes his granddaughter's hand. "Let us say no more in front of the child. Come, we will meet with the elders to discuss this tragic news."

With that said, he turns and walks back toward the Maroon camp. His granddaughter goes a few steps then breaks away and runs over to John and Brandy.

"John Edwards, the last time I saw you, you promised to teach me another game you played as a little boy. Did you forget?"

John grins, reaches inside his trouser pocket, and pulls out a small, leather bag with a string sewn into the seam that allows one to pull the opening closed. He opens the bag and pours out some small, multi-colored glass balls into his hand. "No, Jada, I did not forget. These are marbles, and I will show you how to play a game with them." He puts the marbles back in the bag and hands them to her. "Right now, I will meet with your grandfather, then we can find some of your friends and we'll play."

She holds out her hand and John drops the bag into it. Excited, she opens it, holds up one marble to the sunlight and looks into it. John ruffles her hair and turns to follow Desomond to his home.

"Thank you, John Edwards!" she says as she runs off to show her friends.

Brandy steps up beside John as they make their way to Desomond's home, grabs his hand and walks with him. She looks back at Ralphie and Davonte and flashes them a wicked grin as she recognizes their astonishment at how she is behaving. "What? You think you two are the only ones around here that get to have a little romance in your lives?"

Davonte buries her head in Ralphie's shoulder and giggles, holding her hand to her mouth. Ralphie smiles sarcastically, "That's fine, Brandy. Just don't let it impede our mission."

"Ralphie!" John says without turning his head. At that, the young couple reins it in a little and follows the others into Desomond's home.

Thirty minutes later, Desomond steps out and calls for some elders of the village to meet with him. He tells them about the threat and orders them to make preparations for defense and to send runners to the closest Maroons to warn the rest of the island. He assures John and

Brandy that within three days every Maroon in Jamaica will be prepared; and within two weeks, most if not all in the Caribbean will be as well.

An hour later, John and Brandy are sitting on the ground outside Desomond's home with Jada and several of her friends. John takes one marble and places it in the crook of his index finger with his thumb behind it. He aims at the rest of the marbles that are seated inside a circle drawn in the dirt and uses his thumb to shoot the marble in his hand at them. It directly hits a marble on the edge and propels it out of the circle. He looks at Jada. "You use your cue marble to knock out someone else's marble in the circle, but if your cue goes out, then you lose the point."

Jada takes her cue and shoots it at the marbles in the circle. Somehow, she gets it to spin around as it rolls forward, which causes it to knock two of John's marbles out as hers stays inside the circle, spinning in place.

John stares at the spinning ball in the circle for a moment and raises an eyebrow. "That's some good English you put on that marble there, Jada. Who taught you that trick?"

Jada giggles. "John Edwards, don't you remember that the last time I saw you, Captain Joshua promised my grandfather that he would have a billiards table shipped here? It came a few months later. Grandfather and I play all the time. We're the best players in the whole village. Grandfather figured out that if you hit the cue ball just right, it will stop almost immediately after hitting the first ball. I figured out that if I put a different spin on it, it would hit one ball and then another. Then I started to get more than one ball in the pockets at a time. Now, I beat Grandfather almost every time we play. These marbles seem to be just miniature pool balls, and my thumb is just like a cue stick."

John stares incredulously at Jada for a second, dumbfounded at the girl's intelligence.

Brandy sees that he is at a loss for words. "Jada, men always get a little dumbstruck when we girls show them how smart we really are. The key is not to do it too much or we'll wind up damaging their fragile male egos."

Jada smiles from ear to ear and looks back to her grandfather, who is standing in the doorway of his home, watching them. "Oh, I already know that, Brandy, believe me!" Desomond rolls his eyes and turns back into his home.

John grabs his cue marble and is setting up his next shot when he hears Ralphie's voice. "John Edwards, Zhang Yong knows almost everyone in this village. He comes here a lot and trades with the local healers for their herbs and stuff."

John and Brandy look up and see Ralphie, Davonte, and Zhang Yong walking up to them. They stand up to talk. "John Edwards, it is time for us to go back to Kingston," Zhang says. "One healer Zhang trades with was just there. He told Zhang that *The Morning Star* came into port the same day we left. Captain Joshua will want to see you right away, yes?"

CHAPTER 10

ALL THINGS MANIFESTLY DECLARED

One Day Later, Kingston

Because they did not have to follow the same path by which they came in order to throw off their pursuers, John and the group take a more direct route back to Kingston that only takes a day. They stop at *Katrina's* first to drop off their gear and get freshened up. When they arrive, Davonte has a very pleasant surprise waiting for her in Katrina's dining room. Her foster parents, Ben and Elisa, are there waiting for her. She runs up and hugs them both. "Momma! Poppa! I heard you were coming home on Captain Joshua's ship!" She looks over to Ralphie, then back at them and continues, "I have something very important to tell both of you. This is …"

"Whatever you have to say to us can wait, Davonte. Elisa and I have something very important to tell you," Ben says as he places his hand on her shoulder and motions for her to sit.

The fact that he did not refer to Elisa as her mother is not lost on anyone. Davonte feels a cold chill go up her spine as she sits down in a chair. She knows that when Poppa gets like this, he has something very serious to say. She looks over at Momma, who immediately reaches over to her and grabs her hand, holding it tightly. "Please, Davonte, just listen to Poppa. This is very serious."

Ben takes a deep breath. "Davonte, since you were just a little girl, I took you in and loved you as my own. We both have. Your real mother was a great lady. She taught us both to read and write in the white man's tongue. But more than that, she taught us things about the Christian God and His Bible that we never knew. She converted us to have faith in Christ, and that is how we raised you. Before she died, she told us who your father is, and that he would come looking for you. Seven years went by and he never came. We thought he did not care. He is a famous and a very respected man in England, and we judged him wrongly. We thought that since you and your mother were dark-skinned, he had abandoned you. But then he came looking for you. He did not understand what had happened to you and your mother.

"After you and your mother sailed for Jamaica, his king made him stay and fight one war after another for him. After many years, he finally let him go. He gave your father his fastest ship and told him to go find his family. Since that time, he has sailed to every Maroon in the Caribbean looking for your mother and you. We knew he was here, and we hid you from him because we told ourselves we did not trust him. But the truth is, we just did not want to lose you."

Elisa buries her head in Ben's chest and sobs. Ben holds her as he tries to calm the shakiness in his own voice. "Davonte, can you ever forgive us? We have wronged you. Your real father is alive and here right now. He has done everything in his power to be reunited with you, and we stood in his way."

Davonte is so stunned by her parents' words that she has none of her own to offer. She knows that Momma and Poppa would never intentionally hurt her, but she has never really thought about who her real father is because Poppa has always been there for her. Now she finds out that there is a man who has been looking for her for so long, who is her real father, who can tell her more about her mother. She finally looks up and asks, "Who is my father?"

Ben and Elisa are so choked up emotionally that they have a hard time answering.

John Edwards, who has been standing back listening to all of this, steps forward and places a gentle hand on Davonte's shoulder. "Davonte, your father is Captain Arthur Joshua, one of England's most celebrated naval sea captains and now master of *The Morning Star*. Seven years ago, he asked me to follow him to the Americas as first mate of *The Morning Star* to help him find his family. Since that time until now, I will say this—Captain Joshua has spent every waking moment of his life looking for you and your mother. While in that pursuit, he has also become a champion in the abolitionist movement and has moved more runaway slaves to freedom than any other captain in the Caribbean."

Davonte looks back at her parents and says, "Where is he?"

Ben looks up and points with his chin to the stairs at the other end of the dining hall. "He is upstairs with Dr. Johansson. His heart almost gave out when we told him the news after we left port in New York. He has been bedridden since then. As soon as we made port in Kingston, the doctor was called, and he had him moved here. The doctor and Captain Joshua asked that we all come up as soon as you got back."

Elisa regains her composure and stands up, then takes a deep, calming breath and holds out her hand to Davonte. "John Edwards's words are true, Davonte. Poppa and I have never met a finer man than Captain Joshua. He loves you with all his heart and wants nothing more than to see you. Come, we'll take you to him."

Ben stands up with his wife. They each take one of Davonte's hands and lead her up the stairs to Captain Joshua's room.

When Ben and Elisa told Davonte about her father, Ralphie slunk back with Brandy and Zhang Yong. Brandy reaches down and grabs his hand. "If everything I hear about this Captain Joshua is true, you have nothing to worry about, Ralphie. I do suggest that you let Davonte tell him about your engagement when she is ready."

John Edwards steps back to the two and smiles. "That is good advice, Brandy. But as third mate of *The Morning Star*, Ralphie has a sworn duty to tell his captain that he is now engaged to be married." Brandy is about to object, but John holds up his hand and continues. "But, since he has already told me, and I am second in command, I now have that duty as well. I can choose the appropriate time to either tell him myself or let Ralphie do it."

Brandy looks at John and then at Ralphie and lets out a gasp. "If life on *The Red Witch* was anything close to what you two and your crew have on *The Morning Star* with Captain Joshua, I would have claimed her eons ago. Come on, let's go watch this family reunion."

John and Ralphie are last while heading up the stairs. Ralphie tugs on John's shoulder and says in a hushed whisper, "What is she talking about, claiming *The Red Witch*?"

John is a little flabbergasted that Brandy said that in front of Ralphie, but he shakes his head. "Now is not the time to talk about that. Keep it to yourself, and that's an order, third mate."

Captain Joshua is in the same room that John and Ralphie have used for the last three months. When they enter, they find Dr. Johansson standing next to a bed that Captain Joshua is sitting upright in. He and the doctor are talking.

"Arthur, stay away from the sea for at least six months until we can determine if your heart is strong enough to handle the strain. I am sorry, but fifty years of sailing the world is plenty for any man."

Joshua is about to comment when he notices Ben, Elisa, and Davonte standing at the door. The doctor notices as well and has to push Joshua back down in his bed when he tries to leap out and meet them. "Arthur, please! You promised that you would be calm when this happened. Where the devil is Skynyrd? He was supposed to warn us before all of you came up here."

Before anyone can answer the doctor's question, Davonte steps away from Ben and Elisa and shyly makes her way over to the bed, where Captain Joshua is now sitting straight up with his bare feet touching the floor. When she gets there, she can see that he has a very pale look on his face and his eyes are watery. He bites his lip and tries to say something to her. She gently takes his feet and lifts them back into the bed, then covers him up to his chest with the bedding. She places a hand on his heart, kneels down and leans over to look into his eyes. "Please, Father, do as Dr. Johansson says. I only now have gotten you back, and I don't want to lose you again."

The emotion between the two is so palpable and thick in the room that everyone, including Zhang Yong and Dr. Johansson, is wiping the tears from their eyes. Captain Joshua takes one hand and cups it over Davonte's hand, resting on his heart. He takes his other hand and lays it on the side of her face as he looks deeply into her gray eyes. "How could I be so blind as to not know my own eyes staring back at me? You and I have that obvious physical attribute that we share and I did not see it. There you were, right in front of me, serving me and my officers our food. My own John Edwards stood up for your honor that night. I was in such a hurry to continue my search for you and your mother that I left him here to be cared for, ironically by my own daughter, whom I thought I would find. Fate can be both cruel and kind."

Davonte, openly sobbing now, lays her head on her father's chest. "Tell me about my mother! I know so little."

Captain Joshua looks up to the ceiling as the eyes of his heart stare off into the past. "You match your mother's beauty in every way. Oh, Cassandra—she was my queen. She was a Christian missionary educated at the University of Alexandria in Egypt and then sent to South Africa to teach the tribes there how to read and write and avoid the raiders who would come in and take them away as slaves. The village where she was working was caught by surprise by raiders. They did not care that she could speak their language and read and write better than any of them. They just saw the color of her skin and knew that her skills would just fetch them a better price at the slave markets. They used her to communicate with the different tribes on her ship. That ship was old and out of repair. They hit a vicious storm off the Ivory Coast of Africa. It looked like the ship would sink, so the cowardly crew abandoned her and her passengers.

"My ship and I were part of an armada on patrol with King George IV's brother, Vice Admiral William, in those waters. We came upon that ship and William ordered us to rescue its passengers. William could never stomach slavery and decided that we would move them to a place further south on the African continent where they took in refugees of the slave market. During that time, I got to know Cassandra and we fell in love. Your mother was the most genuine Christian person I have ever met. She taught me more about the Word of God than I ever learned in school or church. She showed me who Christ really is and how he is the only way to the heavenly Father. Her unwavering commitment to the Holy Scriptures is perhaps the greatest thing I still love about her to this day.

"William was sympathetic to our feelings and married us on my ship. Because we were under his command and no one would question the orders of a royal prince, he allowed her to stay with me and she soon became pregnant with you. But King George died, and they called

William back to England to be crowned king. By the time you were born, he knew that I could not be under another admiral's command and have her and you with me, so he arranged for both of you to get passage to the Caribbean. He put you and your mother in the care of a trustworthy merchant and his wife who were to protect you until he could arrange my transfer into this region. Captain Eric Erasmus, the Plague, and his demon wife, the Scarlet Mistress, attacked the ship you were on. They killed the merchant and his wife, and you and your mother eventually ended up here in Jamaica. It pains me that at one point, the two of you were under that idiot Bennets's nose, and had he known about you two, it would have been his duty to protect you when he took *The Red Witch*."

As Captain Joshua is talking, Brandy is standing next to John in the back of the room by the door. She suddenly gasps and holds her hand up to her face, then buries her face in John's shoulder. After a moment, she turns and steps out of the room. John knows something of what is bothering her and wants to pursue, but he holds himself there to be available for his captain. He steps forward and says, "Pardon the interruption, Captain Joshua. Brandy went to find Skynyrd. Please continue."

Captain Joshua waves his hand dismissively. "That's quite all right. It is good to see you up and looking more like yourself, First Mate Edwards. I trust that you and Third Mate Austin's mission was a success?"

"That it was, Captain Joshua. Desomond and his granddaughter, Jada, send their greetings and love. He has already alerted most of the Maroons on the island and will have word sent out to the rest of the Caribbean within the week."

"Did little Jada enjoy the marbles you brought her, John?" He looks around the room with a twinkle in his eyes. "Our John Edwards here has a soft spot for the children he meets at the different Maroons we visit. He always promises them that he will have a new game for them to learn when he returns. What astonishes me and the crew is his uncanny ability to remember all their names."

"Jada, Brandy, and I had quite a nice time playing marbles for a while. What she learned playing on that billiards table you sent to Desomond caused our little friend to easily figure out how to thrash me at marbles very quickly."

"You have never been the best at billiards, John. It's not surprising," Captain Joshua says as he laughs at the thought.

"True enough, sir."

Dr. Johansson steps forward. "Captain Joshua, that sedative I gave you should begin working at any moment. I suggest we postpone this meeting until after you wake up."

Captain Joshua lifts Davonte's hand from his shoulder with his free one and holds it to his lips. As he is about to kiss it, he notices that there is a gold ring on it. "My dear, I did not know that you are betrothed! May I ask who the fortunate young man is"

For a moment there is a very awkward silence in the room while Ralphie and Davonte shyly look at each other. John Edwards steps forward and begins to answer the question. "Sir..."

But then Ralphie puts his hand up and stays him. "Captain Joshua, sir, I had no idea Davonte was your daughter. Neither did she. But I asked her to marry me two days ago, and she said yes. John Edwards said it was okay because he said you allowed him to let me know about my promotion to third mate. I love her with all my heart, Captain. I promise that I will devote myself to her until the day I die."

Ralphie is in front of the bed now and doing his best to remain calm as Captain Joshua stares at him with his now teary gray eyes.

"Calm down, Mr. Austin. This is wonderful news ..." Captain Joshua says. Before he can finish the sentence, he falls asleep with a wide grin on his weathered face.

Davonte leans in and kisses Captain Joshua on the forehead before releasing herself from his grasp. "Momma, Poppa, I am sorry. I tried to tell you about Ralphie downstairs. Everything is happening so fast right now. I don't know what to say."

Ben and Elisa step forward to take Davonte in their arms and hold her as she cries. Elisa strokes her head for a moment and then looks over at Ralphie. "We met your mother and father in New York City. They are wonderful people and they are so proud of you. Davonte is a lucky girl!"

Ben looks up and steps over to Ralphie as he holds out his hand. "If Davonte said yes to you then you must be quite a good man. Glad to meet you."

Two hours later, John and Ralphie enter the front door of *Katrina's* after having taken a walk to the port to check in on *The Morning Star* and Second Mate Jacob Hind. John knows that Captain Joshua would have expected that from him and will want a status report from him when he wakes up. Ralphie runs off to find Davonte and John walks back to the kitchen to see if anyone is there. As he steps into the kitchen, he sees Skynyrd by the big stove, stirring a pot of stew.

"Brandy tells me she told you all of our dirty little secrets. How's that going to affect how you feel about her and me?" Skynyrd says without looking up.

John steps forward. "I believe that a man should be judged by what he is and what he does in the present more than in the past. Whatever crimes you are guilty of are between you and The Almighty. I do not know of Her Majesty's justice seeking either of you. When I look at you, all I see is the owner of one of the nicest taverns in Jamaica, the best cook in the Caribbean, and the uncle of the woman I love! And by the way, where might she be?"

"She be out back, practicing with Zhang Yong. We found her earlier crying and blubbering in the dining room. She found out that Davonte is the little girl who was with her mum on the boat she and I left on after her parents died. All of that guilt over what she was born into has been welling up in her since that day. Brandy is so much like her mother and so different. God knows I've tried to shield her from things. I'm just an old sea dog and ex-pirate. I ain't perfect, but I try." Skynyrd reaches up and wipes a tear from his cheek and then looks down and stirs his stew, embarrassed that John just saw him cry.

"It sounds like you already knew that Davonte was a passenger with you two, Skynyrd," John queries.

"Oh, I knew all right. I made it my business to find and help any of those wretched souls we had held captive on *The Red Witch* back then. I even went to the slave market where she and her mother were sold, and bid on them, but a rich plantation owner had too much money to spend. When they showed that the mother could read and write, he paid five times as much for those two. Little good it did him. She caught an island sickness and was dead within a year. When the Sailor King freed the slaves, I made sure her adoptive parents had work here in Kingston where I could keep an eye on her and help when they needed me to. Had no idea she was the daughter of someone as fine as Captain Joshua. Makes sense, though. Davonte was always a special girl."

He stops for a moment, then looks up and squints. "Then you two boys join our merry little group here at *Katrina's* and sweep my two best servers off their feet with all this romance. Young Ralphie will have an easy enough time. Ain't a sweeter girl alive than young Davonte. But you, John Edwards, I don't know whether to pity you or laugh at ya. That Brandy, she is as headstrong as her mother was and a lot meaner when she wants to be. Don't get me wrong, I love her like she was my daughter. She has the capacity of greatness in her, but most of the time with her, it's her way or no way. Just like her mother. Zhang Yong has helped her I guess, but she needs to see that what she was born to don't define her. It ain't her destiny to be a cold-blooded killer like her parents were. Maybe between you and Zhang, she'll finally see that."

"I'm going out to the courtyard, Skynyrd. Don't worry, your secret is safe with me. Neither Ralphie or even Captain Joshua will ever hear it from me," John says.

Skynyrd puts the lid back on his simmering stew. "Thank you, John Edwards. Like I said the first night I met you, you're a man whose mum taught him right, and you listened."

John reaches to his chest, grabs the medallion hanging around his neck and says under his breath, "That she did, Skynyrd. And I listened."

As he makes his way to the enclosed courtyard where Brandy and Zhang are practicing, he sees that they had left the gate partially open. He knows that means he can go in and practice himself, if he desires. Sometimes Brandy and Zhang's sessions are private and the door will be closed. Zhang would say that it is at those times that he and Brandy were involved in "Master's Training." He really did not know what that meant, only that it had something to do with those master's swords that Brandy was working so hard to earn.

When he steps through the gate, he sees something that he has never seen before—Brandy and Zhang in some type of sparring session. Before today, whenever John was there, Zhang would occasionally leave off instructing him and step over to give Brandy some constructive criticism on how she was performing her forms with the fan or her two sticks. But today, Zhang is using the master's swords and Brandy is using the fan. Their interaction is so graceful and poetic that it hardly looks like combat training and more like ballet. Zhang is jumping, swishing, and flowing the swords in and out of Brandy's perimeter. She is twisting and turning, using the fan in flowing movements to lightly deflect the blades that come within inches of contacting her. She too is dancing and swishing the fan in and out of Zhang's perimeter.

As John stands and watches the forms of interaction between the two, he realizes that it is the way Brandy is using her fan that allows her to sense where and when the blades will get too close. Although the speed and ferocity of the interaction is not at a level of true combat, John can see that one wrong move could cause some serious injury, especially to Brandy. The interaction goes on for a few more minutes before Zhang motions for them to halt. Brandy stops and bows and goes to the little shed to put her fan away and wipe herself off with a towel.

Zhang looks over at John and nods. "Was it nice to be back on your ship after all these months, John Edwards?"

John's face lights up. "It was like returning home, Zhang! I almost took her out to the bay for an inspection cruise just so I could feel the wind in her sails and the ocean rushing underneath."

"Why didn't you do that?" Zhang asks in his clinical *sifu* voice.

John studies Zhang for a moment. "Because I wanted to get back and see how Brandy is doing. I was worried about her."

Zhang smiles. "So, John Edwards, when confronted with the option of visiting the sea for a moment on your most favorite ship or seeing Brandy, you chose Brandy. Correct?"

"Well, yes, what of it?" John says with a hint of embarrassment in his tone. "What are you getting at, Zhang?"

"Oh, not to worry, John Edwards. It's just that sometimes words need to be spoken so another's heart can be cared for," Zhang says. He turns and walks over to Brandy at the shed. Brandy has a smile beaming across her face as she slyly looks over at John and blows him a soft kiss.

For the next hour, John works on his tai chi forms while Zhang and Brandy work with the sticks. John does not perform the forms like he used to when the monk from Hong Kong showed them to him. After learning the practical application of each form, he now practices them as though he is in actual combat. Zhang drilled into him the imagery of how each move feels when executed against an opponent when they practiced together. He would say, "The key, John Edwards, in making the forms help you get better is to remember how they feel when being used for real while you practice."

Since Zhang is always his sparring partner when practicing, John would imagine that Zhang is the one he is using the techniques on when he mimics a kick, punch, block, or throw. It amazes him how, when his mind makes him "feel" the impact of the punch, his legs would compensate for the extra weight and his feet would "feel" the impact of the kick. He would also feel the punch or kick that Zhang would occasionally give him in practice to show him that no move is perfect, and that in the fluidity of combat, adjustments have to be made.

When everyone is finished, the three are standing next to the shed. Zhang, though having done as much physical exertion as Brandy and John, looks no worse for wear. Unlike the other two, he is not drenched in sweat and his clothing is neat and in place. He looks at them and nods slightly. "I have to play instruments tonight in *Katrina's*. Must prepare for all music-loving sailors who come to hear Zhang." He turns and walks out of the courtyard.

After Zhang leaves, John notices that he shuts the gate behind him. He gets a wicked grin on his face and grabs Brandy, pulls her into his arms, and kisses her. At first, she responds, but then she pushes him back and snarls, "Good god, you're sweaty! You need a bath."

John laughs and pulls off his shirt. "I left my change of clothes by the shower booth. I won't be but a little while."

Brandy sees his mother's locket around his neck, resting on his glistening muscular chest. She longingly adores it. "I'll use the other shower, and then maybe we can go for a walk before *Katrina's* opens."

"I would love that, Brandy. See you soon." He races out the gate and to the showers.

Brandy puts her things away in the shed. As she is closing the door, she looks briefly at the locked drawer that contains the master's swords she has been working for and is momentarily tempted to pick the lock and pull them out to admire them. When she first started training with Zhang, she did that a lot, but she began to notice that every time she did that, the next training session with Zhang was always rough. She closes the doors to the shed and walks over to the shower.

After they are finished showering, Brandy and John walk hand-in-hand toward the dock where *The Morning Star* is berthed. The September Caribbean sunset is especially beautiful with its golden flakes of light twinkling off the gentle ocean, which rolls and ripples as it kisses the waters in the western horizon. John pulls Brandy close as they stand at the top of the steps that lead to the dock area. Brandy gently leans her head over and kisses him on his cheek as she sees him adoringly looking at the silhouette of *The Morning Star* at the end of the dock. "Thank you for not taking her out right away, John. After learning that Davonte was the little girl we had captured, along with her mother, then finding out that she is Captain Joshua's long-lost daughter … well, it was a little much!" Brandy wipes a tear from her eye.

John takes his hand, turns her head toward him and gently kisses her on the lips. "Yet, you have befriended and protected her for many years. Who's to know what would have become of Davonte and her family if you and Skynyrd had never taken care of them? It just may be because of you that Captain Joshua has been reunited with his daughter."

Brandy gasps slightly and looks straight up into John's eyes. "How do you do it, John? You always see the good in a situation."

John puts both hands on her shoulders, shakes her gently, and looks into her mesmerizing green eyes. "It's not hard when I am standing here beholding the best thing I have ever seen in my life."

Brandy reaches forward and places her hand on John's chest. She can feel his mother's medallion beneath his shirt, and she caresses it softly through the cloth. She leans in close and places the side of her face against his chest where she can feel him breathe and hear the beating of his heart. "I am in love with you, John Edwards. I never thought I would ever love anyone like this, but I love you."

John softly strokes her hair with his hand and with a quiver in his voice says, "And I, you, Brandy. I love you too."

CHAPTER 11

NEW PATHS

Late that Evening, *Katrina's*

Davonte took the night off from serving tables to care for her father. Captain Joshua was in and out of consciousness throughout the day. Dr. Johansson told her that he believes he will make a good recovery, and with proper care and enough rest he will live a long, healthy life. When she asked about her father returning to the sea, the doctor said that for all practical purposes, that part of his life was over. Somehow that news was welcome to her. She did not remember much about her mother, but she knew that she died a sad and lonely woman. Perhaps if fate had been kinder, her mother could have had Captain Joshua at her side where he belonged.

She will always think of Ben and Elisa as her momma and poppa, but she now realizes that her heart has an open place for this kindly man who never gave up looking for her. It did not go unnoticed by her how happy he was when he found out that she and Ralphie were to be married. All the stars were lining up for her in her life and she feels very blessed. As she is wiping her father's forehead with a damp towel, his eyes open and he slowly sits up and smiles. "I am very thirsty. May I have some water, please?"

"Of course, Father." Davonte goes over to the table, where there is a tub of drinking water with a ladle in it and a cup to the side. She fills the cup and takes it to her father.

He takes a few swallows and hands the cup back to her. "Thank you, my dear. Would you mind telling me where John Edwards and Ralphie are right now? I have some business I need to discuss, especially with John."

"It sounds like they just closed down the dining hall a little while ago, Father. I suspect that they are in the kitchen helping Skynyrd and Brandy clean up."

"Well, when they are done, I need to see them. There is the matter of *The Morning Star* and her mission to discuss. The good doctor has clarified that being her master is not in my cards anymore, but she needs a master, and John is uniquely qualified for that position." He looks over at his daughter. "With John moving up to captain, your Mr. Austin will move right into second mate. Which, I might add, is a proper position for a young officer to be in when he is planning for matrimony soon."

Davonte beams with pride. "You really love Ralphie, don't you, Father?"

"That goes without saying, my dear. A pure-hearted boy that one is. Strong and determined. Doing the right thing is his nature, and I long ago accepted him as family. Albeit, when he discovers the dowry he will have to share with you, I think he might go into shock and perhaps collapse from it." A mischievous gleam flickers in Captain Joshua's gray eyes.

"Dowry! Captain Joshua, Momma and Poppa are good, hard-working people and I think they can afford a nice but simple wedding for us, but a dowry is out of the question," Davonte gasps.

Captain Joshua chuckles and reaches over to take Davonte's hand. "My dear, I am not talking about Ben and Elisa. They already have given so much to you and me. No, you see, I am Arthur Joshua, of the London Joshua family. We own the biggest ship building house in London Harbor. My older brother, Christopher Joshua, your uncle, is the principle master of that firm, holding sixty percent of the stock. I own forty percent, and you are my only heir."

Davonte sits down on the side of the bed and stares at her father. "I am your only heir! What does that mean?"

Captain Joshua leans back against his pillow. "It means you are the richest girl on this island, perhaps in the whole Caribbean." He leans toward her. "I only ask that you let me tell Ralphie this in my own good time. I dearly love that boy and I think of him as family already, so this will be so much fun!"

Davonte takes a little time to help her father get into his proper attire to meet with his officers. Afterward, she sends word to *The Morning Star* for Jacob Hind to join them, then goes downstairs and tells John and Ralphie that once all of *The Morning Star* officers were available, they were to report to Captain Joshua's room to discuss ship's business.

One hour later, John Edwards, Jacob Hind, Ralphie, and Davonte are in Captain Joshua's room.

Captain Joshua and Davonte are seated at the table, where he has several documents spread out and is signing them. John, Jacob, and Ralphie are standing in front of the table waiting for him to say something. Joshua hands a piece of paper to Davonte and shows her where to sign. Once she is finished signing, he takes the paper back and looks up at the men. "John, Jacob, Ralphie, you know that *The Morning Star* was a gift to me from His Majesty King William IV, but there is more. John and I never left active duty in the Royal Navy. I secretly keep the rank of Rear Admiral of the Blue, which the king promoted me to when we left. Few know this, but his niece, Queen Victoria, and John Edwards are among those few. When we left, the king gave *The Morning Star* to me as personal property but commissioned us both to aid the freed slaves in the Caribbean. This was the official commission that we were to hold until I could locate my family. Queen Victoria never rescinded that commission, so it still holds the weight of a royal decree."

He takes a document and hands it to John Edwards. "First Lieutenant Edwards, I hereby promote you to the rank of captain in Her Majesty's Royal Navy. You have fulfilled all that I have asked of you these last seven years and are free to return to regular service. I have included with your promotion papers a letter of recommendation that you be given command of the first man-of-war that becomes available in the fleet. I believe this is what we agreed on when I asked you to come help me in my quest."

John salutes and looks at the papers for a few moments. "Indeed, that was our agreement, Captain … uh … Admiral Joshua. Might I ask if there are any other options left to me at this stage?"

Joshua's relief is emphatic and noticed by all in the room. "Yes, John, of course there is. *The Morning Star* needs a master, and our commission is still active, albeit only for a while. I would offer you command of both."

John steps forward and offers Joshua his hand. "I accept, sir. What are your orders?"

"First things first, Captain Edwards. I think we better explain our situation a little more thoroughly to your two senior officers." Admiral Joshua directs John's attention to Jacob Hind and Ralphie, standing next to him.

John suddenly remembers the two are there and looks over to see the utter confusion written on each of their faces. He then looks back to Joshua and says, "May I?"

"By all means, Captain, go right ahead," Joshua replies.

"Gentlemen, His Majesty commissioned Admiral Joshua and myself to first locate his wife and child, and second, to aid the freed slaves of the

British Empire any way we see fit. *The Morning Star* is officially a British merchant ship and falls under British maritime law. Admiral Joshua and I brought her to the Caribbean and put together a civilian crew that was in agreement with the abolitionist cause to aid in our commission. Admiral Joshua funded the activities of our missions from his private fortune. Though he does, as you now know, hold the rank of an admiral in the Navy, his title as master of *The Morning Star* is that of captain. Admiral Joshua has stepped down from that position and has offered it to me, which, as you saw, I have accepted. Now, knowing all of this, I would like to ask both of you if you will continue on *The Morning Star* as my first and second mates?"

Ralphie and Jacob Hind look sideways at one another for a moment and then burst out in laughter. "We want to continue on with you, Captain Edwards!"

"I am curious about something, though, Admiral Joshua. What will be your involvement with us at this point?" Jacob asks.

"I will send an official announcement to Her Majesty Queen Victoria that I have found my daughter, and I will relate the tragic news about my wife, Cassandra. Since she knew of my commission under her uncle, King William, and has honored it to this day, and now that John has decided to carry on as master of *The Morning Star*, I will request of Her Majesty that I be allowed to set up a special naval office here in Jamaica officially designated to helping all the freed slaves in the Caribbean. Davonte and I will continue to fund *The Morning Star* in all her abolitionist activities, and as an admiral in the Caribbean, I will protect her to a point."

"Why doesn't the British government just come out and help us abolitionists officially? Wait a minute ... did you say that you *and Davonte* will continue to fund our missions?" asks Ralphie.

Joshua and John both look at each other and smile. "To answer your first question, Ralphie, Her Majesty is very sympathetic to the abolitionist's cause in the United States. But there are powerful elements in the empire that are not. The queen's husband, Albert, has stated in some circles that if a civil war were to break out in the United States, he would support the southern slave states. I believe he would do this because he looks for an opportunity to see your country weaken itself enough that he could take it back into the British Empire once that war has taken its toll on the population. But another point to consider is that Great Britain has tried twice to bring the colonies back under British rule and failed. The queen will not openly risk opposing either side for fear of bringing Britain into another war. Therefore, what *The Morning Star* and her crew accomplish for the abolitionist movement must appear to be separate from all British dealings in this area."

Joshua reaches down and picks up two official documents from the table, one of birth and citizenship and the other a last will and testament, signed by Admiral Joshua and witnessed by Dr. Johansson, and hands them to Ralphie. "To answer your second question, Ralphie, these documents make it official that Davonte is my only child and therefore my rightful heir. Everything that I have is now hers also. And once you are married, it will belong to both of you."

Ralphie's cheeks turn beet red and his eyes swell like a blowfish as he plops down in a chair next to Davonte and looks at the documents in total disbelief.

Davonte smiles and rubs Ralphie's back. "Is this why you wanted to be the one to tell him?" she asks her father.

Admiral Joshua tries to hold a straight face for a few moments, but he cannot and bursts out with thunderous laughter so infectious that John, Jacob, and lastly, Davonte join in.

"This says your name is Daphne Joshua. Is that what I call you now?" Ralphie asks Davonte.

She looks at the document then back at her father for an answer.

He shakes his head. "My dear, you use whatever name you want. Daphne was the name your mother and I gave you when you were born. But if you want to be called Davonte, that is your choice." He leans back and lets out a sigh. "Now, Captain Edwards, it is almost the middle of September, and we are fast approaching the hurricane season for this part of the world. I have already scheduled *The Morning Star* to be at the Maroon on the tip of Florida in one week. I am told there are at least forty runaway slaves there, and many of those are families. Our old friend, Neseem, is now chief of a new Maroon near La Plata in Argentina and will take them into his settlement. Sail as quickly as possible and get them to safety. With Governor Bennets's and Don Lomoche's treachery afoot, you will need to be especially vigilant."

John thinks for a moment. "Admiral, *The Morning Star* is the fastest ship of her size in the Caribbean. I think we can do this and still be back to Kingston by the first week in October. If not, the lads and I will just hunker down in South America until the storm season passes. *The Morning Star* still has its thirty-six guns, and we should not be under threat by any local pirates. As for *The Red Witch,* unless they have an armada and can push us into the coast, she is no threat to us. We will always be able to outrun her. We will port nowhere that is not protected by British naval forces."

Admiral Joshua sits back in his chair and rubs the crest of his brow. "I think you are right, Captain Edwards. This should be a mission with little consequence. Make your preparations and be ready to leave within two days."

Two Days Later, Kingston Harbor, *The Morning Star* Main Deck

Though the sun is out and the Caribbean sky is crystal blue, Captain John Edwards can feel the beginnings of the storm season in his bones and knows he will be in for some rough weather.

Brandy is grateful that John has included her in every stage of his preparations to launch his new command this morning. She really was not surprised when he explained to her that he was still an active British naval officer and that Admiral Joshua had just promoted him to captain. When he explained that he had the choice to go back to England and wait to be assigned command of an English man-of-war or stay and assume command of *The Morning Star,* and that he had chosen the latter, she was ecstatic. She and Skynyrd volunteered to buy and stock the ship with everything they would need for their voyage. When Admiral Joshua offered to pay, Skynyrd refused, saying that he wanted to be a part of *The Morning Star's* missions from now on.

While Ralphie and Jacob Hind are overseeing the crew carrying the goods onto the ship, Brandy and John are by the gangplank going over lists and checking off items as they are being loaded. As the last of the supplies are loaded, Ralphie steps up to John. "Captain Edwards, permission to go ashore and say goodbye to my fiancée."

"Permission granted, Mr. Austin. Make it quick, though. I want to launch in half an hour."

Ralphie belts out a quick, "Aye aye, Captain," then runs down the plank and to the dock where Davonte is waiting for him.

Brandy sets her stack of documents down, walks over to John and cups his cheeks with her hands. "You know, after he marries Davonte, you'll practically be working for him?"

John thinks about it for a moment, then smiles and nods. He clasps one of her hands, brings it to his lips and brushes it with kisses. "This is true. But once out to sea, the captain is the master of the vessel and all else are subject to his commands, even the owner." John is holding Brandy in his arms and as he is about to kiss her, they both hear someone loudly clearing their throat. He turns to see Admiral Joshua and Davonte standing near them. "Admiral, I am sorry, I did not see you. Come to see us off, sir?" John says as he releases the embrace with Brandy and turns to greet him.

"Well, yes, and there is one last order of business I want to conclude with you before you go. Davonte, Ralphie, and I talked this over last night and we are all in agreement. We want you to have ownership of *The Morning Star*. I am headed to the Kingston garrison to introduce myself as an admiral in this district after we see you off. I could not find out where Admiral Thompson is. My sources say that he has not been to his office at the governor's mansion in weeks. I hope that Captain Walters can enlighten me to his whereabouts. When I'm there, I will register you as the new master and owner of *The Morning Star*."

"This is stunning news, Admiral! Are you sure you want to do this? I know what this ship means to you."

"John, no one loves this ship more than me, except for you. If you command her, you should have final say in everything about her. Oh, and now that I have officially recognized Davonte as my daughter, she will be the one to fund all your missions from her private fortune. No one will question her motives, and I will be above political and military scrutiny."

John shakes Admiral Joshua's hand. "As always, Admiral, you have thought of everything. Now, with your leave, we will launch and be on our way."

"You have my leave, Captain, and Godspeed to you and your crew." He offers his arm to Davonte and moves toward the gangplank. "Brandy, would you care to join us?"

Brandy smiles slyly, looks at John, then turns to Admiral Joshua. "I will be along in a bit. Captain Edwards and I were just finishing up the inventory."

She waves to them as they walk away. "So, you will be gone for almost six weeks, and if storms hit, you might have to winter down there. It'll be a long wait."

John pulls her in close. "There won't be a moment that I will not miss your beautiful face and those intoxicating green eyes of yours. You know, you should come with me. This is not a military vessel." He holds up the ownership papers and continues, "And now I set all the rules for this ship, at sea and in port."

Brandy wraps her arms around John's shoulders then gently pulls his head down and kisses him. She releases her hold and moans into his shoulder. "I will miss you, my love. I can't go with you now, but please come back to me soon."

She pulls back a little, places her hand on his chest and feels the imprint of the medallion. She caresses it with her fingers, then looks up into his eyes, expecting him to do something. He reaches down and kisses her fingertips lightly. "Wish me fair winds and following seas. I will be back before you know it."

Brandy stands there for a moment and looks deeply into his beautiful blue eyes, waiting for him to say something else, but no more words come. She smiles sadly. "Okay, John, we will talk when you get back. Have a safe trip. Bring Ralphie back safely to his fiancée." She turns to leave.

"Brandy, is everything all right? Are you angry over something?"

Without turning, Brandy says, "We'll talk when you return, John. Stay safe, and Godspeed." Before John can reply, she runs off the ship and up the dock to join the others. When she gets far enough away that she can barely see John standing by the gate where the gangplank has been drawn, she reaches up with her hand and waves them off. She thinks silently, *All you had to do, John, was give me that medallion.*

Kingston Garrison, Office of Captain Walters

Arnold Walters sits at his desk, astonished by what he is holding in his hand. A few moments ago, a special envoy from a British naval frigate that ported last night arrived at his office with an official message from

Queen Victoria herself. He has read the letter five times and still can hardly believe the contents:

My Dearest Captain Walters,

It is my sincere desire that this message finds you in good health and soundness of mind. We have been deeply concerned with the state of affairs in Jamaica for some time. It has been brought to our attention that Governor Bennets may be consorting with known pirates and illegally allowing the practice of slavery within the British Empire. We have dispatched a special parliamentary envoy who will have our royal leave to assess and pronounce judgment in all these matters. You can expect him in Jamaica within three to four weeks after receiving this message. Until that time, it is our desire that you keep the contents of this message quiet. If you find you need help and guidance, we give you permission to reach out to our faithful Admiral, Arthur Joshua. He has been operating under a royal assignment in the Caribbean for several years as our agent. He has, as of the writing of this message, been advanced to the rank of Vice Admiral and therefore supreme military commander of all British assets in the Caribbean. You are to answer to him alone until our representative joins you.

Her Majesty Queen Victoria in the year of our Lord, 9 July, 1844

He finishes reading the message for the sixth time when he hears a rap on his office door. "Come in." When the door opens, his heart almost explodes in his chest. He jumps out of his chair and stiffly salutes. "Vice Admiral Joshua! I was just about to go to *Katrina's* to show you this." He holds out the document for him.

Admiral Joshua is taken aback by the garrison captain's strict adherence to military protocol, especially since Joshua is not in his British naval uniform and no one in this area is supposed to know he is an Admiral. Military discipline kicks in, and he returns the salute. "At ease, Captain." Then it dawns on him. "Wait! Did you just call me Vice Admiral?" He takes the document from Captain Walters's trembling hand and reads it.

Without looking up, he motions for the captain to have a seat while he settles down in the chair in front of the desk. "It would appear that Her Majesty received my last communication and has responded. Apparently, what I said about how Bennets is administering his duties here did not sit well with her." He finishes reading the letter and hands it back to Captain Walters.

Walters takes the letter, puts it in a drawer in his desk and then pulls a key from his pocket and locks it. "Would you care for some refreshment, Admiral?"

"Some tea would be welcome. Thank you, Captain. My daughter and Brandy are waiting outside. Do you mind if I invite them in? At this point there is little they do not understand about my situation, and I vouch for both of them on my honor."

"Admiral, you are the supreme commander of Her Majesty's forces in the Caribbean. You hardly need my permission to do anything."

"That is where you are incorrect, Captain. In a civilized military, respect given for another's command must always be adhered. Bennets is a tyrant, full of nonsensical political ambitions. He has run roughshod over Her Majesty's citizens and government long enough. Anyone subject to my authority will maintain strict adherence to the common protocols and decency expected of any officer or steward in Her Majesty's service." He looks over his shoulder. "Davonte, Brandy, would you both come in, please?"

Captain Walters and Admiral Joshua stand as the two women enter the office. Joshua walks over to Davonte, takes her hand and places his other on her shoulder. "Captain Walters, may I present my daughter, Davonte Daphne Joshua." He reaches in his jacket breast pocket, pulls out some documents and hands them to Walters. "If you would be so kind as to register these documents with Her Majesty's government, legitimizing that Davonte is my daughter and sole heir."

Walters takes the documents and looks at them for a moment. "Certainly, Admiral, I will have these registered and notarized immediately." He then looks at Davonte. "Davonte, how wonderful! To think that you are the long-lost daughter of Britain's most loved sea captain. This must be quite overwhelming for you."

"Thank you, Captain Walters. Yes, it was a little much to take in." She smiles and looks adoringly at Admiral Joshua. "But Father has told me so much about my mother that I did not know. The more he reveals, the more I see how much of my parents I have in me. It is so wonderful!"

"I am so happy for you both." Walters studies the other documents. "What's this? You are transferring ownership of *The Morning Star* to John Edwards? This is incredible!"

Joshua reveals a devious grin. "That's another thing I think you should be aware of, Captain. John Edwards is also still a British naval officer. As of last night, he is a full captain, and yes, now master and owner of *The Morning Star*. That ship has been one of the great blessings of my life, but for me it has served its purpose in aiding me to find my daughter. Anyway, Dr. Johansson tells me my seafaring days are over."

Walters takes the documents and starts to place them on a pile on the corner of his desk. Brandy, who has been standing quietly while the others converse, notices that the document on the desk that Walters is about to cover says, "Title of Ownership for Man-of-War: *The Red Witch*." Brandy points at the document. "Captain Walters, is that the ship that was stolen by the pirate Faustin Reece, who attacked Ralphie and John last June?"

Walters pulls the title from the stack. "Yes, it is. When Faustin hijacked it after escaping custody, I dug this out because I remembered that there was some discrepancy the governor contested when the taxing office tried to levy customs against its worth, while it was being used in British-controlled waters. The governor argued that he had commandeered the vessel but did not own it, so he refused to pay any taxes on its worth, only on its use."

Brandy asks to see the title and Walters hands her the document. "It says here that Eric and Katrina Erasmus transferred full ownership of the vessel to their daughter, Brandy Erasmus. The title is witnessed by Skinner Erasmus and Don Lomoche. Tell me, Captain, how would the rightful owner go about claiming that ship?"

Walters takes the document and places it on his desk. "Well, first she would have to come back from the dead. The crew of *The Red Witch* killed Brandy Erasmus after she took Don Lomoche's hand and poked out his eye. Then she would have to prove that she was who she said she was."

"How would she go about proving herself?"

"Well, one good way would be to have one witness of the document identify her to a British government representative with the authority to acknowledge her."

"Would you or Admiral Joshua have that kind of authority?"

Walters raises his eyebrows and then looks to the admiral for guidance. Joshua nods his head in the affirmative and Walters looks back at Brandy. "Well, yes, Brandy, we could. Where are you going with this?"

Brandy takes a deep breath and looks back at Davonte, who is now staring at her with a perplexed look. "Okay, Captain John Edwards already knows this, and since you two seem to be able to protect my uncle and me from Bennets and Lomoche, I will say it. I am Brandy Erasmus. My Uncle Skinner and I snuck off *The Red Witch* with the rest of the prisoners after Bennets boarded it. My mother knocked Lomoche unconscious and had three of the crew promise they would swear to him and Bennets that they slit my throat and threw me overboard. She feared that since Lomoche had already killed my father and she fully expected Bennets to immediately execute her, that they would also kill me so that they could confiscate *The Red Witch* with no dispute. Skinner shaved off his beard and his hair. They cut mine short and dyed it black. We made it here to Jamaica undetected, and my uncle used what fortune he had saved over the years to buy and open *Katrina's*. We have been here ever since."

Brandy feels icicles going up and down her spine, wondering what Davonte's reaction will be. She walks over to her and grabs both of her hands. "I am sorry, Davonte. I had no idea you were one of those prisoners on *The Red Witch* until the other night when your father explained what had happened to you and your mother. We rode in the same skiff over to the English man-of-war that brought us here. There was a mother with a young girl sitting right next to me and my uncle that I now know was you. My uncle told me a few nights ago that he tried to buy you and your mother when Bennets had you turned over to the slave market back then. He was outbid because the plantation owner wanted your mother, as she could read and write. When the slaves were freed, my uncle made sure that you and your new family were always with gainful employment and he did his best to watch out for you. I am so sorry for what we did to you, Davonte. Can you ever forgive me?" Brandy takes a deep breath and looks into Davonte's eyes for her response.

Before Davonte can respond, Admiral Joshua steps forward. "Brandy, it wasn't you who ordered *The Red Witch's* crew to attack and sink my wife's ship. Nor was it you who took her passengers prisoner to be sold at pirate slave markets. My dear, a ship runs on the direction of its captain and his officers. Tell me, was Skynyrd—I am sorry, *Skinner*— an officer on your father's ship?"

Brandy thinks for a moment. "Well, no. He was the head cook, and in the morning, he would man the lookout nest. But Father never gave him much responsibility. Father and Mother ran the ship, the first mate was Don Lomoche, and he had two others besides. Come to think of it, Skinner never really took part in any raiding or boarding. He was always assigned to protect me. At the time they killed my father, my mother was training me to fight, but they had not given me the opportunity to be a part of things yet. My father promised me that by my sixteenth birthday I would be ready. They murdered him just after I turned fifteen."

Admiral Joshua nods his head and sighs. "That makes sense, Brandy. I have been a warrior for more years than I care to admit. I have seen and fought many men. Some were good lads just flying a different flag than I, and some were cold-blooded killers, like your father and Lomoche. You get to know the difference after a while. The man that I know as Skynyrd has a good heart and has never really been a cold-blooded killer. You, my dear, have never been that either. This can be a wicked and cruel world and sometimes it puts us in dark places. But you and your uncle held on to some light while surrounded by that darkness. Now, tell me, why do you want to claim that cursed ship, *The Red Witch?*"

"Yes, Brandy, why? I don't blame you for anything. You've been like a sister to me. And Skynyrd, like my uncle too. Why would you want that horrible ship?"

Brandy takes a deep breath and looks around the room. "The crew, I guess. My mother cursed them to stay on that ship and wait for my return. Skynyrd says that after she ran off the plank and killed herself, the crew thought they were bound by her blood to stay there. They have no love for or allegiance to Lomoche, or anyone he would set up to captain it. I could make them turn on him and Bennets, and they would follow me. They have been wasting away aboard her for fifteen years. If you and Captain Walters here were to make my claim official and show that I am alive, we could get word to *The Red Witch's* crew, then they would mutiny and bring it wherever I wanted it. Once with us, I could order them to tell you all of Lomoche's and Bennets's dirty little secrets."

Joshua quietly thinks for a moment as the others wait. "Captain Walters, what is the size of your regiment here at the garrison compared to the governor's guard? And can you count on all your men's loyalty?"

"Admiral, all my men are loyal to me and therefore loyal to the crown. We have fifty enlisted men and five officers. The governor has two hundred under his control that are loyal to him; and his assistant, Lomoche, who also has almost three hundred private mercenaries under his command."

"How many British naval vessels are docked at Kingston, and how many more are close enough to Jamaica that they will be here within the next two weeks?"

"Besides the frigate that arrived last night with your message, there's only one local frigate in port. The newly arrived frigate is a fifth-rate two-decker with fifty guns and a complement of 150, and the other frigate is a local patrol sixth-rate with twenty guns and a crew of 110. There is also Bennets's former command, a second-rate three-decker ship of the line. She has eighty guns and a crew of 675. She is not scheduled to be back for another five weeks."

Joshua puts his hand to his chin and mulls over the information. "I am afraid we will have to hold on to your secret at least until that man-of-war docks or the parliamentary envoy arrives from England." He points to the desk drawer where Walters put the letter from the queen. "We have ample proof of my promotion from rear admiral to vice admiral, and under normal circumstances, it would be received without question. But let's not forget that as far as Bennets knows, I am a retired British naval sea captain. I don't know Admiral Thompson, and without this promotion, he would be my senior, even if my admiralty was revealed. The governor is not an honorable man and would use the circumstance of my secrecy against us. If we had that man-of-war in dock, I know that I could convince them of my legitimacy of rank and have them help us arrest the governor. But as it stands, we are outnumbered, and I won't ask men to risk their lives without a chance to win the day. For now, we wait."

Next Evening, Secret Maroon, Southern Tip of Florida

Captain John Edwards can't get his last conversation with Brandy out of his mind. He tried to convince himself that he did not understand what had unsettled her so much that she would run away from him like she did, but deep down in his heart he knew. His mother's medallion still hangs around his neck, and he knows that after telling her its story, she had every right to expect him to give it to her before he left. He was planning to give it to her soon, but with the excitement of Admiral Joshua finding his daughter and turning over *The Morning Star* to him like he did, he felt the old, exhilarating pull of life at sea and had held back the medallion. The conflict in his heart was so real that he felt ill. He could not deny that it was not *The Morning Star* or all of his adventures at sea that he saw when he closed his eyes. No, now all he can see is Brandy's intoxicating green eyes staring back at him, as her beautiful full red lips whisper, "This is where your heart lives now, John. Come home!"

"Captain Edwards, we are about to enter the harbor. What are your orders, sir?"

John shakes the reverie from his mind and focuses on his first mate, standing in front of him at the helm. "Bring her in, Mr. Hind. Slow and steady. Mr. Austin!"

"Yes, Captain?"

"Be ready to dock and deploy planks to receive passengers. Have all available hands on deck to assist. Stay vigilant. They have spotted raiding parties all over southern Florida looking for runaway slaves. I want ten men with rifles on deck for guards, and cannon manned and ready."

"Aye aye, Captain!" comes the simultaneous replies from Hind and Ralphie.

John goes to the front of his ship, takes out his spyglass, and scans the shore. The sun has not quite set behind him in the western Caribbean sky, and he can still make out the silhouette of the grass and coconut wood huts built back around the tree line. The small dock they are porting at is hardly big enough for a class three, double decker Baltimore frigate like *The Morning Star*, but they have been here several times before without incident, and he expects none today.

A flash of light catches the periphery of his spyglass and a second later the sound of gunfire pierces his ears, then screams of women and children erupt. As he focuses on the area where the sound is coming from, he sees a large group of dark-skinned people running toward the dock being chased by armed men on horses and on foot. Without hesitation, and with a burning anger coursing through his gut, he looks back at his mates. "To arms, men! I want cannon fire trained on the middle and rear of those pursuers. Mr. Hind, gather twenty armed men and be ready to move as soon as we dock. Mr. Austin, send one cannon volley into those bastards and cover our retreat with rifle fire. Make ready to repel boarders!"

"Aye aye, sir!" echoes in John's ears as he grabs his pistol and sword belt, straps it on, and heads to the first gangplank to be ready to charge ashore with Jacob Hind and his men.

As *The Morning Star* edges closer to shore, a loud volley of twelve 8-pounder cannon fire erupts from the stern of the ship. John looks to the raiders and sees that it was a fairly accurate hit. The rear section of the pursuers erupts in confusion as horses and men are cut down and blown apart by cannon balls exploding in their midst. The shockwave that it sends to the front of the ranks has the desired effect. Men leave off their pursuit and head for cover in the trees.

The Morning Star pulls into the dock. Ralphie and some men tie her off and deploy the planks, and John, Jacob, and twenty others run to aid the people of the Maroon.

John spots the man he is looking for. He is a tall, slender individual in his fifties with a bald head and a white mustache and beard. He runs in his direction. When the man sees John, he waves him over to where he is aiding an elderly woman.

"John Edwards, it is good you came when you did. It was only a matter of time before they found us. It is one thing to have a Maroon. Quite another to be a pickup point for runaway slaves. I'm afraid we'll have to leave this village now."

"Josiah, get your people to *The Morning Star.* We'll take all of you to safety," John says. He draws his revolver and fires on the raiders, who are now mounting a counterassault. John looks over to Jacob. "Move the men to cover the rear of the villagers. As far as I can tell, the raiders are using single-shot muskets and pistols. Most of them have fired and not reloaded. If we rush them, we can weaken their numbers. Have your sword ready. This will get up close and personal fast."

Before Jacob can respond, Josiah shouts, "John Edwards, this is only a small raiding party, but they are a part of a much larger unit sent to look for us! Many more will be here soon!"

John nods his head. "Hurry! We'll make sure all of you get to the ship before we leave." John and Jacob form a line, raise their weapons, and fire. Several of the raiders who were trying to reload fall from the volley.

John raises his sword and yells, "Charge!" and takes off in front of his men. As he races into the enemy, he encounters a man a head taller and larger than he is. The man attacks with a bayonet on the end of his musket and John barely parries the thrust. He steps in close and hook-punches him across the jaw with his left hand, then tries to reposition his sword with his right to run him through. The man barely acknowledges the punch and takes his own left fist and hammers down on John's forehead.

The power of the blow brings John to his knees. John's eyes water and his head spins. The man brings his rifle up and makes ready to jam the bayonet into John's eye. Before he can make contact, John slaps out with his left palm at the barrel, deflecting the rifle from his face. He then rolls to the side and comes up on one knee. Still holding his sword with his right hand, he thrusts out and impales the man through his kidney. The man falls over sideways and bleeds out.

John gets to his feet, and before he can figure out where his men are, he hears someone yell, "Captain Edwards, look out!"

From somewhere behind him he feels two hands grab his shoulders and throw him down again, then he hears musket fire and looks up to see Jacob behind him. Jacob looks at John, first with relief, but then his eyes go glassy. He grabs his stomach and collapses to his knees. Blood starts to seep through his fingers and comes out of his mouth as he falls over and dies.

A shot from behind John rings in his ears, and he looks up to see a man—who had been coming at him with another bayonetted rifle—fall to the ground with a bullet hole between his eyes.

He looks toward the ship and sees Ralphie on the aft deck, lowering his rifle. John then hears horses and men's voices in the distance and his military instincts kick in. "Retreat! Back to the ship! We need to leave now!" He hoists Jacob's body over his shoulder and carries him as he makes his way back to the ship.

As John and his men enter the dock, they are preceded by what is left of the village occupants and runaway slaves boarding *The Morning Star*. He turns to see over a hundred men on horseback charging in their direction from the far side of the village. John knows it will only be a matter of minutes before they are at the dock, and if he does not launch right away, they will be overwhelmed and boarded. Ralphie has every available man on deck armed with a rifle, ready to fire once they are in range; but what happens next makes him see his young former midshipman in a whole new light.

As the last of John's men board, Ralphie orders the crew to push off and make sail. Once the ship is free and turns into the sea, the starboard side of the ship is facing the pursuers and Ralphie yells "Fire!" Fifteen cannons and thirty rifles fire, exploding into the pursuing raiders. The explosions are ear-splitting as men and horses are cut down and torn apart by the volley. Sand, dirt, blood, and gore mix in the air over the beach. *The Morning Star* glides out to sea. John takes control of his ship and orders his men to set course for Argentina.

Back on Shore at the Tree Line

Don Lomoche sits on horseback a quarter mile inland from the Maroon village, holding a spyglass to his one good eye. He did not expect *The Morning Star* to make it to the Maroon so fast. His reports told him that the ship had left Kingston only two days ago. It would have taken *The Red Witch* three days to make that trip. He knew that Captain Joshua's ship was faster, but he had no idea it was *that* fast. The information he gave to the plantation association was accurate, and they should have been able to recover an estimated fifty runaways in this one raid, and also should have been able to trap *The Morning Star* in the Maroon's harbor. As it stands now, they lose both prizes, and he finds himself in a precarious circumstance—having the leader of the south Florida raiding parties sitting next to him on a horse, viewing through his own spyglass the catastrophe that just took place.

Lomoche puts his glass in his pocket. "Captain Forrest, I apologize for this unfortunate turn of events. We did not foresee *The Morning Star* getting here before the morning. None of my armada will be here until that time. Believe me when I say that Governor Bennets will fully compensate you for your losses here, and—"

The man reaches across his own belly with his right hand, pulls his sabre from its scabbard and puts it at Lomoche's throat. "Not only has your incompetence cost me what looks like twenty to thirty of my men, but now I have to report to my superiors that they died in vain. We were going to take this whole Maroon. Now we have nothing. Are you sure that your Governor Bennets can afford to pay what we will demand, Lomoche?"

Lomoche dare not move an inch for fear that the razor-sharp blade against his throat might slice through his Adam's apple. While holding his chin high and looking sideways with his one good eye at the captain, he says, "Not only will he meet your price, Captain, but we will bring back to you all the slaves we recover from *The Morning Star*. When *The Red Witch* docks here in the morning, I will take our armada and pursue that abolitionist ship all the way to Argentina. We'll overtake her, and capture her and her crew."

Captain Forrest puts his sabre back in its scabbard and shakes his head. "Lomoche, I studied warfare at West Point Military Academy, and I have served under General Lee himself. I know good soldiering when I see it. The man who commanded that ship is an expert soldier and his crew is well trained. That is not a bunch of bleeding-heart pacifist abolitionists you will pursue, but men who know how to fight and kill. Anyone who goes up against that ship and its commander better know what he is doing and have a huge advantage in fire and manpower, or he and his crew will be obliterated. As for payment, I'm sure that my associates will send word to Bennets about this disaster and give him a price tag for its reparations."

Forrest turns his mount and gallops down to his men to more closely assess the damage. Lomoche stays up in the camp for the night, waiting until *The Red Witch* docks in the morning and he can leave.

Back on *The Morning Star*

After clearing the harbor, Ralphie finishes his preliminary checks of all the sailors' duty stations and helps to set the sails per Captain Edwards's instruction. He has not processed that they lost Jacob Hind; but he knows when it hits, it will hit hard. Jacob was closest in age on the Morning Star to Ralphie and they had become good friends. He makes his way over to the head man of the Maroon they just rescued. "Captain Edwards will want a count of how many of your people got aboard. Can you have that for me in a quarter hour, Josiah?"

"Of course, Ralphie. I am sorry for Mr. Hind. He gave his life for John Edwards and my people. If it is any consolation, I do not believe Captain Joshua could have done any better than you and John. You have been our guardian angels today," the elderly man says with tears glistening on his cheeks. "My people will not forget what you are doing for us."

"It is what Captain Joshua taught us to do, Josiah. Your cause is just, and the oppression of your people is a sin. Thank you." Ralphie turns and takes a deep, calming breath that doesn't work, and he makes his way to John, who is manning the helm. They stand next to one another and look out to sea for a few moments as Ralphie endeavors to work out the words he needs to give his report to his captain.

John looks over at the young man and sees that he can hardly keep himself together. "Mr. Austin, whatever you have to say can wait. My quarters need some tidying up, and since we do not have a midshipman or cabin boy to fill your old positions, you will have to continue with that responsibility until we do. Take no less than one hour and report back to me when you are done."

Ralphie thanks him and makes his way to the captain's quarters. As expected, when he opens the door, he finds the quarters in the most pristine and immaculate condition he has ever seen. It has been a shipboard joke for some time that whenever John Edwards makes captain, the need for a cabin boy will be almost nonexistent. John Edwards knew exactly what he needed, and Ralphie thanked God for the man. He sits on the big sofa next to the captain's desk, puts his head between his knees, and sobs for a good half hour.

John stands at the helm wishing he could trade places with Ralphie. Today was not the first time he'd lost men in battle and probably will not be the last, but that does not make it hurt any less. This is the first time Ralphie has ever lost someone close like Jacob Hind, and the first time the young man ever had to take a life. The boy's mettle was tested today, and he came out sterling. Not only did Second Mate Austin save his captain's life but also that of the whole landing party and the people of the Maroon. He kept his head and thought through exactly how to defend the retreat with professional precision.

He and Captain Joshua have lost men in similar skirmishes since joining the abolitionist cause in the Caribbean. Unlike so many of their comrades on land and sea that hold to the pacifist belief, John and Joshua know that if one truly wants to make a change and free the enslaved, blood might have to be spilled. All the battles in Her Majesty's Navy that he has taken part in have never inspired the kind of fervor he feels in the depth of his soul when he helped—and yes, sometimes fought—to see those who were enslaved gain their freedom. He knows it is a worthy cause to dedicate his life to, but he also knows he does not want to do it alone anymore.

He reaches up and pulls out the Spanish silver chain hanging around his neck, then takes out the medallion he gave his mother all those years ago and looks at the image of himself. Just a boy of fourteen, wearing his three-pointed midshipman's hat, looking off into the distance. He can still feel his mother's arms wrap around him and pull him in as she kissed his cheeks. He can still feel her tears on his face and hear her cries in his ears when she thanked him for the precious gift. She wore it for twenty years, never taking it off. His father told him that when she gave it to John on her deathbed, it was the first time he'd ever seen her remove it from her neck. "Give it to the woman who captures your heart, John. It and you will always be hers. That's how you Edwards men are built and I love you for it." Those were the last words she said to him before she died. John squeezes the medallion in his fist and closes his eyes. He says quietly, "If I make it back to you, this and I will be yours forever. I promise, Brandy."

Next Day, Skynyrd's Apartment at *Katrina's*

Brandy raps on the door to her uncle's apartment, and she hears him tell her to come in. It's morning, so as she expected, he is at the washbasin in front of the mirror, shaving his head and face. Saying nothing, she sits at the table in the middle of the room and watches him shave.

"You still love watching your old Uncle Skinner shave off all his beautiful blond hair, don't you, girl?" he says as he looks up at her reflection in his mirror.

"I guess since I told Admiral Joshua and Captain Walters everything, you will go by your old name again?"

"Well, it never was much of a fake name to begin with. 'Twas the fact that I was afraid I'd forget another name in conversation and use my own. But if that happened, me plan was to just tell someone they misheard me and then say my name is Skynyrd. Clever, if you ask me." He winks at her through the mirror, grabs a towel, and wipes his face clean. He walks to the cabinet and grabs the black dye for Brandy's hair.

She sighs sadly and smiles. "Yes, Uncle, almost as clever as naming our tavern after my mother. God only knows how we stayed out of Lomoche's and Bennets's sight all these years, living here right under their noses."

The melancholy is not lost on Skinner as he steps up with the dye and brushes it into Brandy's long, silky hair. "You still pining away for John Edwards and his medallion, little girl?" he says as he steps in front of her and examines the roots of her front hairline.

"Oh, Uncle Skinner, that's what I love about our little family relationship. I think I would go completely insane if I did not have you to talk to about everything going on in my life. You've been more of a father to me than Eric Erasmus ever was," Brandy says as she watches him work on her hair.

Her uncle tries to cover the huge lump in his throat with some humor. "Brandy, I'm wondering about something. It's been so long since either of us has seen our own natural hair color. Do you think my beautiful, blond hair is still there? And what if all that fire that used to grow out of your own head is now frosty white from our abusing it with this black, oily sap I've kneaded into it every week for the last fifteen years?"

A devilish grin appears on Brandy's beautiful face. She grabs Skynyrd's towel and throws it in his face. He pulls the towel from his face and sees that a little of the dye splatted on his shirt. He takes the dye and mockingly holds it over Brandy. "Now you went and did it! I'll pour this right on your favorite serving blouse, little girl, and you can't stop me."

Brandy jumps sideways out of the chair and runs over to the washbasin that he was shaving at earlier and grabs it. "Try it, you bald-headed old sea dog, and you'll be covered in your own soapy whiskers!" They stare at each other for a moment, trying to maintain their feigned intensity, but then they both burst out laughing as they put their weapons of choice down.

"Speaking of medallions, I have something that came to me yesterday that I have been searching for since we left *The Red Witch*." He goes over to his bed, pulls the chest out from underneath it, and takes out a small, red velvet pouch. Inside is a copper-gold medallion on a chain. "I don't think your mother ever showed you this. She kept it very private, but there was not a day that it did not hang around her neck. She had this made when you were about five years old. Oh, you were a handful back then. She kept finding you getting into all sorts of shenanigans on the ship."

He holds it up in the light and points at it. "This picture is from when she caught you trying to jump into the ocean off the front rail of *The Red Witch*. Some of the crew had convinced you that you could fly into the ocean like a mermaid. It was because of the way the way they talked about the day you were born and how the storm settled as soon as we heard your cries. They made you think you were invincible."

He hands it to Brandy then laughs. "Oh, Kat was so mad I thought she would throw you in just to prove to you it wasn't so. But after she calmed down, she made a drawing of you on that rail and gave it to me to have a craftsman in Florida make this medallion. I thought it got lost at sea, but one of the crew that brought your mother up after she jumped and killed herself took it off her neck and kept it all these years. He finally sent by way of a messenger when he found out about a reward being offered here in Kingston."

She holds it up to the light coming through the window to see it more clearly. The medallion is made of bright, shiny, red copper-colored gold. It shows a little girl of about five standing on the edge of the rail of a ship with her hands held out wide to each side and her long, bright red hair flying in the wind like fire. Underneath it says, *Brandy, My Little Gift from the Sea.*

"She had this the whole time I was growing up? That's incredible! I never saw it once." She shakes her head and plops down on the chair and stares at it. "Half the time I felt like she hated me. I never would have thought that my mother could be so sentimental. She always seemed so ruthless and brash, like my father."

Skinner smiles, walks over to her, puts his hands on her shoulders and gives her a light shake. "Brandy, there be a lot you don't understand about your mother. A hard woman she was, but it be the only way she could survive in your father's world. She searched half the Caribbean to find a man who could protect her like Eric Erasmus could. Believe me, there was a price to pay for that protection. Married her, he did. But that did not keep him out of other women's beds. It wasn't till she had you that she ever really felt whole. You were the most precious thing she had, and she did not want this evil world she brought you into eating you up. So she was tough on you and made sure the crew respected and feared you like they did her. The way you knocked Lomoche on his arse, cut off his hand, poked out his eye, and then took to almost gutting him right there proved that she succeeded at that task. You didn't see them behind you like I did, but those three who stood with Lomoche that day could have got to you, and would have, if you had not scared the life right out of their bones. They froze in fear, and that's what gave Kat the chance to kill them before they saw her coming. The pride and love in that woman's heart for what you did that day gave her the strength to do what she did, and gave us the chance to escape. No, Brandy, Katrina

Erasmus loved her little gift from the sea more than life itself. That's why she was willing to give up her own to save yours!"

Brandy looks at the medallion for a moment longer and then places it around her neck and conceals it under her blouse. "Maybe my mother was not as bad as I remember her to be, but there are still things that can never be undone, uncle Skinner. She and my father butchered and wasted lives. Had they survived; I would have turned out exactly like them." She sighs, stands, and then wraps her arms around him and kisses his cheek. "Thank you for giving the medallion to me. I don't know what I'd do without you. Admiral Joshua said you are a good man with a good heart, and I agree."

Skinner pulls back and looks her in the eye. "Said that, did he now? Well, I can count on one hand how many men I could give a spit in the wind about what they think of me. But he be one of them. Praise from a man like that be a valuable thing. Thank you for telling it to your old uncle. Time to go to work, Brandy. Business is slowing down with the seasons changing. We need to make as much as we can before the storms start and all the ships hunker down for a while. I'll see you downstairs." He walks over to his closet and grabs his kitchen apron.

Good old Uncle Skinner. Always knows what I need to hear, she thinks as he walks out the door. She steps over to his table, blows out the candle, then takes the basin full of his shaving water and heads to the courtyard. Once she empties the basin and gives it to the kitchen crew, she heads over to the gate to Zhang's training area for their daily routine before she has to report to the dining room for her shift.

Zhang has really stepped up the intensity of the drills. His attacks with the master's swords were as real as any combat exercise she had with her parents. First, she uses the sticks. The emphasis was to deflect the blades by striking them anywhere but the razor edge, which would more than likely cut the sticks in two. When he first started training her for this, she thought he was out of his mind. "I will knock those things away from me anyway I can. I can't see whether I am contacting the sharp part of the blade every time I counter one of your strikes!" she would scream as he would reprove her for doing so. But now when they move together in combat practice, it is like she can feel his movements as he initiates them. She knows where the sharp part of the blade is by the position his hand is in, the slant of his shoulder, or the way he steps as he thrusts or slices. Instead of hammering him with parries, she uses a gentle tap that lightly deflects the blade, which in turn leaves a slight opening to strike out with an offensive thrust or slice of her own.

Lately, Brandy has gained a touch here and there. This time she lightly taps his right wrist, and then the back of his head. Zhang holds his hand up to halt the practice, lowers the blades to his side and gives Brandy a formal bow, acknowledging her victory. He leans one blade against his thigh and takes his hand and wipes the beginning of a tear from his eye. "Zhang has waited a long time for this. Brandy has learned balance and control. Sticks are no longer clubs in hands, but now are extension of hands and Brandy can now see and feel with those hands. This is a proud day for Zhang."

He wipes more tears from his eyes and shakes his head vigorously. "Training for today is done. Zhang doesn't want to embarrass himself in front of student too much. We do more tomorrow. I go record this great day in my journal." He turns and picks up the master's swords and puts them in their scabbards. As he leaves, Brandy hears him say, "Five years and she can touch Zhang twice with fight-ending touches. No one ever do it that fast. Zhang is truly greatest teacher of Shaolin. Brandy good student too. Other priests won't believe me."

As he closes the gate behind him, Brandy stands there and smiles. She thinks that even a year ago if she had accomplished this, she would have adamantly demanded that she be awarded the master's swords. But now, much to her surprise, they really are not that important to her anymore. The reward of seeing Zhang Yong so pleased with her performance and with his teaching ability was more valuable to her than any sword could ever be. She looks back over at the equipment cabinet and sees her fan on the shelf and spends another half hour working on her forms with that beautiful and delicate instrument.

Governor Bennets's Private Office

Christopher Bennets's eyes crinkle in frustration as he reads the latest reports from his gubernatorial guard/tax collector unit. He does not like what he is seeing and the man standing in front of his desk is afraid that the governor will blame him for the figures. "Really, Captain? A twenty percent drop in collections this summer over last in the main dock district? How do you expect me to compensate for the losses?"

"Governor Bennets, we had a thirty percent increase the year before, so one way of looking at it is that we are still up ten percent overall," the captain sheepishly replies.

Bennets throws the reports on the floor and stomps on them. "I made you collect thirty percent more to compensate for the extra hundred men I got you last year! How, pray tell, do you expect me to pay for them this year with two-thirds less income?"

The captain steps back a pace and holds out both hands. "Governor, last year we had to strong-arm a lot of the local taverns and fish stands around the dock for more money. You told me to be as subtle as I could and not let Captain Joshua or his first mate John Edwards from *The Morning Star* see us doing it. Captain Walters and his garrison upped their dock presence after that attack on Edwards. That forced us to keep our involvement down there to a minimum all summer. Now Edwards is gone, but Captain Joshua himself is staying in the same tavern, and I've heard a rumor that he not only found his long-lost daughter but also found out what happened to his wife. Because of that, he plans to retire here in Kingston and turn *The Morning Star's* mission over to Edwards."

Bennets sits down and scowls. "Well, that is a horse of a different color. The last thing I need is the Sailor King's favorite sea captain sticking his nose into my business. Tell me, Captain, where else in our illustrious city can we make up for our lack of income?"

The captain grins. "There is the northern dock. It is mainly run by local natives and freed slaves. We've left them alone so far because it's mainly slums there and not worth our time. But we could squeeze them some, I think. There are a few new businesses opening up there. Perhaps a new business tax could be levied. In the short term, we could make up your twenty percent and no one will care that we are up there collecting."

"Excellent idea, Captain. Proceed. But keep it as low-key as possible. If that bleeding-heart Captain Joshua hears about this, it could all blow up in our faces."

The captain salutes the governor and briskly walks out of the office.

"I trust you heard all of that from the other side of the door, Reece?" Bennets says as Faustin Reece steps through the door that leads to the governor's private lounge.

"Yes I did, and I have more bad news. Lomoche did not capture *The Morning Star* in Florida at the Maroon. They evacuated the entire Maroon, took out most of the raiding party, and are within a day of the new Argentina Maroon as we speak. Captain Nathan Forrest of the Plantation Association has demanded full compensation for lost men, slaves, and potential salvage from the Maroon. Don Lomoche sent me back here to report to you. He sent *The Red Witch* on to La Plata, Argentina, and went ahead with his new pirate armada to capture *The Morning Star.*"

"*The Red Witch* could never catch *The Morning Star* at sea. Has Lomoche lost his senses?" Bennets barks.

Reece smugly grabs a cigar off Bennets's desk and lights it with a candle. "He doesn't plan to overtake him at sea, Governor. He plans to let Edwards dock at La Plata, get his passengers off, and then follow him to the new Maroon. Then he'll capture as many of the occupants as he can, kill Edwards and his crew, capture and sink *The Morning Star*, and head back. No one will ever know what became of Joshua's ship or her crew and you will have provided the Plantation Association with twice as many replacement slaves as they bargained for. I'm leaving Kingston this evening on a schooner headed to Barbados to rendezvous with *The Red Witch* later this month and sail her back to Florida to deliver the slaves. Lomoche will return in the schooner. That way it will tie neither him nor you to the incident at La Plata. If anyone figures out what happened to *The Morning Star*, it will be the famous pirate Faustin Reece and the crew of *The Red Witch* credited with her downfall."

"Faustin, you know that as a British governor I will be duty-bound to hunt you and that crew down and hang you on the spot," Bennets says with a hint of sarcastic glee in his voice. "If word ever gets back to Her Majesty, she will make it a royal proclamation and you will be in the same situation that the Scarlet Mistress was. Eventually you could face an entire English armada like she and her husband did."

"Lomoche already told me that. That's why once I deliver the slaves to Florida and Captain Forrest, I am to take *The Red Witch* south and sail around South America and go to the Hawaiian Islands. There, we will set up a new slave trade company to supply the Far East clients. *The Red Witch* will never be seen in the Caribbean again."

"What of Lomoche's plans to bring Port Royal back to its former pirate glory?" Bennets menacingly inquires. "Is he now abandoning that ambition?"

"Of course not, Governor," Reece says as he sucks on the governor's expensive Cuban cigar. "Lomoche believes that your plan to aid the queen's husband, Albert of Saxe, in his ambition to assimilate the United States back into the empire and maintain its thriving slave economy will succeed and bring us all great wealth. His plans with me are merely an expansion of his own pirate ambitions in the South Pacific. Port Royal will someday be Lomoche's base of operations for a pirate network that will span the globe."

"Well, I suggest you get to doing your master's bidding. Be discreet about leaving my residence. You are a wanted man, Faustin Reece. If you are recognized by the wrong people while in Kingston, I will not hesitate to order your death. Now get out!"

Bennets knows it is an empty threat, as does Reece. Once in garrison custody, Reece would simply spill his guts to Captain Walters about everything and the governor would be the one having his head stuck in a hangman's noose.

Faustin smirks, puts the cigar out in Bennets's half-full teacup on his desk, tips his hat, and walks out.

Next Day, La Plata Port, Argentina

The Morning Star takes a little longer than expected to make port at La Plata because of a tumultuous storm engulfing the area. Captain Edwards is at the helm and Ralphie is directing men on the deck with the sails. "I am keeping her angled to port, Mr. Austin. On my word, be ready to drop sail and tie off," John says as he shades his eyes from the wind and rain.

"Aye aye, Captain."

"Okay, now, Mr. Austin!"

Ralphie orders the men to drop the sails and proceeds to the starboard side of the ship where she is bouncing and bobbing toward the dock. Ralphie is the first to lasso a dock tie-off pole. The crew tosses four more lines. Two make their target and two miss and fall, but three are enough to begin. Several more ropes are thrown, and they pull the ship up alongside the dock. Once the ship is secured, they set about offloading their passengers. It is still early morning, and they want to get on the trail as soon as possible to make the fifteen-mile hike to Neseem's Maroon before noon. Captain Edwards said he wanted to be back to the port before sundown and, if possible, launch tonight.

With the entire Maroon evacuated from Florida, plus the forty runaway slaves, the number of refugees John and Ralphie show up to Neseem's Maroon with is just shy of two hundred. John makes his way to the entrance of Neseem's Maroon and is immediately greeted by a very astonished Maroon chief. "John Edwards, I told Captain Joshua that the most I could accommodate was one hundred. It looks like you have brought me twice that number!"

Before John can respond, Neseem recognizes someone in the crowd. "What is Josiah doing here? My God, John, what happened?"

"I am sorry, Neseem," John says as he waves his hand back toward the group. "There are raiders combing the gulf coast of Florida looking for runaway slaves and attacking Maroons. Josiah's was being attacked when we docked to pick up the forty runaways and we had to fight our way out of there. We had no choice but to bring everyone with us."

"John Edwards, that is terrible news! Did many die?"

"We lost Jacob Hind and three crew members. We took out close to fifty of them with rifle and cannon fire, though."

"Let's get these people in the camp then. We can discuss how we can assimilate them all later." As Neseem finishes his sentence, a gunshot rings out from behind the group. They look toward the noise and see dozens of men with muskets and swords advancing on their party.

John draws his pistol and shouts, "Everyone to the camp! Ralphie, get our men in formation and guard their escape!" John points his revolver at the closest of the attackers and shoots him. Ralphie gets the men in formation and gets a volley off that takes out most of the front line of the attackers before they can take cover and return fire.

Neseem puts his fingers to his lips and blows out a high-pitched, earsplitting whistle. Within seconds, hundreds of men armed with muskets, swords, bows and arrows, and spears come running to the front of the camp. Neseem takes a long sabre from his waist scabbard and looks at John. "Neseem has been preparing for this day since I ran away and became a free man. We will teach these slavers what it will cost them to invade my Maroon." Without warning, he points his sword toward the invaders and yells, "ATTACK!!"

John looks back at Ralphie. "Cover them with musket fire!" He draws his own sabre and runs to catch up with Neseem and his men. He sees the attackers have fortified themselves on both sides of the trail and most are reloading. Neseem orders a volley of arrows and spears to the left side of the trail as he, John, and some others attack the ones on the right. The first man John confronts tries to cut him down with a sabre strike, but he easily parries it and stabs him in the gut. The next runs at him with a bayonet. As he moves in, John ducks low, blocks the bayonet thrust with an upward parry of his sabre, then crashes his shoulder into the man's midsection and knocks him to the ground, where he stabs him through the heart.

When he looks up at Neseem, he sees that the Maroon chief has downed two attackers on his own and is chasing a third. As he looks around, he sees that the attackers are in full retreat and are headed back up the trail to escape. He holds both hands up to his mouth and yells, "Neseem, we should fall back in case they have split their force and plan to attack from somewhere else! Your Maroon is wide open right now."

Back behind the Attackers

Don Lomoche stands back up the trail and can hardly believe that he has suffered defeat at the hands of this damn abolitionist twice. When the crew of *The Morning Star* defended the retreat at the Florida Maroon, he thought Captain Forrest might take his head, and if not for the promise of raiding this Maroon and returning with Edwards's head and a complete restoration of all his losses in slaves, he might have. Now, he has neither and must flee for fear of annihilation by Edwards and this well-prepared and fiercely protected Maroon.

He looks at the man sitting next to him. "We must get back to the armada at La Plata and get out to sea. If Edwards gets to La Plata before we do, he might convince the local patrols to engage us, and if *The Red Witch* has not made it here yet, then we won't stand a chance." He shakes his head, shoves his spyglass in his pocket, turns and heads up the trail, mumbling under his breath, "Damn you, Eric Erasmus! I told you that making that ship out of redwood was insane. She's the slowest whale in the ocean."

Once back at the bay where Lomoche's six schooners and two smaller frigates are anchored out in a bay, he takes count of how many men he has lost in the attempted siege of the Maroon. Of the hundred men he brought with him, forty-three did not make it back—a catastrophe by anyone's reckoning. Now raiding the La Plata Maroon will be out of the question. It would take an army of five hundred, and the Argentinian government would consider that an invasion and an act of war. He shakes his head in despair and steps into the skiff that is prepared to take him back to his ship. About halfway there, he sees his ship's captain waving at him and pointing due north out to sea.

Lomoche takes his spyglass out and looks in that direction. At first, he sees just a foggy silhouette in the stormy South Atlantic sea; but as it clears, he sees *The Red Witch* coming in their direction. He smiles and says to no one in particular, "You might have gotten the best of me twice, John Edwards, but tonight I will force you into Devil's Curve and send you and that abolitionist ship of yours to the bottom of the sea."

Back at the Maroon

Neseem and John Edwards stand talking inside the village municipal structure, which is also Neseem's home. John looks at his friend. "I'm sorry I brought you so much trouble, Neseem. They must have known where we were heading and sent smaller, faster ships here to catch us off guard. The number of runaways has exploded since Captain Joshua and I have had so much success in getting your people to safety. It was only a matter of time before repercussions would ensue and they would strike back to stop us."

Neseem laughs. He places his big hand around John's neck and pulls his head to his own forehead in traditional tribal warrior fashion. "John Edwards, you and Captain Joshua are my brothers. We have fought to protect the village together. A warrior's honor is to never apologize for doing what we have to do. These people you have brought me are now a part of this community, a community where you are always welcome. You are a great warrior, John. Your honor is your shield and the truth in your words are your spear. Neseem will always be your friend. As you have been there for me, so will I be there for you. We will guard your journey back to La Plata. Now you must go. Those slavers may attack your ship. Your God will hear prayers from Neseem this day to guard your safety. Now go. We will be fine."

John puts his hand on Neseem's shoulder and shakes it. "Thank you, Neseem." He turns to Ralphie. "Mr. Austin?"

"Yes, Captain?"

"We're heading back to *The Morning Star* right away. Neseem thinks it may be in danger. Get the men ready to leave."

Ralphie nods and then turns to Neseem. "Sorry we do not have time to catch up, Neseem. I want you to know I am to be married to the girl that you know as Ben and Elisa's adopted daughter, Davonte. But you probably did not know that she is Captain Joshua's long-lost daughter. He found out about her from them on the trip from here back to Kingston. It's been a little crazy since."

A brief look of astonishment crosses Neseem's face, but then it comes together for him. "Yes, now I understand. Ben and Elisa did not have kind things to say about Captain Joshua like the rest of us. It perplexed me, but sometimes ex-slaves find it hard to forgive any white people, even those who will fight and die for our freedom. I hope that they and Captain Joshua are friends now?"

Ralphie smiles from ear to ear. "Well, yes, they are. They don't know it yet, but Captain Joshua will offer to go into business with Ben. He found out that while Ben was down here, he started to learn about boat making. Captain Joshua's family owns the biggest ship building business in London, and he wants to open a shipyard in Kingston and do it with Ben."

"Well, no act of goodness by Arthur Joshua would surprise Neseem. You are to become part of a great family, Ralphie. Neseem is proud for you."

Ralphie holds out his hand but Neseem pushes it aside and gives the boy a huge hug.

Chapter 12

Master at the Helm

Three hours later, John, Ralphie, and one of Neseem's Maroon elders say goodbye on the dock next to *The Morning Star.* John can smell the storm in the air, coming from the southeast. "Mr. Austin, check the barometer, wind speed and direction. This storm is going to be fierce, get the men to their stations and get ready!"

"Aye aye, Captain." Ralphie responds and quickly does his checks and organizes the men.

Since he is heading northwest, John feels that he can stay ahead of it in *The Morning Star,* so he continues to press Ralphie and the crew to prepare to launch.

He steps up to the helm to take control of his ship. Once out in the harbor and heading out to open sea, he can feel the absent weight in the ship from unloading the passengers. The buoyancy of the ship is more sensitive to the helm and he feels the pull of the wind in the sails, the drag of the water underneath, and the force of the waves crashing against his ship. *The Morning Star* picks up speed as she glides out of La Plata's harbor on the stormy, late-September sea.

Same Time, Bridge of *The Red Witch*

Despite the ever-present danger of her crew mutinying and killing him, Don Lomoche still loves *The Red Witch* above any vessel. Slow though she may be, she is still the most impregnable ship he has ever been on. For seventeen years, he sailed the Caribbean with Erasmus and the Scarlet Mistress, marauding and pirating. The Plague never lost a fight sailing *The Red Witch* up to the day Lomoche put his sabre through his back.

Juan steps up to him and waves his hand away from his head in a mock salute. "Don Lomoche, why have you brought us down to this part of the world? Were there more runaway slaves than you counted on, or was the raid on the Maroon so big that you need us to take on the extra cargo?"

Lomoche draws his sabre with his good hand and rests the point of it on Juan's chest. "You know damn well that I wanted you to follow us so that we could trap and sink *The Morning Star* and her crew. As for slave cargo, we have none. The captain of that ship is quite the military man and those black devils at that Maroon are vicious warriors. We were beaten back as badly as in Florida. But now that *The Red Witch* is here, we will drive that damnable ship into Devil's Curve and kill every one of them."

Juan ignores the blade and steps a little closer. "Go ahead, Don Lomoche, run me through. See how long you last when the old crew sees what you've done. Most of us hope we'll find someone out here good enough to send this cursed ship to the bottom of the ocean, anyway. As it stands, the only thing keeping you alive here are the words the Scarlet Mistress cursed us with before she died."

Lomoche's good eye darts back and forth across the deck as he notes the familiar looks of hatred written on the faces of *The Red Witch's* original crew. He lowers his blade and sheaths it. "Juan, Juan, you need a vacation from all this. Briskett will be back soon and then it'll be his turn to first mate *The Red Witch,* and you can stay at a port for a while and drink and whore yourself into oblivion, compliments of Governor Bennets. All you have to do is help me drive *The Morning Star* into Devil's Curve, and then we can head for Barbados to meet up with Captain Reece, and he'll take you back to Jamaica." He looks around at the rest of the crew. "If we crash that ship properly, I'll have Captain Reece take the rest of you to New Orleans, where you can whore and drink for two months during the storm season."

Juan looks back at the men and can see that the gesture has merit with them. "Well, Captain Lomoche, I guess you're back in charge. Where to now?"

Before he can respond, the lookout in the crow's nest yells, "Ship ahoy, starboard!"

Lomoche takes his spyglass out and scans the sea until *The Morning Star* comes into view. "Juan, signal the other ships. When we're in range, send a volley of eight-pounders followed by twelve-pounders. Drive her due south. Get her close enough that the tide takes her right into the cliff. If she tries to run, we can sink her."

Back on *The Morning Star*

Ralphie and John are standing at the helm, scanning the stormy sea as they hear the lookout from the crow's nest yell, "Ship ahoy, Captain, starboard! Some schooners and a man-of-war. Headed straight for us!"

John takes out his spyglass and scans in that direction. He sees the silhouette of the man-of-war first and what looks to be three or four schooners fanned out on each side. As the armada gets closer, a cold chill goes up and down John's spine as he realizes what is coming their way. "Mr. Austin, we're about to be attacked by *The Red Witch* and eight schooners. All hands-on deck; ready cannon and musket. Prepare for boarders. Hard to port!"

"Mr. Austin, as soon as our starboard side is in position, send a volley of eight-pounders followed by musket fire at *The Red Witch*. Don't worry about the others right now. Keep the lower deck's twelve-pounders ready for close combat."

"Aye aye, Captain. We're ready. Those eight-pounders are going to bounce right off *The Red Witch*, and the sea is so rough that our musket fire will be next to useless, sir. Shouldn't we wait to use the twelve-pounders?"

"Under normal circumstances, yes, Mr. Austin. But we're going to use this stormy sea to our advantage and if we do this right, those eight-pounders won't be hitting the side of that ship," John says as he works the helm.

"What will they be hitting, sir?"

"Those black-hearted pirate scum on the deck, Mr. Austin."

The Morning Star suddenly rises high on a wave and the starboard side lines up with *The Red Witch's* port side. "Now, Mr. Austin!"

Ralphie gives the order and fifteen cannons go off, sending the eight-pound balls across the deck of *The Red Witch*, immediately followed by 17 muskets firing. It cuts the crewman at the helm of the pirate ship in half, along with nine others. The cannon balls also damage a secondary mast as well.

"Unfurl the flying and storm jib and two fore-stay sails at bow, keep the others furled and battened down, and head directly port, Mr. Austin!" John yells from the helm. Though the winds are high, the rain and thunder has not set in yet. This part of a storm tends to produce large waves and he feels that it could work to his advantage,

Ralphie and two others start to make their way to the bow. He looks in that direction and sees where his captain had just ordered them to go, and his face goes ashen. "John Edwards, that's the Devil's Curve you're steering us into! No one has ever gotten this close and survived it, especially in a storm like this!"

"Remember that wave you and I rode over? The biggest one you've ever seen?" John nods his chin out to sea.

Ralphie's eyes get as huge as saucers as he stares at a wave headed straight for them that is completely blocking the eastern sky.

He grabs the nearest poll to him to steady his feet and holds on as *The Morning Star* rocks and rolls on the sea. With pleading desperation in his voice he yells, "We can't outrun it, sir, and if you want to do what you did last time, we're going in the wrong direction! How can we possibly navigate that and Devil's Curve!?"

"You remember the story of Jesus walking on the water, Ralphie?"

"Yes, John. What are you going to do? Ask Her Majesty the sea to let us ride her past those cliffs on that wave?"

"No, Ralphie. Jesus walked out to his disciples on a stormy night like this one, and I am positive that he did not ask the Sea of Galilee for permission. He got his permission from the One who tells all the seas what to do. Mr. Austin, give the order for the men to hold tight and pray. I will too."

John holds *The Morning Star* in line with the wave that will take them right into the cliffs of Devil's Curve. *The Morning Star* slowly begins to rise as the few sails unfurled catch a good gust and pull it up. Along with Ralphie every man on the deck darts their eyes back and forth between the giganteas wave and deadly cliffs ahead, and the spikey teeth beneath the water that spell certain death if the hull meets them with not enough sea between to separate the two.

As the ship approaches the famous devil's fingers area, the wave moves in and raises her higher. The force of the wind and sea is so great that the ship momentarily dips sideways, but John is ready for that and he steers in the opposite direction. The ship levels and John keeps her behind the front of the gargantuan wave's cresting waters.

When they reach the top of the wave's height a huge gust of wind takes hold on the few sails unfurled and turns the bow of the ship out to sea. John sees the Godsent miracle he was looking for and yells to Ralphie, "***Unfurl the main sail!***" Ralphie and the men respond immediately and unleash it. When the heavy winds fills the canvas a loud groan is heard from the main mast, but miraculously it holds in place and with the power the extra pull of the wind provides *The Morning Star* races out past Devil's Curve and the pirate armada. By the time things settle down, the crew finds itself out at least two nautical miles past the pirates, and when the storm winds have finally abated, John Edwards gives the order to head southwest toward Barbados and then Jamaica. Not a man on *The Morning Star* is ignorant of the fact that God brought a mighty miracle to pass for them. They thank the Eternal Father for it, and for having the greatest helmsman on the seven seas to guide the ship through it.

Those members of the crew left alive on the deck of *The Red Witch* along with Don Lomoche and Juan, stand with mouths agape and in stunned silence as they contemplate what they have just seen. Finally, Juan walks over and points his shaking hand out to sea, then glares at Lomoche. "All my life have I've sailed these oceans. Never have I seen the man who could master a ship through that. That man is a wizard and I want no part of warring with him."

Lomoche, though scared to the depths of his heart, starts to rebuff Juan, but then hears comments coming from the deck crew.

"Did you see that? I swear it was like the hand of God held the ship up and carried her through Devil's Curve! That ship's master must be the greatest helmsman alive. Who is he?" one asks.

"That be Captain John Edwards who sailed with Captain Joshua himself. There be no place on the ocean that man can't sail. He has no equal," another says.

A devious grin manifests itself on Juan's face. "Don Lomoche, while we were chugging along to meet up with you, we spotted an English armada headed for Kingston. It had three men-of-war and a half dozen smaller vessels. One of the men-of-war was flying a British parliamentary envoy flag. That usually means that some governor in the Caribbean is about to be replaced. Looks like your and Bennets's little situation might be falling apart."

Don Lomoche grinds his teeth. "Did we lose any ships in the storm, Juan?"

"The wave engulfed two and it beached one. Should we drop anchor and send rescue for survivors?"

"No. If what you're saying is true, then our plans have changed. We must get back to Port Royal and pick up our hostages from the Hawaiian Islands and head to the Pacific right away. If Bennets is out, we won't be allowed to stay there anymore."

Juan's face turns beet red. "Lomoche, you're insane. No one can sail around the southern tip of South America this time of year. We'd be torn up by the ice and wind!"

At first, Lomoche is taken aback by Juan's statement, but then a wicked gleam appears in his eyes. "We just saw a man pilot a ship over Devil's Curve on a tidal wave. If he can do that, he can navigate anywhere on the seven seas. Set course to follow *The Morning Star.* We'll recruit Captain John Edwards to get us to Hawaii and freedom."

Juan throws up both hands to object, but Lomoche stays him with his hooked hand. "We will not engage her again. One of our twelve-pounders penetrated her hull just above the sea line. She'll have to set into the next port with a shipyard for repairs. The closest is Barbados. Faustin

Reece should be there by now. We'll sneak in there, catch them off guard coming back from a tavern, and shanghai him."

"Why in God's holy name do you think he will ever help you, Lomoche? That kind of man would rather die than help people like us!"

"Because, my old friend, it was reported to me by one of our men who frequents that tavern, that the girl who Faustin Reece got his head kicked in by Edwards for, is none other than Captain Arthur Joshua's lost daughter. Our famous British naval hero rescued and married a slave girl some years ago and sent them to the Caribbean to wait for him. *The Red Witch* met up with the ship that was carrying his wife and daughter fifteen years ago. We sent it to the bottom of the sea, but we kept the mother and daughter to sell. When Bennets showed up with a whole armada, you and Briskett let them join the other prisoners as they left *The Red Witch*. I've had men stalking her since I learned of this and they have orders to kidnap her and bring her to Port Royal as soon as possible. I originally planned to use her as a hostage to ensure safe passage to the Pacific when we leave in the early spring. Now I can use her to make Captain Edwards be our pilot. I'm sure he will do anything in his power to keep the daughter of his beloved mentor safe."

Lomoche turns toward the captain's quarters. "Get this ship's mast repaired and throw the dead bodies overboard. Let me know when we're close to Barbados. It's been a long day. I am exhausted."

Back Aboard *The Morning Star*

While the crew hustles to clean up from the fight and check for damage, Captain John Edwards bows his head and closes his eyes while holding the helm. He thanks the Eternal Father for once again guarding him and his crew's lives for this third time that he has seen combat since leaving Kingston. He takes his mother's medallion out from underneath his shirt and looks at it. A tear forms in the corner of his eye as he acknowledges to himself and God that, besides the safety of his crew, all he could think about when his life was in danger was getting back to Brandy and giving her this medallion and pledging himself to her forever.

He looks up and sees the young former midshipman—whom Captain Joshua entrusted to his care and tutelage three years ago—giving orders and coordinating the crew as well as any first mate or first lieutenant could. A deep sense of pride swells in his chest. He knows that if he must leave *The Morning Star* and her crew to another's care, they will be in good hands. "Mr. Austin, condition report, please," he says as he wipes the dampness from his eyes and face.

"We're taking on water in the lower deck, Captain. One twelve-pounder found its way in. We'll need to set in for repairs as soon as possible. I have a three-man pump team set up and we'll rotate a new crew in every three hours. No other hull breaches found. All crew are accounted for. No major injuries or deaths to report, sir."

"I suspect that those bastards will think twice before ever challenging *The Morning Star* and her crew again, eh, Mr. Austin? We gave them a good bloody nose."

"That we did, Captain. I think those pirates must be shaking in their boots thinking about what *The Morning Star's* captain pulled off at Devil's Curve." Ralphie steps close to John's ear and continues. "You'll not be playing that maneuver down to pure luck, or claiming it's what any competent pilot would do, John Edwards. No, that one's going in the history books!"

One Week Later, Trinidad and Tobago Port

Captain John Edwards and his second mate, Ralphie Austin, sit at the bar in the same inn where Captain Joshua met the pirate from *The Red Witch* a few months earlier. They are both enjoying a cup of ale before they turn in to their rented rooms down by the dock.

"Ralphie, you're a little young, and I want to talk it over with Captain … uh … I mean Admiral Joshua first, but I think that I would like to offer you the position of first mate on *The Morning Star.* We'll be ready to launch in five days, and Kingston is about a seven day's sail from here, so if you're interested, you'll have a firm answer by then. I'm confident that after he hears how well you performed on this voyage he will agree," John says as he stares into Ralphie's now astonished face.

"Uh, it would honor me, Captain. I don't know what to say. My goodness, Davonte will flip! Hey, once we're married, does Admiral Joshua's offer still stand? Can the mates bring their wives with them?"

The question takes John aback a little. "Well, we're seeing a little more combat lately, but our work has always been dangerous. Also, we need to consider that Davonte is Arthur Joshua's only child, and putting her in harm's way may be something he would be uneasy about; but yes, his offer still stands as of now."

Ralphie smiles, spreads his arms wide, and yawns. "I am beat, Captain. Are you ready to turn in?"

John counts some pence, throws it on the bar, and tips his hat to the owner. "Me too. Let's go, Mr. Austin." The two sailors head down the cobblestone road to the dock and the comfort of their rented rooms.

The back corner of the tavern is very dark, and sitting at a table are two of Don Lomoche's men. Both have been keeping a very low profile, sipping their ale and biding their time. One leans over and says, "Get a carriage and get to the dock. Tell Lomoche that they left and are on their way back to their rooms. I'll gather the others and follow from behind." The man nods his head and steps to the door. He finds a carriage for hire on the next street, takes it to the docks, meets up with Lomoche, and gives him the news.

Meanwhile, the other man meets up with Faustin Reece. Once he is outside, he gives a low whistle and ten men, including Reece, come out of the shadows from different parts of the street to join him. "Did you see which street they took?"

"Yes, Captain Reece. They went down the center cobblestone one there. They're not five minutes ahead of us."

Reece displays a malevolent grin. "I'm not waiting for Don Lomoche to join us. I want that arrogant English bastard to understand that it was Faustin Reece who got the best of him once and for all. Let's go."

Like Kingston, the local garrison commander does not allow sailors to wear a sword or gun while in the city, so Faustin and his men carry only small knives and clubs. He doesn't expect a civilian night watch to come to John Edwards's and his companion's rescue in Barbados, so he feels confident this will be easy. As for the garrison, the one in Trinidad and Tobago has only two men per shift, and the night shift at present won't be responding to any alarms because Faustin's men caught them earlier this evening, knocked them out and tied them up.

Faustin and his men move at a full trot around a corner, expecting to overtake John and Ralphie as they come into a clear area where the street lets out into a small lot before entering the dock. They stop and look back and forth, scanning the area for their prey, but they see nothing—until a fist comes out of nowhere and smashes into Faustin's jaw with the force of a battering ram.

John Edwards's danger sense started tingling as soon as he and Ralphie left the tavern. When he heard men running behind him, he took Ralphie and circled around to get behind the group. Once he recognized Faustin Reece, he knew that he was in for a fight.

The street narrowed significantly in the last block before it spilled out into the lot before the dock, and Reece was last in the group, so John attacked him first. After knocking Reece to the ground, he grabs the next one by the back of his head, twists him sideways, and kicks his feet out from under him. There is little space in the alleyway between the buildings, and he and Ralphie use the space well. Ralphie has already knocked one man down and is proceeding to the next one.

When Reece's men see their leader attacked, they turn and try to engage, but John and Ralphie hold them at bay as they proceed to down them. As Ralphie was taking on one at a time, John chops one in the neck, elbows another in the face, and kicks another in the groin. Then he grabs the one he kicked and throws him into another, trying to mount an attack. As he makes his way to the mouth of the street, he leaves behind him several unconscious and injured men. When he steps into the clearing of the field, there are only two left. They are standing and holding small clubs, waiting for him. He can see the fear in their eyes as they gaze at the bodies lying behind him.

He turns and sees that Ralphie is about to down his third man. When he turns back, the two men in front of him begin their attack. The first rushes in and swings his club at John's face, but he ducks low and cracks his fist into the man's thigh. John grabs the attacker's arm holding the club and stands up, pushing it back and into the face of the other attacker. He smashes the first assailant in the face with his elbow and knees him in the groin. The man falls down, unconscious. John steps in and smashes the second assailant across the jaw with a devastating right cross. That man also falls to the ground. But before he can revel in the victory, he hears several musket flintlock hammers being pulled back, and he turns to see a new group. One of them is wearing an eye patch and has a hook for a hand on his right arm. Don Lomoche. John considers the predicament. *They didn't fire. They must want me for some reason.*

He reaches inside his shirt, pulls off his mother's medallion and turns to Ralphie. John tosses it to him. "Mr. Austin, take that to Brandy. She will understand. Sail *The Morning Star* back to Admiral Joshua. He'll know what to do."

Ralphie looks like he's not sure what to do, but John says, "Please, Ralphie. If they wanted me dead, they would have shot me already. Tell Brandy and the others that the man who has me is Don Lomoche."

As Ralphie stares at his captain, inwardly praying for another option, they both hear Lomoche bellow, "Go! Kill the man he's talking to! Then bind Edwards and bring him to *The Red Witch.*"

Three men armed with muskets run forward. Two grab John while the third proceeds to the entrance of the narrow street. John sees that Ralphie needs more time to get away, so he crashes his shoulder into the midsection of the man on his right, grabs the musket, and aims it at the man who is about to pursue Ralphie. He then fires the musket, hitting him in the back and killing him instantly. The man on the other side of him takes his musket butt and swipes John across the jaw, knocking him over. Then he aims the barrel at John's head and pulls back the hammer, ready to fire.

A shot rings out, but not from the man's musket that is aimed at John's head. Still dazed by the blow to his jaw, John looks back and sees Don Lomoche holding a pistol with his good hand. "I want him alive, you idiot! Get him up here now. The garrison watch will have heard those shots and will be down here any minute now." Several others run down and help bind and escort John to a small sloop at the dock, from where Lomoche and his men launch and stealthily glide out into the bay, then start rowing to the northeastern shore of the island where *The Red Witch* is anchored.

Two Blocks Away in an Alley

When Ralphie sees that John is all right, he sprints down the cobblestone path that he and John came down earlier until he is about halfway back to the tavern. He stops and wipes the sweat from his brow, then scans the area with his eyes and his ears. After a few moments, he feels confident that he is not being pursued, and he doubles back down an adjacent street to the dock area, specifically to the shipyard where *The Morning Star* is being repaired. He finds the night watchman for the yard and tells him what had just happened. The man tells Ralphie that the workers won't be there for another five hours, and that he doesn't know how far they are on the repairs. He will have to wait for them to arrive to find out. He tells Ralphie that there is still someone at the small British naval office and that he should go report the incident to them.

By the time Ralphie gets to the naval office, the night watchmen from the local garrison are already there talking to a Lieutenant Smyth about the shots they heard earlier and the two dead bodies they found. Ralphie explains to the two military men what happened and why. Smyth then looks at both men. "Gentlemen, as tragic as this sounds, it would seem that you have a civil matter here and unless I receive proper authorization, I cannot involve Her Majesty's forces." He then looks at Ralphie and sees the cold despair in the young man's eyes. "But perhaps it is a good time to send our patrol sloop out and check for any small boats having a rough time, what with the storms we've been experiencing of late. If they see a pirate vessel like *The Red Witch* lurking about, that would be ample cause for our governor to allow committing more ships."

Ralphie's relief is palpable, and he enthusiastically shakes Smyth's hand and thanks him.

The lieutenant's efforts are to no avail. Don Lomoche sets to sea as soon as John Edwards is aboard *The Red Witch*. He knows that if he does not get a head start, *The Morning Star* will overtake him and force him to fight, and there is also the possibility that Captain Edwards's men have enlisted some help from the local British naval command.

Two Days later

Ralphie takes a deep breath to calm himself down. The shipyard manager at Barbados is good friends with Admiral Joshua and Captain Edwards, and he put round-the-clock shifts on getting *The Morning Star* repaired and back out to sea. Now Ralphie finds himself in command of a ship that he had signed on with as a cabin boy a little over three years earlier. To his relief, he finds that the men respect and obey his orders just as well as when John Edwards was standing there backing him up. He knows that Lomoche has an almost three-day head start on him, and he can only guess that the man is heading for Kingston or an American southern port like New Orleans. But he also has direct orders from Captain Edwards to bring *The Morning Star* back to Admiral Joshua. And come hell or high water, hurricanes, or tidal waves, he will obey those orders. He shakes the panic from his psyche, grits his teeth, and gives the order to make for Kingston at full sail. *What else could possibly go wrong?* he wonders.

CHAPTER 13

LINES DRAWN

Kingston, Six Days Later

Davonte is bubbling with excitement as she strolls down Kingston's cobblestone road to the north part of town, where Ben and Elisa are setting up their new home near the shipyard, where they plan to open the new shipbuilding business with her father. She expects that Ralphie and John Edwards will be back any day now, and Elisa wants her to come by this evening to begin the fitting for her wedding dress. Once Ralphie is in port, she won't want to be away from him, and getting fitted for a wedding dress is not something you invite the future groom to be a part of. She crosses the main square of Kingston and makes her way to the northern docks. Her momma never liked her walking over here this late at night, but she feels anxious about Ralphie returning soon and does not want to waste the whole morning tomorrow getting over to their house. This way, she can get the dress fitted and then make her way back to where *The Morning Star* will dock.

Lost in thoughts about her and Ralphie's warm embrace, she does not notice the shady-looking men walking straight for her until it is too late. The wind is blowing, and the rustle is so loud that no one hears her scream when the three men attack and subdue her. One of them pulls a vial from his breast pocket and opens it, then sprinkles some of its contents on a cloth and puts it to her face. She loses consciousness within a matter of seconds.

She wakes up a day later in a dark dungeon that she later discovers is part of the old fort at Port Royal.

Next Day, Governor's Mansion, Kingston

Governor Christopher Bennets can hardly fathom why a parliamentary envoy of no less than three men-of-war would have showed up last night at the Kingston harbor. The last time something like this happened was after that little indentured servant girl who later became the infamous Scarlet Mistress slit King George's cousin's throat all those years ago. His Majesty was so incensed by the incident that he sent an envoy to hunt down the little vixen and bring her head back to him. They were unsuccessful, of course, which opened the door years later for Bennets to capture and execute the Scarlet Mistress in the name of the king, thus earning him a promotion to regional governor of Jamaica. But that was three monarchs ago, and now this new envoy is here.

All he can think about is Admiral Thompson and the questions that he will incur when he cannot explain the man's absence. He knows that his relationship with the infamous Don Lomoche has always been questionable, but he has also received assurances from sources inside the monarchy that the queen's husband will support him as he helps to further the schism in the United States over the slavery issue. Lost in all these musings, he barely hears the knock on his door and the entrance of his manservant. "My Lord, there is a parliamentary delegation in the court, accompanied by Vice Admiralty, to see you. They are demanding entrance at once."

Astonishment manifests itself across Bennets's face, then he thinks, *the governor's private guard!* His men have standing orders to stop anyone from entering the gubernatorial house without an appointment. "Tell those fools to stand down and let Her Majesty's representatives in at once!" The servant's eyes dart back and forth as he gives a quick nod and rushes out of the office.

Ten minutes later both doors to Bennets's gubernatorial office are opened and an entourage of stately dressed men and soldiers steps in. Bennets recognizes only one of them, and his heart goes into his throat at what the man is wearing. Former Captain Arthur Joshua is wearing the distinct uniform of a vice admiral of Her Majesty's Navy. On his right is a man who appears to be in his late twenties or early thirties; but by the way everyone in the group is acting, he can tell that this is the official representative from parliament who was dispatched to handle state business with him.

Admiral Joshua can't help but savor the panic he sees run across Bennets's face as he and his new friend step into the governor's office. He steps forward. "Governor Bennets, by the authority of Queen Victoria I am informing you that I am now supreme commander of all British military assets in the Caribbean. You are hereby ordered to disclose the whereabouts of Admiral Thompson so that word can be sent for him to report to my new office in this building as soon as possible." He then turns toward the young official and says, "May I present the newly elected Speaker of the House of Commons, Alexander Walters."

Bennets is so stunned that he can hardly force himself to talk, but then it dawns on him who this man really is. "You are Captain Walters's son, aren't you?"

Alexander Walters steps forward and glares at Bennets. "That I am, Governor. Once we received my father's last report about how you have been using your own personal guard to collect illegal taxes from the peoples of Jamaica, I met with certain members of the queen's staff to discuss how to proceed. They authorized no action, but then a special envoy arrived with a letter stamped with a royal seal granted by the Sailor King to Arthur Joshua. The letter for the queen's eyes only contained Joshua's testimony, exposing that you have been sponsoring and working with known pirates and wanted men in the area. When she read that, she sent me." Alexander stops for a moment and looks around the room, then at Admiral Joshua. "Where is my father? Were they able to locate him yet?"

Before Admiral Joshua can speak, Captain Walters comes running through the door and straight up to Bennets's desk, out of breath and brimming with excitement. He turns and salutes Admiral Joshua, who returns the gesture and then motions with his eyes toward Alexander, who is standing behind his father. Walters turns around and stares at the man who now replaces the five-year-old boy he last saw almost a quarter of a century ago. "Alexander! Is it really you?"

"Father! Yes, it is me. We have a lot of catching up to do, but let's take care of state business first."

The Speaker of the House of Commons then turns and points an accusing finger at Bennets. "Christopher Bennets, you are hereby charged with gross misuse of your gubernatorial powers, aiding and sponsoring known pirates, and forcing unlawful taxes on the peoples of Her Majesty's colony of Jamaica. In the name of Queen Victoria, I arrest you to be brought back to England to stand trial." He waves his hand and two English dragoon soldiers step around Bennets's desk, bind his hands behind his back and escort him out. As they are walking through the door, one of them leans in close to Bennets's ear and whispers, "Mention one word of the queen's husband's involvement with you, and you won't make it out of this house alive."

When they are gone, Alexander turns back to his father. "Captain Arnold Walters, for your long and faithful service to Her Majesty's crown, she would like to offer you the position of Jamaican regional governor. If you accept, you will have her extreme gratitude."

Before Walters can respond, Alexander holds up a hand to stave off his answer and continues. "Father, Her Majesty also has a personal request for you. It has been brought to her attention that a member of our family has been a little too busy trying to influence both your and my service to the crown. Her Majesty would therefore consider it a deep personal favor to her for you to take custody of this individual and keep her here in Jamaica, where she will have no more opportunity to meddle in state affairs." He then turns to Admiral Joshua. "Please have my mother brought in, if you would, Vice Admiral Joshua."

Admiral Joshua turns and motions, and a few moments later two naval officers escort Ramona Walters into the gubernatorial office. Walters stares at his wife for a few moments. Though she is twenty-five years older than the last time he had seen her, she has not changed a bit, albeit if only in his eyes. Strawberry blonde hair, rosy cheeks, deep gray/green eyes, and still sporting a striking, full figure. Despite his anger at her for using her influence to keep him away for so long, he has to admit that she can still take his breath away when he sees her. He shakes his head, walks up to her, takes her in his arms, and kisses her. At first, she resists and tries to free herself from his embrace, but he has always erupted deep passions in this woman, and she eventually settles in and returns the kiss. After a few awkward moments for everyone else in the room, Walters releases his wife and looks at his son. "Mr. Speaker, it would be my humble honor to oblige Her Majesty and become governor of Jamaica. Please tell Her Majesty that I will also take up my husbandly duty to care for my wife, and that I promise she will do no more meddling in state affairs."

Father, mother, and son stand in the middle of the governor's office, awkwardly looking at one another, when Admiral Joshua steps forward.

"Mr. Speaker, with your permission, I will dismiss my men and leave you to talk with your parents. Also, I would like your permission to interrogate Bennets and find out where Admiral Thompson is."

"Oh, by all means, Admiral. This is your command now and I am sure Governor Walters would agree that finding Admiral Thompson is of the highest priority. Am I right, Father?"

Walters looks away from gazing at his wife, Ramona. "What? Yes, yes, of course. Please, Admiral, find out where he is. If you need any help, the garrison is at your disposal."

Admiral Joshua nods and turns to leave, wanting to give the newly united family some privacy, but Alexander holds up his hand. "Admiral, remember the parliamentary envoy has to leave in twelve hours. We are still endeavoring to fix diplomatic relations with the United States, and we have the newest of Her Majesty's envoy extraordinaire and Minister of Plenipotentiary, Lord William, whom we must deliver at best speed to New York City. You will have until then to learn what you can from Bennets. After that, he comes with us to face judgment before the queen." After everyone leaves the office, the Walters family then has a very robust, albeit brief, family reunion.

Admiral Joshua learns that Don Lomoche has murdered Thompson. After more rigorous questioning, he also learns that Lomoche has been secretly rebuilding the fort at Port Royal, and that is where Faustin Reece bases his operations with *The Red Witch*.

The parliamentary envoy departs from Kingston Port exactly ten hours after the meeting in the gubernatorial house. Four hours after that, *The Morning Star* sails into Kingston Port on uncommonly calm seas for an October day.

CHAPTER 14

RETURN OF THE PIRATE PRINCESS

That Evening, Kingston Port

As soon as they told her that *The Morning Star* was spotted sailing into Kingston Bay, Brandy asks Skinner to cover for her, and she quickly changes out of her work clothes and makes her way to the dock. With all the excitement of a parliamentary envoy showing up and Governor Bennets being arrested and then replaced by Captain Walters, she and Skinner have barely had time to catch their breath. She knows she is putting a lot of pressure on her uncle, seeing how Davonte is at her foster parents' house being fitted for a wedding dress. She was supposed to be back before the shift started that evening, but something probably came up. Brandy thought it was kind of silly that Davonte still wanted to work at *Katrina's* after finding out that Arthur Joshua was her father and that she is an heiress to a fantastic fortune; but in a way, it also made sense. Since John Edwards and Ralphie showed up, the whole group around *Katrina's* was growing into a funny little family unit.

Brandy makes her way to the steps leading to the dock where she and Zhang Yong rescued John and Ralphie earlier this past summer. She is finding it hard to breathe as she anticipates her reunion with John.

She made the decision that if he could not leave the sea, then she would join him. She knows that she loves him and wants to spend the rest of her life with him. She tells herself that when he is ready, he will give her his mother's medallion. She sighs, yearning for the day when he will take that final step and commit his whole self to her as she has already done in her heart to him.

As she spots that tall, blue-white ship that bears the name of the savior of the world, she notices the fresh repairs on the fore port side and knows immediately that probably means that they have been in combat at sea. Panic courses through her as she sprints to the access plank and runs across it to find John and ask what happened.

Ralphie would have preferred to make it to the Kingston port earlier in the day while it was still light out, but he had to lie out in the ocean off port to wait for the weather to calm down. As he was making his way to dock, they passed an English armada of ships and he is eager to ask his future father-in-law what their purpose was. He is giving the final order to the crew for securing *The Morning Star* to port and dock when he sees Brandy running across the gangplank with panic in her intense green eyes. Brandy spots Ralphie standing at the helm. "Ralphie, what happened? Where is John?"

Ralphie lets out a long sigh. "Brandy, we saw combat three times on this mission. Twice on land and once at sea. Captain Edwards saw us through all three engagements. We lost Jacob Hind and three others at Florida and two men at Neseem's Maroon. We lost no life at sea."

Ralphie explains John's superhuman maneuver at Devil's Curve, and how Almighty God saved their lives from sure death. He further tells her about how *The Morning Star* suffered damage from cannon fire and had to set in at the port in Trinidad and Tobago; and that while there, Don Lomoche ambushed him and John that night coming home from a tavern and, for reasons he cannot fathom, shanghaied John and took him away on *The Red Witch*.

"You should have seen John Edwards fight, Brandy. He took on eight of those scummy pirates bare-handed and downed them all. When some of Lomoche's men tried to shoot me, he disarmed another and killed the man who was trying to kill me."

Ralphie pauses and delicately returns Brandy's stone-cold stare. He can't help but notice that her intense green eyes are taking on a fiery red hue as they burrow into his own. He reaches inside his vest pocket and pulls out the medallion that John ordered him to give to her. "Captain Edwards gave me two orders before they took him. The first was that I get this to you and tell you that it is yours forever. He said you would understand what that means. The second was that I am to get *The Morning Star* back to Admiral Joshua and that he will know what to do."

As she reaches out to receive John's mother's medallion, all the fiery rage that threatened to overcome her drains away like boiling water emptied from a teakettle. She holds it in the palms of her hands, beholding all that it means. As the realization dawns that John has promised himself completely to her in every way, she feels the last vestiges of her stony, cold heart break away and crumble to the ground. In its place comes a new, bigger, and more powerful sensation than she has ever felt in her life.

Suddenly her mind is clearer and more focused than it has ever been. She knows exactly what she must do. She puts the medallion around her neck and kisses Ralphie on the cheek. "Thank you, Ralphie. Vice Admiral Joshua is at the governor's mansion with Governor Walters. He is waiting to hear from you or John, and his men have orders to let either of you in immediately."

"Brandy, where are you going? Don't you want to come with me?"

"I am going for a swim in the ocean, Ralphie. Then I am going back to talk to my Uncle Skinner. If you get a chance, tell him I'm taking that midnight swim I've threatened to take over the years," she says as she walks off the plank and onto the dock.

"Brandy, that water is a little too cold for a swim, and what about sharks attacking? With the seas being so rough this time of the year, they can sometimes breach the reef wall."

Brandy turns and with a mystical twinkle in her eyes. "They wouldn't dare!"

The stars are clear and bright, and Brandy walks far enough down the beach away from the city lights that she feels she has some privacy. She takes one final pan around her area of the beach to make sure she is alone and then strips down to nude, save for the medallion John gave her. She places her clothing far enough up on dry sand to ensure they don't get wet, then walks out into the cool October Caribbean water until the depth brings the water up to her chest, and then she dives into the first wave that comes.

About an hour later, Brandy is sitting on her knees in the water rubbing her hair with the salty ocean water that each new wave brings in. She does not have a mirror to check her appearance, but her Uncle Skinner said that he spoke with an apothecary once regarding how long it would take to remove the dye from her hair in saltwater, and he told him that one-half hour should be sufficient.

She wrings her long, silky hair out one last time then stands and walks over to her clothing. Much to her delight, the ocean is bringing in an unseasonably warm breeze that has just enough force to it to make her wet hair sway in its embrace. By the time she is fully dressed and walking back to the dock, Brandy Erasmus's long, silky, red hair is swaying in the increasingly violent winds of a coming storm. With the stars and the moonlight moving in and out of cloud cover and reflecting off her bustling red hair, if one were to see her from a distance the effect would be like that of a torch of fire being carried across the beach on a dark and windy night.

Later at *Katrina's*

Skinner can hardly believe what he heard. Ralphie, Admiral Joshua, and Governor Walters told him everything that had happened to those on *The Morning Star,* and then Ralphie related Brandy's reaction to what had happened, and told him what she said she would do. When he heard that, he immediately excused himself and went to his room to retrieve some items, then took them to Brandy's room and rejoined the group. Knowing what to expect when Brandy gets back, Skinner excuses his guests and closes the tavern early, save for Admiral Joshua and his companions.

As the four men are talking the front doors to the tavern burst open from a blast of wind and makes them all look up. When they do, they see the silhouetted form of a woman with her hair flying in the wind. As she steps forward, Skinner takes a big gulp of air. Brandy's silky red hair falling around her beautiful face and her intense green eyes brings tears to his own. "Bless my soul, Brandy! If I did not know better, I would have sworn that it be the Scarlet Mistress herself that stands before me."

Brandy stares at all four men. "Where is *The Red Witch!?*"

Skinner takes a calming breath. "I put some things upstairs in your room for you. When you are ready, I'll take you to talk to someone who can help us locate your ship." Without saying another word, she walks past the men and ascends the stairs leading to her quarters. When she gets to her room, she finds a white cotton blouse, some black leather leggings, a leather vest, tall black boots, and a pair of rapier swords and scabbards that are worn on the back instead of at the hip. Next to the swords is a dagger that takes her breath away as she remembers which one it is.

"That be the same dagger you took Lomoche's hand and eye with fifteen years ago. And those rapiers are the same two you and your mother were dueling with that very day—the ones she used to kill those bastards who sided with Lomoche. And that is the outfit your mother took you out of when we cut and dyed your hair. It took me almost this whole time we've been here to find all these things, but I did. I been keeping them for when you be ready for them."

Brandy turns to see her Uncle Skinner standing in the doorway. He steps up and places a hand on her shoulder. "She always dressed you the same way she did. She wanted the men to see you like they saw her. If you really want to claim *The Red Witch* and her crew, you better show up looking the part."

She reaches out and embraces Skinner. "I don't want it or them back. All I want is John." She leans back and bores into his eyes with an intensity that nearly stops his heart from beating. "I will do whatever it takes to get him back. If it means ramming that evil ship and her crew right up Don Lomoche's arse, then so be it."

Two Hours Later, at a Small Tavern on the Other Side of Kingston

Juan sits in the same tavern that Briskett has been at for the last three months, doing the same thing his shipmate was doing before him—trying to drink himself to death. Don Lomoche was not going to let him take the skiff that Briskett had rendezvoused with *The Red Witch* on back to Kingston until it looked like the whole crew would mutiny. Lomoche tried to convince Juan to go with them to the Pacific after they collected the rest of their pirate companions from Port Royal, but the crew said that he had promised Juan his break, and no one cared that *The Red Witch* would never be back to collect him. The crew just looked at it as a victory of another being freed from that cursed ship.

Juan had heard that the British armada had already collected Governor Bennets and sailed, and he figured that if Skinner found out about John Edwards and Admiral Joshua's daughter, Davonte, being kidnapped, Skinner would lead the authorities to Juan and he would either be executed or jailed. He really feared neither. He would just tell them everything he knew about Lomoche's plans, and hope for the best.

He lifts his glass of ale to his lips and swallows the last couple of gulps, then pounds it down on the table and yells, "Inn-keeper, my glass is empty! Bring me another—" Before Juan can finish the demand, the door to the tavern opens and the individual who steps inside from the windy, black of night causes him to lose his breath and turn as ashen as a dead man. He looks up in horror as he sees that her hair is still the same fire red he remembers, and her eyes are as intensely green as when she stared down the whole crew of *The Red Witch* and cursed them all before taking her life.

She is silent for a few moments as she stands there and bores into his soul with those eyes. "Hello, Juan."

With the silence broken, Juan falls from his chair to his knees and bends over with his face to the ground, groveling and crying. "Please, Mistress, don't damn me anymore. I've done all that you asked. Pablo joined you in hell many years ago when he jumped into the ocean from madness whilst we were coming back from Africa with *The Red Witch's* hull full of slaves, but Briskett and I have never stopped. We swore allegiance to Lomoche like you ordered and kept your ship for your daughter to come and claim someday. It is out of my control that Lomoche plans to force that sea wizard of a captain, John Edwards, to sail your ship around South America and into the Pacific Ocean ..."

While he is still groveling, Brandy reaches down and yanks the gangly man to his feet, then takes the dagger Skinner gave her earlier and places it at his throat. "I never wanted to come back and claim that wretched ship or you bunch of cutthroat pirate scum. What do you mean, force John Edwards to sail it down there at this time of year? Has Lomoche lost his mind?"

Juan opens his eyes wide in astonishment as he sees the woman before him more clearly. Though she resembles the Scarlet Mistress more than anyone living could, he sees that it is not a ghost he is being confronted by but a living, breathing woman, a woman he has known since the day she was born. He wipes the tears from his eyes and exclaims, "Brandy?!"

She sucks in her breath and lowers the knife from his throat. "Yes, Juan, it's me. Now, what are you talking about? How could they possibly force John to do something that stupid? No one in their right mind sails those seas now!"

She lets go of his collar and steps back. She understands why he mistook her for her mother. Although she has been dyeing her hair for fifteen years, Skinner told her on the way over that he forbade all three of the original conspirators from getting anywhere close to her. He said that if any of Lomoche's men spotted them lurking around *Katrina's*, it would have brought too much suspicion on the place.

Juan gulps. "Lomoche told me that he has had some of his men stalking a girl named Davonte and that she is the lost daughter of the famous British sea captain, Arthur Joshua; and once they grab her, they will use her to make John Edwards do what he wants." He shakes his head and continues. "Brandy, I faced that man at sea. He could have sunk *The Red Witch* if he wanted to. Never have I seen a man handle a ship like he did. If anyone could navigate a ship down there, he could."

Brandy barely hears Juan's reply about John. She turns and yells, "Uncle Skinner, Lomoche has Davonte!"

Skinner hurries into the tavern and over to Juan. "Where be *The Red Witch*, Juan?"

Juan tries to steady himself as the shock and adrenaline finishes clearing the rum from his mind. He sniffs back tears. "She still has to be anchored out past Port Royal. There is a big storm coming and Lomoche can't bring her in to that port because of all the wreckage and debris from the earthquake. Either he'll leave her out there to fend for herself or he will try to get your John Edwards to take her out and try to survive the storm. My guess is that he hunkered down in the old fort with his prisoners, and the crew is out there waiting for death to free them.”

“What kind of storm are we talking about, Uncle Skinner?”

“I haven’t been sailing much these days, Brandy, so I’m not as tuned in as I used to be about such things; but my bones tell me it will be a bastard of a storm out there and it’s coming fast.”

Brandy stands there for a few moments fiddling with the dagger in her hand and thinking. “Let’s go back to *Katrina’s*. Admiral Joshua and Ralphie need to know about Davonte. If anyone can figure out how to get her and John back, Admiral Joshua can.”

Back at *Katrina’s*

As soon as Brandy, Skinner, and Juan walk through *Katrina’s* door, Ralphie runs up and exclaims, “Brandy, Davonte never made it to Ben and Elisa’s house yesterday! We don’t know where she is!”

“I have ordered the garrison to wake all the men to begin a search at once,” Admiral Joshua booms from the rear of the room. “If anyone has harmed my daughter, they will rue the day they were born! Ralphie and I are leaving now to help in the search.”

Ben and Elisa look like they have not slept in a day. Brandy holds up two staying hands to block Ralphie and Joshua from leaving. “I know about Davonte, and we know where she is.” She tells them everything she knows.

Admiral Joshua shakes his head in frustration. “To think that that Spanish demon Lomoche would use my daughter to force John to do such a foolhardy thing! But to keep her safe, he would do anything in his power, including make that treacherous journey. We have to get there as soon as we can. Mr. Austin, return to *The Morning Star* and gather the crew and prepare to launch. Ben and Elisa, go to the governor’s palace and inform Governor Walters what is going on and ask him to send whatever ground forces we have to Port Royal." He then looks over at Brandy and Skinner. "If I get you to *The Red Witch,* can you persuade her crew to join us in liberating John and Davonte?"

Before Brandy can respond, Skinner says, "Admiral, once the original crew sees Brandy here, they will do anything she tells them to do, and kill anyone who gets in her way."

Admiral Joshua nods and motions his chin in Ralphie's direction. "Then I think you should come along, Brandy. You, Skinner, and Juan can go with Ralphie and help him."

"I also would be honored to join your force, if Admiral Joshua permits it."

All eyes turn to the back of the tavern near the kitchen and they see Zhang Yong standing there.

Admiral Joshua smiles emphatically. "We would be honored and humbled by your help, Master Shaolin Priest Zhang Yong."

Zhang gives a slight bow and says over his shoulder, "Brandy, please join Zhang Yong in the courtyard before we leave."

It is about two o'clock in the morning when Brandy goes to the gate of the training area. She sees Zhang in his traditional Shaolin priest battle robes and sporting a pair of master's swords strapped to his back. Brandy looks closely at the swords and does not recognize the design on the handles.

Zhang sees the confusion in her expression. "I entered Shaolin Temple when I was five years old. Twelve years I trained before master Shaolin priest give these to me. I take them out only when they are needed. Tonight, I need them." Zhang reaches over Brandy's shoulders and grabs her two rapiers from their scabbards and huffs. "A master does not go into battle with meat cleavers better designed to cut off chicken heads." He walks over to the storage shed and retrieves the pair of master's swords that Brandy recognizes and holds them out to her. "For five years, Zhang Yong has been perfecting these for his student, Brandy. I watch you and see how you move and how you react. Zhang fit and form these in little ways to make perfect for Brandy's hand. They are ready for you and you are ready for them. Honor teacher now and take these master's swords into battle and use them as only you can."

Despite the urgency she is feeling to get on their way, she recognizes the solemn importance of this moment. She bows her head and says with a quiver in her voice, "Sifu, you have been my great teacher and friend. I promise that I will only use these in the way you taught me to. I will carry them in my hands, but it will be you who will be in my heart when I wield them."

Zhang lets the tears flow and takes Brandy in his arms, and with a parental gentleness, softly caresses her silky red hair as she lays her head on his shoulder. He then releases her and steps back. "Come, the great Admiral Joshua will lead us to victory and we will free our friends. Tonight is a glorious night. Zhang can feel it."

One Hour Later on the Deck of *The Morning Star*

Ralphie and Admiral Joshua are aboard *The Morning Star* discussing what they are about to do. They see Zhang and Brandy coming up the boardwalk and the admiral waves them aboard. "It's too bad the English armada left when they did Capt … uh … Admiral Joshua. We could have used their help right now," Ralphie says.

Admiral Joshua pats his future son-in-law's shoulder. "Not to worry, Mr. Austin. I sent one of our local schooners to Cuba earlier this evening. I believe the armada will endeavor to seek port there to wait out this storm. I've requested Speaker Walters to order his fleet to form a blockade and be on the lookout for *The Red Witch* should she escape us this night. I am confident he will be sympathetic to our cause and comply as quickly as he is able."

Brandy and Zhang Yong come aboard, and Admiral Joshua tells Ralphie to gather the rest of the crew to discuss their plan. A few moments later, Ralphie comes back with Skinner, Juan, and an officer from the Kingston garrison. Admiral Joshua looks everyone in the eye and nods as he takes a calming breath.

"I'll be frank with you all. I have been a naval battle commander for most of my life. I have seen more death than any man should, and I thought I left that life when I came in search of my family. When I sailed into hell, it was always for king and country. But this is different. This is personal. I pray that Almighty God helps me keep a clear head and calm heart so that I can lead you to victory.

"But I have to be honest—fear tempts to control my heart. Davonte and John Edwards are two of the people I value most on this earth, and to lose either would tear my soul from me. Governor Walters is leading a ground force of 150 men to Port Royal as we speak. They should be there in twelve hours. It is a three- to four-hour sail from here depending on the seas. We have only *The Morning Star* and her crew, and maybe *The Red Witch* and hers, at our disposal. Lomoche has Governor Bennets's personal guard and an unknown number of pirates at his disposal. This won't be an easy assault. My guess is that we will face a force of at least three hundred, and we will have barely half that if *The Red Witch* crew joins us.

"We do have a few advantages, though. The element of surprise. The storm that will keep them hunkered down, and the hand of the Lord God to guide us and strengthen us."

Admiral Joshua takes his hat off, bows his head, and thanks God for a successful outcome. When he finishes, he looks up with a steely gaze. "Mr. Austin, take her out, and Godspeed to all of us."

Four hours later

It is hardly noticeable that dawn has already come. The clouds are so thick and the seas so tumultuous that one's vision is left to only a tenth of a mile in any direction. When they do spot *The Red Witch,* they barely have time to weigh anchor to avoid ramming into her. Skinner tells Admiral Joshua that he, Brandy, and Juan should be the only ones who go over to the pirate ship, but Zhang Yong insists that he be allowed to go over as well. Grudgingly, the admiral agrees and has Ralphie and the men prepare a skiff to take them. Ten minutes later, the four are rowing the stormy seas and making their way to the ship where Brandy was born.

Aboard *The Red Witch*

Briskett sees the sails in the distance and has already ordered the crew to man the cannons on the port side of the ship. He really has no stomach to fight—not because he's afraid, but because he just has no passion for it. He hates Lomoche and wants no part of angering a man like Arthur Joshua. When the famous sea captain first showed up seven years ago in the Caribbean, he thought for sure the British government had sent the man to deal with illegal slave trading going on in this part of the British Empire. It was a relief to find out that he was only interested in supporting the abolitionist movement and finding new homes for runaway slaves. Now, he knows that there is no place on earth a man like that will not go to rescue his daughter or avenge her death.

Then there is the mysterious Captain John Edwards. He had heard that the man was called the greatest navigator and helmsman on the seven seas, but what Juan and the rest of the crew told him about what the man accomplished at Devil's Curve was too fantastic to fathom. And now he finds himself part of a group trying to force the man to sail a pirate ship in some of the most treacherous waters on earth. "Ready the cannons! As soon as she is close enough, sink her," Briskett orders as he shakes the reverie from his mind.

"Belay that order, Briskett. This is my ship, and you will do as I say from now on." The voice comes from the port side, where the ladder to access skiffs is located. When he turns to see who just spoke, his eyes almost burst from astonishment. Standing there at the rail with her fiery, long, red hair blowing in the wind, wearing the same white blouse, black leather vest and leggings, and tall black boots, and sporting an exotic-looking sword in each hand, is an apparition that robs him of the ability to move. He barely finds the strength to utter the single word, "*MISTRESS?*"

As Brandy steps toward the petrified man, others on the deck fall on their knees and wail, frantic with the thought of what she will do to them.

When she gets close enough to the man who showed loyalty and fidelity to her mother all those years ago, a deep sense of pity over-whelms her and she throws back her head and yells, "Stop it, all of you! I am not my mother. I have not come to damn you but to free you from her curse. I am Brandy Erasmus, daughter of Eric Erasmus, the Plague, and his wife, the Scarlet Mistress. This ship and her crew are mine and I claim you!"

When she finishes, Skinner, Juan, and Zhang ascend the ladder and walk over to stand next to her. Juan holds up a hand. "It is true. When I first saw her, I too thought she was the Scarlet Mistress come back from the grave to take vengeance on me for failing. But this woman is her daughter, Brandy, and she has come home to take what is rightfully hers. The mistress's curse is over! We are free!"

The crew of *The Red Witch* tentatively approach Brandy to get a better look at her. An older man whom Brandy recognizes as someone who used to help Skinner in the galley comes up and places a shaky hand on her shoulder. "Brandy, is it really you?"

She smiles. "Yes, Jorge, it's me. I do miss those buttery biscuits you always made for me."

He turns around and holds up both hands. "It is her! Brandy has come home. *WE ARE FREE!*"

Briskett, frantic with excitement says, "Brandy, shall we leave Lomoche stranded in the fort? I am sure the British already know that he has Joshua's daughter and the new captain of *The Morning Star*. He'll hang for sure. If we leave now, we might beat the storm if we head straight for Mexico."

Brandy's intense green eyes bore into Briskett's for a moment, then she walks over to the stairs that ascend to the helm, climbs them, and turns to face the crew. She sheaths her two master's swords and takes out her father's dagger that Skinner had given to her. "Fifteen years ago, I took Lomoche's hand and eye with this. Now I will finish the job and shove this straight up his arse. We are not leaving. We will attack Port Royal and free those two prisoners." She looks around the deck and sees that her words have deflated the good mood that her return had caused.

"Brandy, when you and Skinner left there were more than a hundred and a half of us on this ship. Now we number eighty-nine. Lomoche had all who weren't part of the original crew get off, and they went to the fort with him. There are over four hundred armed men there. Let the Royal Navy deal with them. Storming that place will just get all of us, including you, killed."

The shock of hearing there are even more men than Admiral Joshua had estimated gives her pause, but she shakes off the hesitation. "Briskett, men, listen to me. We all have our concerns, but let me ask this. When my father captained this ship, was there not a man on her that would not invade hell itself if he so ordered it? Am I right?"

Slowly, each man nods his head affirmatively.

She continues. "I have been away for a long time, and in that time, I have met and known many a sailor and many a sea captain. This I tell you from the depth of my soul—in all that time I have only met two men that I would follow as captain." She takes the dagger and points it at *The Morning Star.* "One stands at the helm of that ship, Vice Admiral Arthur Joshua." Then she points the dagger at the fort. "And the other is Captain John Edwards, who is being held prisoner in that place. Either one of them are ten times the captain my father ever was. Admiral Joshua has a plan. He has won more battles and led more men than my father ever did. We can do this! Follow me in following him!"

Briskett looks around the deck at the ragged crew of *The Red Witch* and sees something in their eyes he has not seen in a long time—excitement and dogged determination. He turns around and throws his hands in the air. "We are with you, Brandy! Where you go, we follow, right boys?"

They all cheer and clap.

She looks over at Skinner. "Send the skiff back and tell Admiral Joshua what they said and let him know we await his signal."

Fifteen minutes later, a flag goes up a pole on *The Morning Star.* Brandy looks at Briskett. "Full sail, Briskett! We are heading straight in, hard and fast."

"Brandy, a ship this size can't safely navigate that port. Our hull could be torn up with the debris under the water!" Briskett answers frantically.

Brandy walks up to the old pirate, puts her hand on his shoulder and gives him a gentle shake. "Briskett, *The Red Witch* will never leave Port Royal. We are counting on her getting stuck in the debris. When she does, *The Morning Star* will go around her and Admiral Joshua will dock. With both ships in that port, no one will be able to leave and we can hold them until Governor Walters's ground forces get here. Then we take and free John and Davonte."

"Aye, Brandy, you're captain now." He looks around at the men and shouts, "You heard her, full sail! Head for Port Royal. Make her go as far as she can!"

CHAPTER 15

THE POWER OF LOVE

The Red Witch's bow heads straight toward the old dock of Port Royal. As she pulls ahead of *The Morning Star,* she picks up momentum but so does the storm. Both ships are about two miles out to sea and the raging winds and seas of the hurricane slam into both ships, making them almost uncontrollable. Each vessel is now engaged in a panicked effort to keep afloat in the storm.

Brandy looks around the deck of her ship and sees nothing but panic on everyone's faces save for Skinner and Zhang. She knows that each man of the old crew has fought storms like this before and survived, but she fears that their superstitious natures will cause them to believe that some twist of fate is judging them all worthy of death.

She makes her way to the bow of the ship and leans out against the rail as she did when she was five; but instead of throwing her arms out like she wants to dive in, she grasps the master's swords and points them both at Port Royal. From the depth of her soul, she lets out a guttural scream, God Help Us! That cuts through the wind and the rain, the thunder and lightning. So loud and voracious is her voice that they even hear it on *The Morning Star.* Brandy's eyes are closed and the blackness that she sees behind her eyelids is almost absolute, but miraculously the rain stops and the winds die down.

Brandy stops screaming and opens her eyes, only to be greeted by the early morning sunrise shining on the left side of her face from the eastern sky. Both ships have passed right into the eye of the hurricane.

Brandy turns and faces the crew, noting the awestruck look on the faces of every man standing on the deck of her ship and the profound silence that hangs in the air. The old sailor, Jorge, steps up beside her and says to the rest of the crew, "It be the same as when the Scarlet Mistress gave birth to her in the bowels of this ship thirty years ago. The Almighty Himself heard her cry and passed her on safely." He reaches down and grabs his old, chipped rapier and holds it high in the air. "If Brandy says there be a better captain to rescue over there and Don Lomoche stands between him and us, then let's take this cursed old pirate ship and run it straight up that Spanish peacock's arse!"

The old crew turns back to their posts with a dogged determination and a sense of purpose they have not known in a long time.

Port Royal Dungeons

John Edwards opens his eyes from another fitful night of sleep in the damp and dark dungeon Don Lomoche put him in two days ago. The whole trip on *The Red Witch* after they captured him is a bit of a blur. He remembers being led aboard and Lomoche telling him that he would force him to guide this ship around the southern tip of South America within the next couple of weeks. When he rebuked the insanity of such a request, someone struck him from behind and gave him another concussion. He spent the rest of the trip in a small cabin in the bowels of the cursed old ship, in and out of consciousness. The blow was not as serious as the one he suffered on the dock with Ralphie this past summer, and he is almost feeling normal again. He scans his surroundings, looking for some way to gain his freedom.

Suddenly the cell door opens and Don Lomoche steps in, and panic attacks his heart as he sees Davonte in tow. He is immediately on his feet and ready to help her. Lomoche holds up his hook. "Captain Edwards, you asked me how I could persuade you to take my ship to the Pacific Ocean by sailing her around the tip of South America at this time of year. Well, as you can see, I have the only child of your beloved Arthur Joshua. Do what I say and nothing happens to her. Give me any trouble and …"

"And she becomes my property." Faustin Reece walks up behind Davonte and rubs her shoulders as he bends down and smells her hair. "English, I hope you don't do what Don Lomoche says, because I've had an itch for this one for a while now." He then kisses her neck and uses his tongue to lick the side of her face.

John bolts from his cot with such force that he knocks Lomoche out of the way. He grabs Reece by the hair and pulls him away from Davonte. He wraps his right hand around Reece's throat, and with a vice-like grip lifts him off the floor and hurls him through the cell door into the hall. He is about to grab Davonte and run, but he hears the hammers of Lomoche's pistol and several flintlock rifles in the hall. Don Lomoche stands and sneers at John as he aims the pistol at Davonte. "Come here, my dear. It's time to leave Captain Edwards to himself so that he may contemplate the hopelessness of his situation."

John briskly walks over to Davonte and places himself in Lomoche's aim. "She is not going anywhere. If you want my cooperation, Davonte does not leave my side." He points out in the hall and continues. "If that black-hearted bastard touches her again, I will break his neck."

Lomoche stares at John, contemplating what he will do next. "Captain Edwards, be reasonable. I can't leave her in here with you. What would her father say …?"

BOOM!

The sound reverberates throughout the entire fort. It is not cannon fire, but more like what a giant tree sounds like when it falls.

Lomoche backs out the cell door. "Lock it. We'll deal with them later."

Davonte turns to John. "John Edwards, What was that?"

"I'm not sure, Davonte, but if I had to guess, I would say that your father is here."

Bridge of *The Red Witch*

Brandy scans the area to make sure that everyone is okay. Although it is a lot calmer inside the eye of a hurricane, the winds are still boisterous and *The Red Witch* hits the debris surrounding the dock of Port Royal hard. She walks to the rail at the bow and looks down. The ship is firmly lodged in place and although there are huge, gaping holes in her hull, the rocks and rubble are holding her up and in place, even though she is taking on massive amounts of water. As Brandy looks back, she sees *The Morning Star* glide in beside *The Red Witch*, miraculously unscathed. Admiral Joshua found the right access and avoided any obstacles. As he docks, Brandy sees that he has ordered his crew to tie off the ship not only to the dock but also to *The Red Witch*.

Admiral Joshua holds his hands to his mouth and yells over to *The Red Witch*. "Brandy, get your men over here so we can muster for the attack!"

Brandy, Skinner, and Zhang get everyone organized and set up planks to access *The Morning Star*. When the last of them are there, Admiral Joshua quickly lays out his plan to invade the fort. The structure of the old fort is like that of a medieval European castle. Just off the dock is a wall that rises two stories and has walkways where men can line up to defend it. There is one large gateway with doors that open in the middle, probably held in place by a large wooden beam set in brackets on the inside.

He divides the combined crews of each ship, totaling 175 men, into three groups. The first group is to stay on the ship and man the cannons and cover the assault. The second will scale the wall, and the third will go through the gate after the cannons blow it open.

Admiral Joshua stands near the helm. "I am sure that they know we're here by now, so at any moment those walls will be crawling with armed men. I'll stay aboard and cover both groups with cannon fire after we take out that door. Once the second group scales the wall and engages the defenders, the third will penetrate the interior and begin the search for Davonte and John. Mr. Austin, you and Brandy will lead the frontal assault. Skinner and Zhang will lead the party scaling the wall. Juan and Briskett, you and your men will go with them. If there is one thing I know, pirates are good at climbing things."

Admiral Joshua has his eight-pounder cannons trained on the large gate at the center of the wall and gives the order to fire. After the second volley, there is nothing left of the gate. Skinner and Zhang lead their group to the wall, using ropes with grappling hooks, throwing them up and climbing as quickly as they can. When they gain the top of the wall and engage the defenders, Brandy and Ralphie vault over the side of the deck to the dock below, along with the rest of the men.

Brandy reaches back for her master's swords as the men fall into formation. Muskets and pistols are in short supply, but Ralphie is sporting John Edwards's revolver and five of her men have rifles. The rest are using rapiers. She gently sways her swords back and forth in the air in front of her. She marvels at the intricacies of the design. Zhang was right—they are perfectly fitted to her hands. So delicately sharpened and honed is the metal of the blade that the very feel of the air being cut as she waves them is instantly transferred to her hands. The more she holds them, the less they seem an instrument to wield and the more they become an extension of her very being.

As she sees the enemy forming beyond the pulverized doors of the gateway, it is not rage that fills her consciousness but an all-encompassing desire to protect and rescue those she loves. Her senses are heightened and amplified as she and Ralphie lead the men into battle. Like the mother cat in the streets of Kingston being confronted by the pack of dogs, she sees, feels, and hears everything, like the sound of a crossbow bolt launched from above them. She instantly reaches out with one of the master's swords and slices it in half so that it falls harmlessly to the ground in front of Ralphie's face.

Then she hears the familiar sound of Zhang's wrist slingshot launching a metal ball at the enemy who had just fired on them, and then sees one fall from a window in the fort above and behind the wall where Zhang is now standing. She is completely aware of her allies as they all work together toward their objective.

Once through the doorway, they engage the first of Lomoche's men on that level. Like Brandy and Ralphie's group, they only have a few muskets. Thankfully Ralphie's men are much faster to take aim and fire, and they take out most of them with the guns. Brandy leads the charge and engages the first man armed with a sword. As she confronts the man, she sees him not as someone to obliterate and demolish, but only as an obstacle to get through to obtain her objective. She easily outmaneuvers and downs the man and goes on to the next.

She is in awe at this new strength she feels. She confronts two and even three attackers at a time. The realization that there is great power in love and an indomitable strength found in caring for others and wanting to protect and save people enfolds and settles her whole being. When she sees one of her men in trouble, she is instantly at their side, aiding them. She looks to the side and sees that Ralphie is motivated in the same way. He is not trying to conquer an enemy—he is trying to rescue his loved ones. He too is fighting with precision and awareness.

They quickly dispatch the men on their level and gain entry into the old fort.

Once inside, Skinner, Zhang, and the crew of *The Red Witch* come down the stairs from the wall access and join them. Their combined force numbers 125 men. They see only one access to the interior of the fort, and Ralphie sounds the charge as they proceed to the doors. When they open them, they find another group of men armed with swords and rifles, but the ones with the rifles only have muskets, and they are busy reloading.

As they stop to assess the situation, Ralphie sees someone he recognizes. There, standing in the middle of the group, is the man he remembers from *Katrina's Tavern* who attacked Davonte.

Faustin Reece sees the look of recognition on the face of the sailor from *The Morning Star* who was with John Edwards the night he ambushed them. With a deep rasp in his voice caused by his previous encounter with John Edwards, he yells, "So, you're the one who is engaged to Joshua's daughter!" He rubs his throat where John Edwards's handprint can still be seen and taunts, "I warmed her up good earlier. If you can get through me and my boys, she should be prepped and ready for you."

Faustin steps behind three of his men who are still reloading their muskets, and draws his rapier. Cold icicles go up and down Ralphie's spine as he raises his revolver and kills the three in front of Faustin then rushes him with his own rapier. Ralphie is shorter and slighter of stature than Faustin, but he is also faster. The pirate tries to hammer down on the boy, but Ralphie manages to dive to the side and avoid the strike.

Skinner begins to step forward intending on aiding the boy, but Zhang Yong reaches out and grasps his shoulder. "Not to worry. Brandy and John are not the only ones Zhang has been training. The boy will defeat that filthy animal." Skinner looks up, not totally convinced he should wait, but what he sees next brings a huge smile.

Ralphie manages to kick Faustin's knee as he comes out of his roll, which causes the pirate to stumble. He then attacks with lightning-fast slashes and stabs that quickly and completely overwhelm the disoriented pirate. Ralphie brings his rapier down on his opponent's sword, knocking it out of his hand, and then runs the man through the abdomen. Faustin goes to his knees and stares bewilderingly at Ralphie as blood begins to drip from his lips. As Ralphie is removing his sword, Brandy runs up, vaults over his back and takes out three men coming up from Ralphie's blindside to bushwhack him. As she drops the third man, she looks over. "We do this together, Mr. Austin. Davonte would never forgive me if you died while trying to rescue her."

The force they face now is mostly comprised of Bennets's private guard, and they are trained soldiers. The hall in which they are fighting is huge and Brandy estimates that Lomoche's forces number closer to two hundred. Ralphie, Skinner, and the others are doing fine, but they need an edge.

Zhang steps up beside Brandy with his master's swords. "Is my student Brandy ready to fight alongside her sifu?"

Brandy nods then mimics Zhang's posture, and the two of them, armed with their master's swords, hit the enemy like a raging tornado. Master and student engage the enemy in the middle of the room at lightning speed, each totally focused on the other and the enemy at the same time. Their combat style almost looks like a dance as they use their swords, knees, feet, elbows, and foreheads as weapons while twirling and swaying around one another. The whirlwind of motion makes it all but impossible for the enemy to penetrate their perimeter. Those that try are automatically downed as Brandy and Zhang move through the heart of the enemy forces. By the time they reach the other end of the room, they have downed more than twenty men. Ralphie and the rest dispatch what is left of the remaining force in the hall.

When they open the next set of doors, they enter a part of the fort that looks like it has been recently refurbished. There are several doors to the right down the long hall, and they hear a scream coming from the last one and head that way. Ralphie and some of his men are the first to make it through. What lies on the other side of the door takes Ralphie's breath away and turns his blood ice cold. There, standing in the middle of the ornately decorated banquet hall, is Don Lomoche, holding his hook to Davonte's throat, and a hundred of his pirate companions are there with him. He looks at Ralphie and sneers. "Tell Admiral Joshua that if he ever wants to see his daughter alive, he will surrender his ship to me and allow me and my men to sail away from here."

At the sight of this villain holding his beloved like that, Ralphie feels pure rage threaten to take hold. He holds up his rapier and begins to sound the charge when he feels a gentle hand on his shoulder. He turns to see Brandy's intense, green eyes gazing into his.

"I'll get her. Trust me."

She steps out from behind Ralphie and his men, and stands within ten yards of Lomoche. She pulls out her master's swords, holds the left one at her side, and puts her right foot forward while holding the other sword point down in front of her right foot. She had seen her mother take the same stance many times when the Scarlet Mistress met a challenger. She bores into Lomoche's one good eye with her intense gaze.

"Hello, Don Lomoche. Are you ready to die?"

Don Lomoche loses all awareness of Davonte and drops his grasp on her. She immediately dashes across the room into Ralphie's arms. Lomoche cannot control the awestruck terror that fills his heart. He looks back and forth to the other pirates in the room and sees that they too are awestruck and terrified. The tale of the Scarlet Mistress and her curse of *The Red Witch's* crew is sacred legend. He can barely control himself to utter one word, but he does. *"Mistress!?"*

Brandy rolls her eyes. "I am not my mother, you pathetic sea slime. Tell me, does that miserable stump from which I took your hand still itch?"

Lomoche looks closer at the woman standing before him. He now sees that she looks exactly like the Scarlet Mistress, but then again, she always did. *"BRANDY!!"* He throws back his head and lets out a beastly roar, and thrusts forward with his rapier.

Brandy sees the move almost before he executes it and brings her two master's swords up and then down on Lomoche's rapier, breaking his wrist and knocking the sword out of his hand. He screams in agony, drops to his knees, and holds his left arm to his chest. Brandy kicks him in the chest with the heel of her boot, knocking him on his back. She then sheaths her master's swords and kneels down on his chest, pinning his arms to the ground with her knees. She reaches to her side and retrieves the dagger that Skinner had given her, then waves it in his face. "Remember this?"

Lomoche screams in terror as Brandy holds it high in the air and brings it down on his good hand. At first it looks like she used it to cut off the hand, but then it appears that she had expertly stabbed it between two of Lomoche's fingers into the floor. She jumps to her feet and takes her two swords, crosses them, and places them at his throat "Yield!" she demands.

Before he can respond, all of his men drop their weapons and put their hands on their heads. Brandy hears a commotion from behind and turns to see Admiral Joshua step in with Jamaica's largest Maroon chief, Desomond. They are followed by hundreds of armed men. Most of them are dark-skinned citizens of Desomond's Maroon.

Admiral Joshua steps up to Lomoche. "Don Lomoche, in the name of Her Majesty Queen Victoria I arrest you for treason, illegal slave ownership, and the murder of Admiral Robert Thompson."

Brandy still has her swords at Lomoche's neck. "I should just remove your miserable head from its shoulders and save the hangman the trouble of executing you."

As she presses in, she feels a hand on her shoulder and hears a familiar voice say, "You'll not be staining those beautiful swords with this bottom-feeding scavenger anymore, Brandy. Let the admiral have him."

Brandy turns to see Skinner standing beside her. She lets go of the rage and releases her hold on Lomoche.

Two men step over and stand Lomoche up and begin to take care of his wrist. Though still in shock from the confrontation with Brandy, he manages to look up at the pair. "Skinner, you two really fooled me. I was sure you were both dead. Tell me, old friend, does she know who her real father is?"

With the speed of a shark in water, Skinner steps up and backhands Lomoche across the face so hard that his eyepatch and hat come off. "Shut up, Lomoche, or I swear I'll finish what Brandy started."

Brandy grabs Skinner's hand before he hits Lomoche again. "What is he talking about, Uncle?"

Lomoche is on the ground with blood now dripping from his mouth where Skinner had just knocked out his tooth. He looks up at both of them and says through blood-stained teeth, "Tell her!"

All the fight drains out of Skinner's old face and he shrugs his shoulders. "There be no way to tell for sure, Brandy. But I loved Kat, and she loved me. Eric Erasmus whored at every port starting a year after he married your mother. He always made me stay on *The Red Witch* to guard it and Kat, not that she needed any guarding. He just didn't want her coming in and killing every wench he wanted to whore with.

I stayed and we grew close. We could talk. She knew I never wanted to be a pirate. My cousin promised me that if I sailed with him long enough, he'd stake me in gettin' a tavern of me own." He nods his chin over to Lomoche. "This bastard came back early one night and caught me and your mom together. He threatened to tell Eric if we didn't pay him. That's when I took to arm-wrestling and gambling in port. Always been good at both. Then your mom got pregnant with you. When you was born, you were her mirror image and we just did not know who your father was. When we was out to sea, your dad still demanded that Kat take care of his needs and she did. So, Brandy, I don't know if I be your father. But this I know—there be not a man alive that could love a daughter more than I love you. And that be the truth of it."

Brandy places her swords in her scabbards, and cups Skinner's face in her palms. "This is the happiest news you could ever tell me. I love you, Father!"

While father and daughter embrace, Admiral Joshua motions for the men to take Lomoche away. Brandy pulls back from her embrace with Skinner, then throws back her head. "Now will someone please tell me where John is?!"

Davonte releases herself from Ralphie. "He's all right, Brandy. When Lomoche found out that you wrecked his ship, they came back for me. There were eight of them. John Edwards beat four of them unconscious before they could grab me and threaten to kill me if he did not stop. They still wanted him to pilot a ship to the Pacific Ocean, so we knew they would not kill him. They took me and the four men he beat up out of his cell. He should still be there. It's at the end of the hall and down the stairs in the cellar."

Brandy bolts out of the room and down the hall to the door. She practically vaults down the stairs and sees the doorway to the dungeon straight in front of her. She runs up, takes both the master's swords and strikes the lock on the door with them. The hardened, tempered steel cuts right through the old lock mechanism and she lifts the lever and opens the door. Sitting in front of her on an old stone slab for a bed, looking beat up and dirty, is the man she has already pledged her whole heart and soul to.

He looks up at her with those majestic blue eyes and flashes a brilliant smile at her. Brandy steps forward, doing all she can to calm her pounding heart. "I hear that there is an opening for a first mate on *The Morning Star.* I would like to offer my services for that position to her captain."

Just as she finishes speaking, Ralphie and Davonte come running up to the doorway and step into John's view. John Edwards looks over at Ralphie, then back at Brandy. "It would appear that I already have a first mate." He slowly shakes his head and laughs. "No, Brandy, the only position I can offer you is that of being a full partner in mastering *The Morning Star* with me as my wife."

Brandy stands there for a moment in blissful joy. She pulls out his medallion from inside her blouse and softly kisses it. "You drive a hard bargain, Captain John Edwards of *The Morning Star,* but I accept."

With a quiver of joy in his voice, John Edwards looks into Brandy's eyes. "Brandy, my little gift from the sea."

Brandy reaches inside her vest pocket that contains her mother's locket and puts it around John's neck. She kisses him passionately, then leans into his powerful embrace. "Aye, Captain. That I am."

One Month Later

John and Brandy are facing Vice Admiral Joshua at the bow of *The Morning Star* after releasing themselves from their wedding kiss. Admiral Joshua looks out to the audience with a huge grin on his weathered old face as he gives his benediction after performing their wedding ceremony.

"My soul rejoices at this solemn occasion where two souls destined to be with one another have pledged before God Almighty their sacred vows of matrimony. Please stand and welcome for the first time Captain John Edwards and his beautiful Bride Brandy Erasmus Edwards!"

Ralphie and Davonte are up with John and Brandy as best man and matron of honor. Two weeks prior it was they who were being introduced in this very spot as husband and wife for the first time by the man that performed their wedding, Captain John Edwards.

Seated in the front row on the Bride's side is Brandy's father Skinner, Zhang Yong, Ben and Elisa, and the crew of *Katrina's*. On John's side is the crew of *The Morning Star*. As they walk down into the crowd, cheers and hollers can be heard all over the ship for the happy couple. They make it to the back where some refreshments are set up. Brandy has been so frantic all day with the wedding that she forgot to eat, so she excuses herself from John's side and hurries over to the table. As she is filling her plate with food, Zhang Yong steps up behind her and says, "Brandy, Zhang have something to say to his most beloved student."

Brand quickly chews and swallows the tiny sandwich she picked up and turns to him and smiles. "Yes, Zhang?"

"Before Zhang go to play exquisite Chinese wedding music for Brandy and John, I want to tell you that I know it was good thing we decide to rescue John Edwards when we did. John Edwards has great destiny in the Caribbean to fulfill. He and this honorable ship have much work left to do." Zhang just stands there and solemnly looks into Brandy's eyes as he notices he's caught her completely off guard by his words.

She bores into him with those piercing green eyes. "And what is it that Zhang Yong believes is my destiny then, oh all wise sifu?"

Zhang does not hesitate to answer. "Isn't it obvious to Brandy? She is to guard, protect, and sometimes rescue John Edwards!"

Before she can rebuff him, Zhang chuckles, turns, and walks away. Brandy stares a bit longer, consumed by the urge to yell at him for saying such a stupid thing. But as the day goes on, she continues to think about his words and they start to make sense.

Onward

John and Brandy spent their honeymoon camping at a little waterfall close to Desomond's Maroon. Through the years, they grew quite fond of the place and purchased it from the Maroon leader and built a small home there where they could stay when not out at sea on *The Morning Star*.

Some of *The Red Witch's* crew joined that of *The Morning Star*, others went to work for Skinner at *Katrina's*, and a few went to work in Admiral Joshua's new shipbuilding yard that Ben managed. None went back to the pirate's life.

Speaker Walters brought Governor Bennets and Don Lomoche back to England to face a myriad of charges, including illegal ownership of slaves in the British Empire. Both men were executed by order of the queen.

John and Brandy spend the rest of their days sailing *The Morning Star* on the Caribbean, aiding in the abolitionist movement, and supporting and supplying Maroons. They also spend a considerable amount of time rescuing each other from all sorts of predicaments, though Brandy is always quick to remind John that she will forever be the first one to have rescued the other, and not just once but twice. They have two children, a boy named Arthur and a girl named Katrina Rose. Arthur goes on to join the union army in 1861 and fights for the freedom of the slaves in the United States. He later joins the railroad and is assigned to the northwest to help build the railways in the territories of Wyoming and Montana. Their daughter, Katrina Rose, meets and falls in love with a Mexican wine vineyard owner's son by the name of Thomas Gonzalez, and moves to southern Mexico, where she and her husband raise a family.

New, more efficient types of ships begin to take over the waters of the Caribbean and they eventually retire *The Morning Star*. But if you ever stand on a beach somewhere in the Caribbean —and especially in Jamaica near Kingston —and listen very closely to the waves coming in off the ocean, soft whispers and gentle songs can still be heard about a green-eyed, flaming-haired angel of mercy who, along with her husband, John, sailed the Caribbean in a tall blue and white ship, fighting for freedom and giving aid to those in need.

THE END